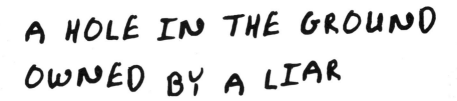

A HOLE IN THE GROUND OWNED BY A LIAR

DANIEL PYNE

COUNTERPOINT

Berkeley

This is a work of fiction. Names, characters, places, and incidents are the product of the author's imagination or are used fictitiously. Any resemblance to actual persons, living or dead, is entirely coincidental.

Library of Congress Cataloging-in-Publication Data
Pyne, Daniel.
  A hole in the ground owned by a liar / Daniel Pyne.
    p. cm.
  ISBN 978-1-58243-797-2
  1. Life change events—Fiction. 2. Colorado—Fiction. I. Title.

  PS3616.Y56H65 2012
  813'.6—dc23

                          2011039680

Cover design by Ann Weinstock
Interior design by Tabitha Lahr

Printed in the United States of America

COUNTERPOINT
2560 Ninth Street, Suite 318
Berkeley, CA 94710
www.counterpointpress.com

To Katie and Joe. My gold mine.

"Circumstance is incommensurable: let none essay to measure men who are its creatures."

—Douglas Southall Freeman, from his biography of Robert E. Lee

PROLOGUE

A small mountain airport, shrouded in fog, dusted with summer snow. Visibility of about twenty feet, butt-cold, but no wind.

"July in the Rockies. What the fuck."

"Is it safe to fly?"

Three businessmen in heavy, hooded, fur-lined coats waited, stamping their feet on the tarmac, near a slutty red Bell 206L-3 Longranger helicopter, just warming up. Stan Beachum—salesman, squat, fit, gym-sculpted, hair-deprived, slicker than a non-stick pan—squinted up into the cerulean sky, tugged the brim of his baseball cap, and made a well-considered and thoughtful downturn of mouth.

"She's just ground fog, this soup," Beachum observed. "Once we're airborne, it's blue skies to X marks the spot. But . . . Freak weather indeed. Coupla slides have closed Colorado 5, so . . . Lucky we got your whirlybird, huh? Unless you wanted to wait a couple days and chance there's a quick thaw and a frisky road repair."

The Slocumbs, Paul and Saul, Pakistanis by–way–of–Jackson Hole, Leadville, and Beaver Creek, with flawless walnut complexions and thick, flapjack-flat west Wyoming patois, didn't want to wait, no. Fraternal twins of a single mind. Saul looked at his watch. Tag Heuer. Swiss avant-garde since 1860. The crystal was fractured, and

Saul made a point of not having it fixed. He wasn't really interested in the time, just dramatizing his irritation.

"Is he always late?"

"Yes," Beachum drawled, laconic. "They say it's the surest sign of genius."

"Who?" Paul asked sharply. "Who says that?"

The Bell engine fired up, whining, high-pitched, its rotor blades whirling and whorpling to life, a quartet of disorganized samurai swords, drowning out any attempts at continuing the conversation.

The men stood, hands in pockets, shoulders hunched, pricked by the icy crystals whipped up by the helicopter's mad frenzy.

A quarter of a mile away, out in the nether-reaches of the empty Garfield County Regional Airport parking lot, forty(ish) Lee Garrison, slumped in the front seat of an old, classic black Chevy Camaro, was hyperventilating. There were Band-Aids on three of his knuckles and his forehead, somewhat diminishing how uncommonly guileless, almost boyish, Lee really was. He took a brown paper bag off the seat beside him, shook it out, and jammed his face into it to settle his breathing but all the while giving him the ungainly turtled posture of a gluehead huffing EZ-Off.

"Ohgodgodgodohgodohgodoh—"

Lee shouldered the door open and lurched out, unfolding himself from the car, awkwardly, and yanking an old black briefcase off of the backseat. He balled up the paper sack and sucked in the cold, thin mountain air. He wore the same fur-trimmed winter coat as the Slocumbs (a testament to the twins' foresight and perennial devotion to the End-of-season Skiwear Close-out Sale at Dick's Sporting Goods in Longmont) and some sooty, fleece-lined rubber boots he'd found in the front closet at home, but didn't think were his. His feet scudded around inside them as he came running across the tarmac to where the three men were waiting for him, wind from the flight-ready helicopter rotors whipping their parka hoods and flogging Beachum's lucky Sky Sox cap and tangling Lee's uncombed mop of hair.

"Where've you been?"

Beachum's lips moved, but Lee couldn't hear him. Blah blah blah. Lee smiled and they all shook hands and traded pleasantries lost in the turbulence and got into the Bell Longranger and, like a miracle, Lee thought, it lifted skyward. Science rules. In less than a minute they were above the fog, and the famous liquid blue, sun-shiny, seemingly limitless Rocky Mountain sky yawned above them, dwarfing them.

Western slope thermals rocked the chopper like rolling ocean waves. The men bore due east under that bleached canopy, follow-ing an intermittent dark ribbon of Interstate 70 as it snaked through high country calicoed, where the fog cleared, with conifer forests, low slate clouds, and drought-scarred plains. Lee gazed down on the badlands beyond the Bookcliffs and Rifle Gap and remembered his merit-badge survival hike for Scouts, seven days in the wild with a knife and a bedroll and a box of matches. He lost six pounds; ate pine needles boiled; sought shelter from an electrical storm in a cave on the banks of the Green River and surprised a fellow Surviv-al Pledge getting blown by Mr. Pilgrim, the assistant troop leader. Pants down, chapped asses. Sad. Lee never told anybody, passed Survival, and became an Eagle Scout. Mr. Pilgrim died of some kind of cancer and the Survival Pledge was now a family-values conser-vative assemblyman in the Colorado State Legislature. Third term.

"How's it feel to be a rich man, Lee?"

Lee looked at Beachum, riding shotgun beside the pilot, and took a minute to assemble the individual words and make sense of them. His mind was thick, leaden. His heart was pounding. Lee was mashed three abreast with the Slocumbs in the backseat, the black briefcase in his lap, sure that they could feel his heart, too, pound-ing, and it would give him away.

"I wouldn't know yet."

Saul Slocumb assured him they'd wired the money to Lee's bank first thing that morning.

"Prolly put a ten-day hold on it, though," Saul's brother opined darkly. Beachum laughed.

"A ten-day hold on a million bucks. Yessir. Ain't that hysterical. They clear your check overnight through the Federal Reserve, then get to use your million bucks free for nine days. Banks suck."

Lee squirmed. "I'm hot."

"Understatement," Saul observed. "From a man sitting on quite possibly the biggest goll durned gold strike since Cripple Creek."

"I would say you're boiling, sir," Saul added.

"I can't breathe," Lee said.

Beachum, a joke: "Want me to open a window?"

"No. Um. You know what? Lemme just—yeah, if I could just—"

Lee unbuckled his seat belt and tried to stand up. The pilot glanced back. "Sit down, sir."

"Air. I need air."

The pilot let the chopper veer as he turned his whole body and reached back with an arm, grabbing at the empty space around the moving Lee. "Sir, I need you to take a seat."

Lee stepped on feet, groped for the door handle, clambering over Saul Slocumb. Icy, thermal wind slapped them hard. Beachum yelled. Lee threw his briefcase out the open door and followed it, headfirst.

Those remaining in the helicopter saw a black tumble of a man dropping away from them, coat blown up, flapping, arms windmilling, as if to fly. A fluffy bird, with thin Gore-Tex wings and a briefcase.

Smaller and smaller.

Plummeting into the soft, white fog.

For a long time nobody in the cockpit of the Bell Longranger said anything. The helicopter spun stunned circles. Sunlight glowed off the slut-red canopy and trim, giving them all a hellish glow.

"Je-sus," Beachum said finally. "Hell-o. Lord God in Heaven."

He threw up.

THE WILDERNESS

ONE

*H*e stopped on the sidewalk even though he promised himself he wouldn't—not that tired cliché; he stopped, took a deep breath of the fresh air, and squinted up uncertainly into an ashen sky burned partway through by an uncertain sun.

It was true, he thought, what they said about getting out.

Light mist slicked the buff stone walls of the Colorado Territorial Correctional Facility and caused the chain link to glisten like polished silver. Next to the big wire-cage drive-through gate, a smaller pedestrian passageway had opened for him, and the stolid guards in the tower had made a passing note of him as the system kicked him free, debt paid.

He crossed the road and didn't look back.

"My brother bought a gold mine."

Allie, waitress at the Whistle Stop, leaned on the counter, her long legs pulling the stretch hem of her uniform, one sneaker foot turned in, swaying absently, and she gazed, ensorcelled, into the icy eyes of the coffee-black-lots-of-sugar man who smelled faintly of soap and regret and wore the boxy secondhand pants and shirt and navy pea coat of a day laborer (which he totally wasn't) but that nevertheless worked on him, and she decided, then and there, he had that kind of dreamy, dangerous electricity that women tend to ruin themselves over.

Allie was always looking to get ruined.

"A lot of people thought it was midlife crisis," the coffee man was saying, "triggered I guess by this prank his senior shop class played on him with their midterm woodworking projects right after Lorraine moved out."

"Your brother teaches high school?"

"Two dozen or so sanded and shellacked head-racks of wooden antlers," the coffee man continued, ignoring the interruption. "Handmade with varying skill. He sent me a picture." The waitress just stared at him with a retriever's empty hopefulness. "You know. As in: cuckolded. Having the," he made two points on his head with his fingers, "horns hung on you?"

"What's your name?"

"Grant."

"Grant. What kind of name is that?"

"Famous general."

Her face, blank again.

"Civil War? My parents were . . . " he began, then stopped. "Anyway. It's a long story, and I'm telling you a different one now, okay?"

"Okay." She cracked her gum, flirty.

"It was kind of funny," Grant resumed, "and snarky but droll, in that arrested adolescent way that weblogs and reality TV and comic book pop culture reduces other people's pain to a punch line; it was funny if you weren't my brother, Lee, or you'd never read *Ulysses*, which, of course, his senior boys hadn't, but my brother Lee has . . . four times, front to back."

"I'm Allie."

"But people are so wrong, Allie. That old backhoe from hell he took home from the highway department auction after Lorraine moved out? *That* was his midlife thing."

Allie thought: *Lorraine?*

"Rumbling through those shake roof split-levels of Hiwan Meadows like, I don't know, a mutant mustard-yellow shellfish in a Japanese horror film or something, all dust and exhaust, the one big scorpion-tail shovel-claw thing poised to make hash of all the terrified mole-people Priuses multiplying in every driveway."

"Oh."

"Personally, I expected a boat, but . . . "

"A boat?"

"Oceangoing vessel. Something with a motor, not sails. Lee's got a seafaring bent. Maybe a trawler. He belongs to a boat club."

"Does your brother live near the ocean?"

"No. Evergreen."

"Evergreen, here in Colorado?"

"Yeah."

"Oh." The waitress frowned.

"They get together in Broomfield the third Saturday of every month and talk about nautical stuff."

"They live in a state that gets, what, gee . . . about, oh, three inches of rain, annually?"

"Some can dream."

"I guess."

"Anyway, the mine is, was, well—could just be that Lee believes happiness is something you gotta dig for. I don't know," Grant said.

"You got a way with words, Grant."

"I kissed the Blarney Stone, Allie."

"Oh." Again, she had no idea what he was talking about.

"Ireland. I was eight. It's a stone, actually part of the wall in this iron-age castle; you lean back over a gaping hole, turn your face upside down, kiss the stone, and you get the gift of gab. It's about a hundred fifty feet up—the hole you can fall through—so some fat Mick, who smells of Guinness and old jeans, sits there and for, say, a euro, buck and a half U.S. thank you very much, he holds you up over the drop, and then washes the stone off afterwards with this scuzzy rag and some Scrubbing Bubbles cleaner. We were there with our parents. Lee wouldn't do it, but I did, and, ever since, you actually can't shut me up. True story."

"Huh. More coffee?"

"Yes. Thank you."

Allie's ass was her best asset, and she could tell, pivoting to the coffee machine, that Grant's grey eyes were on it.

"Where you from?"

"I just got out of Territorial Prison."

Allie nearly spilled the coffee. Grant reached out, steadied her hand. His fingers were warm and unexpectedly soft.

"Yeah. Everything you think, don't even ask. And yes, I am horny as a dandy, but you, do not worry, are safe as milk."

Not surprisingly, Allie was conflicted about whether she wanted to be safe as milk. She put the coffeepot down on the warmer. How long was he in—?

"Can we, um, talk about something else? Because . . . well, I am my brother's brother, and he—"

"Snap. Horny as a dandy!" she said. "Now I get it! Mousse T. and the Dandy Warhols! I have the 'So Phat!' mash-up; it's off the hook. I can't believe you knew about that!"

Grant didn't. It was just the way his life worked, things always falling into place. Allie felt his eyes on her again, eyes you could drown in, a sweet, soft, long, wet goodbye, worth it. Totally worth it, she supposed.

Although.

Prison.

Grant sipped his coffee, stirred in more sugar, tasted it. Now, he realized irritably, it was too sweet. And it was as if he could read Allie's look:

"Assault," he told her. "I did just two years of a possible five. Look, Allie, we're just here talking, okay? I'm not angling for anything, just some civilian conversation, with a pretty girl is good, it's been a long time, but—"

"Okay."

"Okay?" Grant thought: *Okay*. He slipped into neutral. Okay.

"You don't look like an ex-con. We see a lot of them coming through. You know. You're different."

Grant just stared at her.

"I get off in an hour," she said.

Grant just stared at her.

She shifted her hips, self-conscious, the hem of her skirt stretching, and again she was aware of her ass. "What happened to Mr. Sweet Words?" she teased him. "I mean, a minute ago you were yakking like a talk show, and now . . . ?"

"There's this Navajo superstition about balance in the universe, Allie. Well, actually, it's probably Zoroastrian, which predates the Navajo by about fourteen hundred years if you want to get all formal about it—but, hey, we're in Navajo country so—well, actually, no, Colorado, what, Pawnee? Arapaho? Ute? Ouray? I can never keep the Southern Plains tribes straight. It doesn't matter. The Navajo, they have this superstition, it goes: If you're evil, you've got to do some good. But if you're too good, well, you gotta get a little evil. You know. Just to even things out."

Allie was thinking about where they could go after work. Motels were depressing; her sister was probably already at home watching *The View*; she most certainly was *not* going to do it in the car, her Scion, with an ex-convict, on the fabric seats and the stale smell of her boyfriend's cigarettes. *Oh Allison, please, no, no, that would be, God, so low.*

And condoms. She was definitely going to insist on using protection.

"But Lee?" Grant shook his head and pushed the coffee cup away. "Lee. My brother. Has spent just about his whole fucking life being good. So . . . I suppose . . . that's where I come in."

He looked up at Allie, and his beautiful, sad, apologetic smile torched all that remained of her self-respect.

Two

A land listing on eBay:

COLORADO GOLD MINE.
$32,300.00 USD
Buy It Now!

What a sensational opportunity for the right person!

Forgive the casual nature of my pitch, but I'm not one who goes in for all that fussy, starched formality, which may be why I'm in the mining business, under open skies, and not some windowless box behind a desk!

THE PITCH: My Blue Lark Mine is a United States Patented Gold Mine that received its certificate way back in 1878. Technically, it's three overlapping lode claims: the Phoenix, the Griffin, and the Unicorn—all mythical beasts, but there's no myth in these mines; they're the real thing.

WHAT THE PATENT MEANS: In order for a mine to be patented back in the old days (and even now), prospectors had to prove to the U.S. Government that there

was, as they used to say, in fact, "gold in them thar hills."
Uncle Sam eyeballed all claims pretty carefully since tax
money was at stake. These poor miners had to pull something to the tune of one thousand tons of ore out and
process it right there in front of a federal patent agent
to prove there was a viable opportunity for an ongoing
business of mineral extraction and not just some devi-
ous landgrab going on.

THE LAW OF THE LAND: All U.S. citizens eighteen
years or older have the right under the Mining Law of
1872 to locate a lode claim (hard rock) or placer claim
(sand or gravel, usually along a river or stream) on
federal land. Locatable minerals include, but are not
limited to, your gold, your silver, your platinum, copper,
lead, zinc, uranium, and tungsten ores. Patent approved,
the mine became the property of the person who first
applied for it, and the proved patent, and the land that
was the government's, becomes the *personal* property
of the person who claimed it, in perpetuity. Even if you
later build a house on the land and live there, the land is
still considered mine property and the taxes will reflect
the *unimproved* property status. In other words, you
could have a many-acred parcel of land for the incredible
yearly tax of maybe $200! (Don't you wish your property
taxes were that low? I do!) The only way for a patent to
be removed is to have the land revert to the government
by the owner selling it or trading it to them.

I KNOW WHAT YOU'RE THINKING: You're thinking
the same thing any sane, sensible person would: If the
Blue Lark Mine's loaded with gold, then why are you
looking to sell it, ya doddy old coot? Well, let me just
say that owning a mine and mining a mine are two completely different propositions. Mining, without a doubt,

is a young man's game! The work can kill ya! I have been a miner for fifty-three of my seventy years, and I have made some hay, raised a family, put food on the table, and can say with all humbleness that I have had my fair share of good fortune. But the Blue Lark was a recent purchase, made in the flush of excitement that follows the rush of discovery, by a gentleman who wakes up most mornings feeling all of eighteen until he looks in the medicine cabinet mirror and sees the grizzled old coot staring back at him. Me! And, sad to say, but true, I have come to realize that that old coot will not be the man to make the Blue Lark pay.

I have, admittedly, not sunk my good money into the engineers, engineering firms, and geologists. But others have been there and done that, and let's just say, an analysis done by the School of Mines in '46 is encouraging. Very encouraging. Cut through the high weeds, what it all boils down to is a measured, indicated, and inferred gold yield of 1.63 OPT (gold per ton) or approximately 774 thousand ounces! It also showed silver running about three to four ounces for every one ounce of gold in the Blue Lark, so it's conceivable you could also have about three *million* ounces of silver down there. That's closing in on half a billion dollars, all told!

Sound too good to be true?

Well, they always say that if it seems too good to be true, it usually is! Me, I don't trust those numbers, and, I'll be honest with you, my expert guess is the Blue Lark Mine dump will show more like 0.59 OPT, on the high side. That's half an ounce of gold per ton of ore. Now, this is still a pretty respectable figure. A few years back, when commodity gold was priced at $500 an ounce, professional speculators were reopening mines on the promise of as little as three *grams* a ton! Now it's what? $1500? $1800? Sweet Jesus. And what did the Rev. Sen. W. J. Bryan say? "You shall not press down upon the brow of labor this crown of thorns, you shall not crucify mankind upon a cross of gold." That old windbag didn't know what the hell he was talking about.

A WORD OF CAUTION (AND I DO MEAN *CAUTION*): Do not presume to go out and locate my mine and think you can do your own assay or a little weekend prospecting on the sly. First off, you would be trespassing, and I would be hard-pressed not to prosecute or worse (a load of double-aught buckshot upside your hairy ass, for example). Secondly, this is an underground mine. Yes, veins may come up to the surface of the property (you will have to tender a real offer to have that disclosed), BUT (and this is the certified lifesaving "but") all the exploration and blasting that have occurred over the last hundred and thirty–odd years have left the property highly unstable. I will tell you I near lost my brother-in-law down a hole that I couldn't see the bottom of with a high-beam halogen spot aimed straight down it. (When you drop a rock down something like that and you don't hear it hit the bottom, you know death is very close to your feet! I'd not have missed him, my in-law, but my sister would not have abided it, and she's considerably meaner than me, so I managed to hook his belt with my claw hammer and haul him back from the brink.) Stay Out and Stay Alive! It's not worth it; trust me, it's really not.

FOOLS NEED NOT APPLY: Anyone that is a scammer, crook, charlatan, land shark, thief, felon, yuppie, illegal immigrant, liberal Democrat, con man, or otherwise unsavory of character will not get anywhere with me. I've seen it all. I've been hustled by flimflam artists, and even the FBI couldn't believe what these characters were trying to pull off! Furthermore, if you have no sense of humor, I really don't care to truck with you. It's serious business, surely, but I say if you can't have fun with it, then go to hell.

You think I'm sniffing glue? The numbers speak for themselves. Just as a for instance, without revealing too much, let's say that the Blue Lark offers 0.59 ounces per, and let's say you put a 300-ton-per-day mobile stamp plant on the property to process the ore; you should, on average, come out with around 175 ounces of gold and 500 ounces of silver per twenty-four-hour day (three eight-hour shifts of loud, hard labor, but you and your friends are young!). Figure a six-day week, and you'd have, at the end of one month, 12,600 ounces of gold and 36,000 ounces of silver. Sold at yesterday's closing mineral market prices, that's $22,865,220 in gold and $1,469,880 in silver, or a combined gross of about 24.3 million dollars *in just one month*!

You've got to admit, with gold at record prices again, this mine seems ripe for the picking. You would be right. But there is one more thing you might want to know.

FULL DISCLOSURE: The individual who originally prospected it was a Swedish immigrant who hiked back and forth from Silverton, over Loveland Pass, because his wife was sickly and couldn't tolerate the additional altitude. Well, after a couple of seasons, you can guess what happened: He got caught by an early blizzard and that was all she wrote. Six days in, cold and delirious, he tried to walk out, got turned around, and they found his frozen body thirty miles in the other direction, down mountain, clutching a tintype photograph of his bride and newborn child. His widow pulled up stakes and moved back East to her family, and the Blue Lark subsequently lay fallow for forty years. When she passed, a mining consortium bought the claim from her estate, but that operation went belly-up in the Great Depression. The mine was forgotten and fell into tax arrears and got purchased for pennies on the dollar at auction by a Denver man who never even set foot on the claim, bided his time, and sold it at a fair profit, he believed, to me.

I know what you're thinking now: bad luck. There must be a curse on this mine. Well, that's not unheard of. God only knows, gold does things to people, brings out the worst in most. If you're a superstitious person, this is NOT for you, and I would go as far as to propose that you do not belong in the mining business at all because it takes a great deal of faith and optimism to go down into a mountain every day and look for your future.

Not for the faint of heart!

Not for the doubter and his close cousin, Mr. Despair!

Truth is, this mine's just sitting there, waiting for the right someone to come along with a little cash and a lot of gumption and to start pulling that precious metal out.

Maybe it's you.

THREE

$\mathcal{B}$ ut then, gold was never the point.

Barely a blemish in fourteen thousand feet of lumpen igneous and metamorphic rock and thawing tundra sprawled under thunderclouds roiling up in a liquid sky, the Blue Lark Patent Mine was just another sorry caved-in dent on the western slope of the Continental Divide, north of the old Loveland Pass, and gold was probably the last thing Lee intended to find there. For two months of weekends he hiked the mountainside with a malfunctioning GPS device trying to locate his claim after the escrow closed. At first, it was just something new to do on weekends if there weren't tests to grade or demonstrations to prepare or other high school business needing his attention. Unfortunately, Lee's map (crudely drawn not by the seller, bOOmerbust@gmail.com, as promised, but by one of the original turn-of-the-century patent holders as if in the throes of delirium tremens, and then repeatedly photocopied until it had taken on the greasy, translucent quality of a tamale wrapper) had the plat located slightly below a scribble of timberline and directly above a township collective of box-and-triangle cabins and buildings that was quaintly named Basso Profundo by some alcoholic nineteenth-century opera-loving wag.

But, missurveyed, caved in, hidden, grown over, one of the dozens of jutting chins of strangely beautiful red-orange and mustard tailings that spilled down into the aspen and bristlecone pine on either side of Horseshoe Basin, the Blue Lark stubbornly refused to reveal itself.

Perhaps predictably, bOOmerbust had disconnected his phone and stopped answering Lee's emails as soon as he had his money; Lee imagined some slick thirty-five-year-old land speculator crafting the grizzled, baked-bean narrative in a Denver wine bar with a couple of friends, and he fully intended to give strongly worded, bad feedback on the online auction site, and a zero-star rating. His outrage was short-lived, however, because just finding the mine was a huge part of the voyage, as far as Lee was concerned. Finding it, opening it, exploring it, imagining all the immigrants and hard, desperate men and all the dreams that had been there before him. Finding it. An indifferent woman who worked at the Summit County Assessor's office had assured him that the land existed, and that the land was Lee's, and, let's be honest, *caveat emptor*, not the seller's responsibility to locate for Lee unless he specifically made that a condition of sale, which he had not done.

It was a sullen, muggy Saturday when Lee finally poked his way carefully around and through the collapsing mine buildings he'd somehow missed on his first six trips up the mountain. Exploring the ruins of blackened sluice planking, rotted post and beam, silvery wood siding, and squandered hope, Lee wisely tested the floorboards before he walked on them; shadows and empty spaces implied an elegiac history that may have been, in fact, simply brutal days of pointless labor ending in failure, the whole array probably one gust away from total collapse. An early summer squall was rumbling and gathering itself in the thermals around Torey's Peak, promising to come in hard from the south, its stiff new winds tugging at the plat map Lee tried to keep flat in his hands.

This time, Lee had hiked straight up from where he parked his Jeep at the switchback instead of walking the rutted road that snaked through the National Forest. This tumble-down collection of ruins hidden in the stunted trees was not anywhere near where the map appeared to have the mine sited, but Lee knew from his casual library reading on gold-rush mining claims that it was common for the old surveys to be done purposefully wrong in order to conceal, from the unsavory characters a gold mine was likely to attract, the true location of the strike. Or, even more likely, that it had been made in an office, site unseen, by a couple of rummed-up Federal Homestead Act office staffers and the original patent holder himself, based loosely on the claim staker's description because, if it hit, he'd have it all done over professionally to protect his rights, and if it didn't, well, who would ever care?

Fat raindrops smacked Lee as he walked out to the edge of a wooden deck that hung out over the mountainside. He could see over the treetops, across the valley to the skeletal ruins of the St. John's Mine stamping plant, once the richest lode on the Front Range, with over three hundred employees and a foreman who had all his teeth capped gold with just the leavings that sluiced out of the placer troughs. Lee watched the grey and black whorl of the gathering storm. A drapery of rain hung down from the clouds five miles south. Forest stretched unbroken to the ski slopes of Keystone, then west to Dillon and the shores of the reservoir. The few scattered structures that comprised Basso Profundo Township were directly below him: the peeling asbestos shingles, the dry-rotted steeple of the old Baptist Church, the dark opening of the abandoned mechanic's bay at Shorty's Conoco, a sliver of its luminous white sign. The patched aluminum rooftop of the General Store glinted crenulated sunlight back up the mountain. Once this town had supported thirty-five hundred people. Now there were, maybe, twenty-three.

A rushing stillness overwhelmed him, as it always did when he hiked in the Rockies. Wind untiring in the trees, relentless, the breath of God across the rock and grass and crooked fingers of drizzling snowmelt. And sky. Colorado was all about sky, everywhere, the yawning vault of heaven, the infinite blue of it. Lee wiped away tears. The altitude, the mountains, their immutability, his own insignificance, and that sky. Strangely, everything seemed possible here. Life opened up before Lee like an unfulfilled promise, left him breathless, dizzy, yearning, unmoored.

For what?

Not gold.

Meanwhile: Thunder. The wind rising; the trees hushed. A Clark's nutcracker's shrill khraa khraa khraa.

Lee tucked the map away, turned to go, took one step, and the wood planks gave way beneath his feet. He yelped and disappeared down into the dark splintering hole in a clatter of debris and obscenities as the rainstorm came hurrying in.

The cashier behind the General Store counter looked to be completely enthralled by the latest *National Enquirer*, and the unplanned pregnancy of another underage and auto-tuned pop singer she'd never heard of, when Lee came in, warning bells tripped by the open door and sounding more like a loose collection of metal parts than anything remotely musical. Outside, the rain fell in fuzzy sheets. Lee ducked behind the sunglasses rack and was halfway down aisle two when Rayna Lincoln finally glanced up from her tabloid. She could see just enough of her new customer in the concave security mirror mounted high on the back wall. He didn't appear to be a robber or a shoplifter or a mass murderer, so she resumed reading until boxes of Band-Aids spilled out on the checkout counter in front of her.

"Do you have antibacterial topicals, besides the gel kinds?"

Rayna was pretty enough, and knew it, and had made her peace with it, and the steady cast of her hazel eyes said she didn't want to think it mattered much, but understood that, in this world, it did. Lee was all scraped up, wet, dirty, his forehead was bleeding, but she liked him right away.

"Whatja do to yourself?"

"Oh." Lee's hands fluttered meaninglessly. "You know."

"No." She saw the wedding ring on his finger but none of her usual alarms went off, which, she thought, was weird.

Lee just tried to wait her out.

"No, really."

"I fell," Lee admitted finally.

"Fell."

"Yeah. Down," he added unnecessarily.

A short, awkward silence ensued. This was all the explanation Rayna was going to get, she guessed.

"You got something against gels?"

"They're oily," Lee said.

Now Rayna waited.

"I have rips and tears all over," Lee said.

"There might be an old case of Mercurochrome in back," she told him. "It's not legal for me to sell it to you," she advised, "on account of the trace mercury content which the FDA got nervous about—Hunter-Russell syndrome, acrodyinia, Minamata disease, and so forth—but I don't see why you can't just use it. At your own risk. You know. If you want."

Rayna pretended to go back to her magazine as Lee frowned and then told her that his mother had used Mercurochrome on his and his little brother's perennial failed-Ollie lacerations and abrasions, "without any long-term toxic effects."

"Yet," Rayna said.

"I never got the hang of skateboards," Lee admitted. "My little brother got fairly decent."

Rayna hiked her jeans up as she came out from behind the cashier's counter so he wouldn't be staring down her butt crack as she led him into the storeroom; her knockoff designer jeans looked fine in JC Penney's but were not cut to fit anything but the boyish booty of those anorexic fifteen-year-old meth addicts who aspired to be America's Next Top Model—normal gals with standard equipment need not apply. She found the Mercurochrome box where she thought it would be, and by the time she got it down and sliced it open with her box cutter, Lee had his shirt off, revealing more cuts and scrapes on a surprisingly lean, nicely cut torso (not that Rayna dwelled on it) for a straight white man (which at this point she only assumed he was), and she watched, oddly fascinated, while Lee proceeded to dab bright red mercuric iodide on his wounds and then cover them with Band-Aids, as if she wasn't there.

Not exactly a shy guy, but he didn't talk or flirt with her either.

"Does that sting?"

Lee looked up at her, and really looked this time, as though he hadn't even seen her before.

"No. Not (ow) not too bad. It's (ow) just, this dropper, it's a little awk—(OW!)" He flinched, fumbled the applicator, and got dusted pointillist with tiny dots of Mercurochrome when it fell to the tabletop. "Dammit."

"You want some help?"

"No." Pause. "Well, sure. Yes." He fumbled with the idea for a moment longer. "Maybe just here, with my back."

Rayna cautiously took up the Mercurochrome applicator from the mess of Lee's Band-Aid leavings and remoistened it. Lee tensed up, turned, put his back to her, and she resumed the dabbing and dressing of the scrapes from his fall.

Neither one of them said anything for a while. The alcohol of the tincture felt cool against Lee's skin, and Rayna's hands moved lightly. He relaxed.

Lee's gaze wandered across the supplies carefully organized and stacked up in the storeroom.

"You carry mining equipment?"

"Why? You got a mine?"

Lee had to determine first whether she was teasing him. He decided she wasn't. "Well, actually, yes. That's how I got hurt, I—"

"Where?"

"The mine?"

"Yes."

Lee paused. Rayna waited.

"Up near, you know, timberline."

Rayna stopped dabbing and looked at the back of Lee's head quizzically, waiting again for further elaboration, and somehow knowing that none was coming. Lee stonewalled her, gave nothing away. Rayna smiled at the back of his head.

"You don't know where it is?"

"The mine?"

Rayna reinserted the applicator in the Mercurochrome bottle, screwed the cap closed. Lee, turning around and picking up his shirt, couldn't stop looking back at her, as if he was afraid she'd disappear; she easily caught him looking and smiled and he got self-conscious, which made him blush pink.

"Don't put that shirt on, yet, or you'll ruin it."

"Look, I don't—"

"It's totally cool if you don't want to tell me. As long as you know where it is. I mean, some people come up here, they're looking at the old plat maps, which are pretty much useless, and nobody told them that the U.S. Forest Service resurveyed all those old mining claims in the seventies as part of that whole national hazmat public lands cleanup thing that never happened, so they could just go to the County Clerk and, you know, get the exact coordinates."

"*I* know where it is."

"If you had GPS on your BlackBerry, I think you could use that."

"I don't. Have a BlackBerry. Or GPS. To speak of."

Rayna tilted her head in a way that she hoped would make Lee even more self-conscious. She liked his awkwardness. There was a warmth and a truth in it.

"You don't look like a guy who'd worry that I'd steal it, is also what I'm saying," Rayna explained.

She stared at him, waiting. Nicely waiting.

Lee twisted the wedding band on his finger, baring his teeth, a grimace he tried to bluff into a smile.

"You, ha, no . . . oh, c'mon . . . you think I'd buy a mining claim without even knowing where it is?"

She did. She knew he had. And while his false bravado disappointed her, it didn't surprise her either.

FOUR

Rain poured down all that day, from low-hanging cast-iron skies, across the Divide and along the long grade to the Eisenhower Tunnel and the guidebook-quaint mountain town Victorians of Georgetown and Silverthorne. Lee's grey Jeep pulled to the curb in front of a small, new, quasi-Brutalist courthouse composed of a lot of concrete and a little glass. Windbreaker up over his head like a deconstructed umbrella, Lee sprinted up the steps to the front door and got drenched anyway.

The County Clerk's office was empty of petitioners when Lee came in. He was dripping water, still shedding pieces of rotted wood from his clothing, his arms and face dotted with the bright red antiseptic that had smeared a little in the rain. Lee was a fleshy candle, melting, sweating red, and the fat man behind the counter put down his can of Red Bull and regarded Lee skeptically, his eyes going eventually, and irritably, to the water puddling on the slate tile floor where Lee was standing. The fat County Clerk cleared his throat.

"If somebody comes in and slips on that floor, I would have to testify that you were responsible."

"Testify?"

"In the legal sense."

"What other sense is there?"

"Aren't you a Christian, sir?"

"I'm looking for someone who can help me locate some property I purchased recently, up near Argentine Pass?"

The fat man drained his Red Bull and just watched the puddling water grow.

"I'm sorry about the water," Lee said, self-conscious and polite. "Do you have a mop or something, I could use it to . . . ?"

"No, I don't. Have a mop. My point, completely. I have to wait until janitorial arrives. Five-thirty, six o'clock. And in the meantime? Georgetown resident breaks her neck."

Lee nodded and thought about it, and carefully backed out of the office, closing the door behind him.

The fat man, county employee Douglas Deere, of Idaho Springs, heard rustling sounds out in the hallway and two dull clunks. Then Lee came back in, sans windbreaker and boots. He did a soft-shoe dance, sopping the water off the floor with his stocking feet, and explained:

"It's property I acquired recently, on, well, from the previous owner who lives out of state, so . . . And the documentation is not so good, I mean, the legal description from the original claim, but there's no posts or markings up there to indicate a lot line and I'd rather not pay for a full-out survey if I can help it. Being strapped for cash . . . and so forth."

He finished sock-mopping, then crossed to the counter, feet slapping on the cold tile, leaving dewy footprints as he unfolded his sodden plat map for the fat man's inspection.

"I understand the U.S. Forest Service resurveyed all those old mining claims in the seventies."

"Hazmat recon. Early EPA."

"Oh, uh-huh."

"Another federal boondoggle."

"Mmm."

"United *Socialist* States of America."

Lee hoped that by saying nothing the fat man might quickly move off the subject. He was right.

"It's a mining claim?"

"Yes, it is."

"You with the Slocumb Group?"

"Um, no."

"Those bastards are buying up everything like it's a fire sale. I expect they want to strip-mine the mountain the way they did down at Cripple Creek, rat-bastard devil Hindoo immigrants. Now it all looks like landfill."

"Oh."

The fat man glanced up at Lee incuriously, then disappeared down a row of county records and returned after only a moment with a huge, dusty, leatherbound book that he splayed out on the counter and expertly flipped through to find the U.S. Geological Survey's topographical detail of the area around Loveland and Argentine Passes.

"That's the Belmont Lode," he said.

Lee didn't feel the need to respond.

"Gold mine?"

"Well, um, most of the original documentation reports it as a silver mine, but, yes," Lee said. "The initial claim dated 1872 was for gold, though I've heard—"

"The Argentine District was generally known for its silver. First strike in Colorado, matter of fact, 1864. It'd be a drift mine, I'm guessing."

"What?"

"Horizontal."

"Oh." Lee had no idea what he was talking about.

"You've probably also heard how they'd often lie about the mine to keep the criminals away."

"I have. Yeah."

The fat man stared hard at Lee, and they shared a conspiratorial smile Lee all of a sudden wasn't sure he wanted to be a part of.

"Doug Deere."

"I'm Lee. Lee Garrison."

They shook hands.

"How'd you come to buy a gold mine, Lee?"

"eBay."

"'Scuse me?"

"I bought it from this ad on eBay."

Doug was staring again.

"I know that sounds stupid, but the seller seemed legit, the price was fair, and I've hiked and jeeped those peaks, and pretty much everything else up there, for twenty years; jeeped and hiked and camped the whole Divide—it's all so beautiful, in the end it didn't seem to matter."

"Your own private slice of heaven," Doug said.

"I guess."

"A pristine corner of high-country paradise. I gotcha."

"If I could find it," Lee added. Doug sounded like a Coors commercial, and Lee started to wonder about the wisdom of letting him in on the hunt.

Doug Deere studied the map book, marking coordinates right on the page, then drew crisp lines between them with his straightedge. There was a high school class ring wedged on his pinky finger; he smelled like mildew and Old Spice, and his wavy ginger hair was razored up in a low shark-fin fauxhawk. Doug put his ruler against the page and ripped the whole topographical map right out of the county book.

"Put your boots back on, Lee. I'll drive."

It was late afternoon by the time they got back to the switchback, the rain had stopped, and the road turned to Play-Doh. Doug Deere moved with relentless force, like a steam engine, up the steep muddy slope from his embedded Subaru Forester, through the trees, dipping in and out of long shadows, wheezing, always on the edge of breathlessness. Lee tried to remember his Junior Lifesaving CPR because he thought he might need it, but called up instead murky memories of Noreen Finn in a madras bikini at the Platte River Club pool. Pale and willing.

"In the old days," Doug huffed. "When they. Surveyed their mines. They'd. Triangulate the property corners, notch three trees. Or mark with rocks."

Not too far behind him, Lee aimed a big flashlight into the blue shadows where the trees were thickest.

"There we go!" Doug shouted.

The beam found a twisted, ancient, Rocky Mountain bristlecone with two vertical, barkless scars gone grey with age. Doug made a spot check with the survey coordinates on the Blue Lark plat map.

"Ding-dong!"

Lee was just catching up as Doug ricocheted off into the darkness.

"They'd mark the B-cones on account of they live so long. Ho! Cairn of rocks. Here's another one!"

"It's getting dark, Doug. Maybe we should think about coming back tomorrow."

Crashing, stumbling, branch-breaking sounds came from the shadows where Doug Deere had all but disappeared.

"Ow—sweet Mary—OW." Then: "Ding-dong!"

Lee arrived under a low pine canopy as Doug Deere's big hands clawed a man-made mound of stones away from a bigger rock held fast in the mountainside. Lee trained his light over Doug's shoulder.

"There. There. There. *Yes*."

Doug brushed the rock clean, revealing crude numbers carved into its surface. Latitude and longitude. Again Doug consulted the plat map.

"Yes."

"That's three."

"One more." Gesturing vaguely: "Prolly over there. But the mine should be . . . right up here."

"Doug, it's getting pretty dark."

But the clerk was up again, out from under the canopy before Lee could find his feet with the flashlight, moving with surprising quickness for such a big man. Lee's beam washed across the silver siding of a ruined mine building behind which Doug disappeared.

"Five, six, seven, eight, nine . . . "

The ridges of the mountains above them were on fire with light from the setting sun; everything below was flooded indigo, shadowed, dark, massive. Lee's thin beam of light flickered in the trees.

"Thirty-seven, thirty-eight, thirty-nine . . . "

Doug stood just up from the buildings in a treeless, jumbled, rocky clearing with the faint suggestion of an old access road angling through it. Lee stopped and aimed the flashlight up, past him.

"Should be right here," Doug insisted. "By the map. The primary egress, the main opening of the darn thing, a.k.a. the adit, should be . . . right . . . here." He peered into the darkness at the mountainside as if, just by looking, the Blue Lark would reveal itself.

"We can come back tomorrow."

"No sign of an opening of any kind. Be rare to see a shaft mine up here. So."

"I really appreciate your help, Doug," Lee said firmly and sincerely. "Now I know where it is, I mean exactly where it is. I know it's here. I'm not in any kind of rush, I've got time, and I know you've probably got other—"

"Unless they were lying," Doug cut him off. "Because sometimes they lied, so that nobody would know exactly where the mine was."

"Right," Lee said. "We've been over that," he added. He let the beam of the flashlight drop to his side, hoping that would be a signal that it was time to call it a day.

"Or, maybe it's all flopped, like a mirror," Doug speculated, "and you gotta count it backward—they did that a lot—especially with the better strikes."

Doug turned, looked right at Lee, and didn't see him.

"Which means thirty-seven paces southeast in the mirror version."

He walked down the slope, heavy, his boots sliding. For a moment Lee was afraid he'd fall and come crashing down on him, but then Doug was brushing past, lost in calculations.

"I've got to go, Doug. I've, you know, got school tomorrow, and a long drive home."

Doug ducked under the low beam of a framed doorway. The floorboards of the mine building groaned under his weight.

"If this shack held the stamping machinery," Doug mused, "it'd be downslope from the mine proper 'cause nobody's gonna want to heft a full ore cart uphill . . . "

Doug wandered out onto the wooden deck, carefully skirting the place where Lee fell through.

"Doug. That wood's bad."

"Say again?"

The dark made it harder to see exactly what happened, but there was the sound of wood splintering and the windmilling of Doug's arms as he suddenly disappeared down in a shower of rotted pine and pique.

Rayna's General Store was still open, which surprised Lee since it was late, and, from the telltale television-blue light glowing in every front room of every house along the main road through Basso Profundo, the two dozen residents didn't appear likely to reemerge from their houses again until sunup.

The store was, Lee decided, still open because Rayna knew he and Doug were still up on the mountain. He didn't care to speculate what this meant. Rayna worried him in a vague, unexplored-territory way.

Lee plucked more splinters out of Doug's big back and applied Mercurochrome to the wounds. Rayna, peeling the paper off the Band-Aids and handing them to him, just listened while Doug railed:

"How about this: It's (ouch) coded or something. The map, I mean. That used to happen all the time. They didn't want anyone to (ouch) find their (ouch) mine. Which means we may have to get some special equipment up here, like, where we can x-ray the mountain and (ouch) find the cavity within."

"Sounds complicated," Rayna said.

"Everything important is complicated," Doug shot back. "We live in the twenty-first century," he added. "We're not a couple of yahoos from Kansas come to Colorado on a goat with a shovel in 1883 intending to find our fortune."

Lee was on the receiving end of Rayna's worried look.

"What?"

"I'm just saying," Doug said. "I'm just pointing things out."

"I'm sorry." Rayna looked hard at Lee again, and her eyes softened almost imperceptibly as she tried to communicate, well, something, and Lee literally took half a step back from her.

"He doing all the talking, now?" she asked.

"He likes to talk," Lee admitted.

"I thought it was your mine."

"He's helping."

"Is he?"

Lee had never had too much success solving women, including the one to whom he'd been, for a long enough time to make it not an accident, married. Not so much the mystery of them as the calculus, calculus being the one branch of mathematics Lee was unable to get a handle on in school. Lee didn't like change, not integrally or differentially, and particularly not personally.

"Not an x-ray, it's, what, like an MRI machine," Doug wandered on, in a kind of verbal scavenger hunt. "CAT scan. You know. But portable. Looking for the space in the rock where the tunnels are."

Lee put the tweezers down.

"I think we're done, Doug. Wait a second before you put on that shirt, let the Mercurochrome dry."

"You know what? Kinda operation we're talking about here could be a 'Holy Moses' scenario, by which I'm talking about something akin to the tragic story of Nicholas C. Creede, after whom the town of Creede is named," Doug mused. "You ever been to Creede, Lee?"

"Maybe drove through it," Lee said. "Is it up near Fraser?"

Doug looked his same question at Rayna. She frowned and shook her head. Doug nodded, professorial, another lively disquisition imminent; took a deep breath; and before Lee could head it off, launched in:

"Well, Nicholas C. Creede's sad tale ends in suicide by morphine, July 13, 1897, alone, emasculated, in the garden behind his Cherry Creek mansion, wearing stained satin underwear—given to him years before by a Texas working girl—and a single wool sock, following an unhappy encounter with his wife in the taproom at the Brown Palace, where she was attempting to rekindle the matrimonial fires. He'd kicked her out the previous January. Paid her twenty grand to pack her corsets and doilies and whatnot and hightail it back to Fort Wayne, Indiana, surrendering all further claims on him or his fortune, which included, evidently, the family jewels. See, Creede had, in fact, figuratively quitclaimed his junk to the lovely young actress Edith Walters Walker after she gave birth to a love child resulting from a backstage tryst at the Cripple Creek Opera House in the tumble of her assembled costumes for her title role in the popular Victorian melodrama *Maria Martin; or The Murder in the Red Barn*. Based on a notorious crime committed in Suffolk, England, around 1826 or 7, where young Maria Martin was shot dead through the heart by her lover, Wee Billy Corder. Subsequently buried under the floor of his barn, Maria rotted, and Billy sent forged letters to her family from her, implying that she had eloped with him and moved to Belfast: 'sorry we didn't say goodbye.' Unfortunately, about six months later her stepmom had a dream in which Maria appeared and told her she'd been murdered and buried; the body was found badly decomposed but wearing the green scarf Maria had received as a communion gift from her parents, and Corder was arrested in London, where he was running a ladies' boardinghouse with his new wife, also named Mary. Wee Billy pled his innocence until the very end when, with the noose around his neck, seven thousand people watched him die. His body was dissected, and his head was subjected to phrenological examination, the conclusion being that the skull had overdeveloped in the areas of philoprogenitiveness and imitativeness, with little evidence of benevolence or veneration. Later, his skin was tanned by surgeon George Creed, no relation to Nicholas, and used to bind the written account of the murder."

Doug paused to take a breath, and Lee mistakenly supposed that the wrong turn Doug had made into Suffolk, England, offered an opportunity to cut the story short.

"That's fascinating," Lee began, looking at Rayna. "But we should probably get going."

"Anyway," Doug resumed, not hearing him or, more likely, just ignoring him, "thespian Edith, front-loaded in a way that never failed to be enthusiastically remarked upon by theater critics of the time, also had a considerable but lesser-known talent involving her pubococcygeus muscle that Creede's wife could not, in her wildest fantasies, which were decidedly demure, have conceived. Still, Creede's wife was capable of her own apparently serial infidelities, and Creede hired investigators to chronicle and present to her an accounting of her trysts in the form of an eight-page dissertation, resulting in their mutual agreement to end intimate relations. Unfortunately, pregnancy and childbirth did irreparable damage to the actress's love muscle, and since Kegel maneuvers had yet to be invented and actresses are never given to admitting their failings, Creede soon sunk into depression. His estranged wife, meanwhile, had come to learn that the twenty thousand dollars she'd accepted as a marital buyout was an insignificant penalty compared to Creede's aggregate net worth and was insufficient to support her chosen lifestyle, which explains why she was back in Denver meeting with Creede on that fateful July day to suggest that they attempt a reconciliation. She was feeling frisky and had booked the Bridal Suite and had already removed many of her undergarments. For a man who had left his wife for a livelier procreation to now have to reveal to her that the drawbridge no longer rose was simply unacceptable to the proud Nicholas Creede. He wept, rose, excused himself, went back to his own apartment, imbibed in an elephantine dose of morphine, stumbled out into the garden, and died."

Doug took a can of Diet Pepsi from a stack of cases nearby, popped the top, and drained nearly all of it.

"Hmm," Rayna said, numbed.

"So exactly how does this relate to our not being able to find the mine?" Lee asked irritably.

"I'm getting to that," Doug said, and then belched some Pepsi gas.

"I guess being dead would make it challenging," Rayna said.

"That's not the point, no."

"Is that dynamite?" Lee asked Rayna, pointing to a crate in the corner.

"Under the parachute?"

"Yeah. Wait. What? You have a parachute?"

"He was one hundred and fifty percent Western archetype . . ." Doug went on, talking over and around them.

"I know." Rayna shrugged to Lee, ignoring Doug pointedly. "I know."

" . . . who lived a dime novelist's plot's worth of hardship, hell-raising adventure, speculation, and lightning-strike riches. His name was a watchword among western financiers, and his success as a prospector was honored by the naming of one of the richest mining towns in Colorado after him."

"Somebody gave it to me when I broke up with my old, well, ex," Rayna continued to Lee. Her cheeks colored. "Yeah. Parachute. Ha ha, funny and symbolic, right?"

"But it was the Holy Moses that was legend-to-be Creede's coup de grâce, strike-wise . . . "

"Yuck, yuck. Some of Rayna's old so-called friends," she told Lee, chagrined.

" . . . and he kept its location a closely held secret. And even burned the assay documents after they were delivered and the man who performed it mysteriously took sick and passed away. The mine opening itself was blasted and filled in. Creede's intention from the get-go being to wait until the price of gold peaked and then cash in, but before that could occur, his wife showed up with her crafty plan to reensnare him with her charms, and, well, I already relayed to you how that turned out."

"Who says she was there to seduce him?" Rayna asked, suddenly interested. "Creede was dead, and I don't believe that his wife would tell that story."

"Again, that's not my point," Doug insisted.

"What if he was trying to get her back since the actress had lost her, you know, talent?"

"No." The cords of Doug's neck got tight.

"All right."

"No. That's not how it went down."

"Fine."

"Um. Doug? How is the situation we're in a 'Holy Moses' thing?" Lee asked again.

Doug looked at him. "The mine is hidden," Doug told them. "Not just caved in, but hidden." Doug said that, consequently, they needed to think not like men looking for a forgotten, fallen-in maw, but like men looking for a forgotten, *hidden* maw.

"Huh."

"What about tracks?" Rayna asked.

"We need to look where we don't think it is," Doug said. "Where we don't even think it will be."

"No tracks?" Rayna asked, mostly of Lee since asking Doug was pointless.

Now both men looked at her blankly.

"What?"

"Tracks. Mine cart tracks."

"What about them?"

"Mine carts, you know, run on tracks. Tracks. Tracks that run out to the end of the tailings where the mine carts dumped their slag. Even when the mine collapses, the tracks still run out, to the end of the, you know, tailings, and if you can locate the tracks, you can just follow them back to where they go into the mountain, and there's your adit.

"Or so I'm told," she added.

Lee and Doug traded frowns.

"Creede would've had the tracks removed," Doug sniffed, looking somewhat annoyed that the grocery girl was getting involved now, and telling himself: *This can only be a bad omen.*

FIVE

—Grant?

—Yes, sir.

(handshake)

—Hi. Ken Lightfoot. Sorry about the wait.

—It wasn't bad.

—What?

—Don't worry about it.

—Understaffed and underpaid. Follow me. You want some coffee?

—No, thank you.

—Or we've got bottled water here somewhere.

—I'm good.

—'Kay. You've probably figured out we are not a Jefferson County operation; we're a private sector contractor. More and more, local governments are outsourcing parole and probation services to for-profit operations like ours.

(gesturing)

—Sit.

—Thanks.

—So . . .

(shuffling through a file)

—Howzit?

—I'm good.

—Damn straight. You're out.

—What?

—Out. *Out.* Am I right?

—Yes, that's right.

—First time in?

—Yes.

—Hard?

—Yeah.

—You don't want to talk about it?

—No, sir.

—Fair enough. A winner listens, a loser just waits until it's his turn to talk.

(reading:)

—Felony assault. Guilty plea. Three years knocked down to twenty months. Certificates of completion, anger management and substance abuse. No issues inside?

—No. Other than being inside.

—I hear that. You want to talk about the crime?

—I got mad. I hit a guy. More than once. The whole thing just got away from me, and . . .

— . . . drinking?

—No.

— 'Kay. It says here you were under the influence.

—Yeah, well. That's a convenient excuse, but no. The drinking was an afterward.

—So what is the excuse?

—I don't have one. It was stupid. I was stupid.

—Think like a man of action, act like a man of thought.

(a moment's thoughtful reflection)

—Between us. The guy you messed up. He deserve it?

—No.

—No?

—No.

—You didn't even hesitate when you said that.

—No.

—C'mon.

—Categorically no.

(pause)

—I see that you're from around here.

—Evergreen, yeah.

—Family?

—Brother.

—Parents?

—Deceased.

—Right. Yeah, that's here too. I'm sorry.

—It was a while ago.

—Still.

—Okay. Thanks.

—Your brother's a schoolteacher.

—Yes.

—And you're planning to stay with him.

—Until I get on my feet, uh-huh.

—You got a job lined up?

—Um . . . no.

—I see a college degree here.

—Yes.

—Vassar?

—Yes.

—The girls' school.

—Coed since 1971.

—Connecticut?

—Poughkeepsie.

—Gesundheit!

—Ha. Yeah. It's a weird-sounding place all right.

—How the heck'd you wind up at a girls' school?

—They let me box.

—Heh.

—Seriously. I was Eastern Collegiate Middleweight Champion.

—No shit?

—No shit.

—Bachelor of Arts, it says here. Good for you, man. An investment in knowledge always pays the best interest. What'd you major in?

—Women's Studies.

(a spit-take)

—Is that a joke?

—No. Well, yes. It's what I really majored in. But I guess the joke applies.

(Lightfoot's salacious grin as it dawns:)

—Lotta pussy.

—There you go.

(requisite forced laughter)

—Okay, Grant. Okay then. You signed the contract of your parole; I assume, college degree, you read it, you understand what we call the parameters but I'll just go over them briefly anyway: Stay clean, stay sober, stay employed, regular contact with me, no contact with the victim, you can't leave the state for 180 days without written permission. Don't let your victories go to your head, or your failures go to your heart. The only difference between try and triumph is a little umph.

(a perplexed silence)

—How often am I required to call you, Mr. Lightfoot? Or do I come into town for office visits?

—Make it Ken, Grant. Mr. Lightfoot is my dad. And you will be phoning me once a month for the first six months. Unless we, you, got a problem, by all means, let me know, 'kay? Thereafter an email or a text'll do me, just to let me know you're there. I will contact you about a yearly review, and I would remind you that

I am permitted to show up unannounced from time to time to check on you in your environs. But, this being a for-profit enterprise, I carry a pretty heavy caseload, Grant, and you strike me as a one-off, so you'd be doing me a big favor if I never had to think about you again. If you're not part of the problem, you're part of the cure. If you catch my drift.

—I do. You won't.

(the file closing)

—Women's Studies qualify you for any particular line of work?

—No.

—Gynecology?

—Ha ha, yeah, that's another funny variation on that rich double entendre you've already mined, Ken.

—What?

—Nothing.

—What'd you do before you went in?

—Taught some boxing to rich women. Construction. Sales. I biked across Africa, backpacked through Asia, worked in a free clinic in Turkmenistan, couple of winter seasons lift-wrangling at Copper Mountain. Summer camp counselor in Estes Park. You know.

—Follow your bliss.

—I don't think about it. I'm not career-oriented.

—That sounds like an excuse. The only time you run out of chances is when you stop taking them, Grant. Opportunities slide away like clouds.

—I'll keep that in mind.

—Plus the job market's shit right now.

—So I'm told.

—And you got a record. It's not going to be easy, Grant. What I'm saying is, circumstances don't make or break us, they simply reveal us. Don't let anyone make you feel like you don't deserve what you want.

—I won't.

—Make sure the juice is worth the squeeze.

—I will.

—You got a girl? Someone special you been thinking about, thinking she's been faithfully waiting for you to get out?

—No.

—Good. Because they don't. Wait. Typically.

(sigh, stretch, chuckle)

—My old man would of beat me like a redheaded stepchild if I'da come home from Durango saying I was gonna major in Women's Studies.

—Mine was dead, so . . .

—Right.

—Plus I don't like getting hit.

—Right.

—Anyway.

—Mmm. 'Kay, well. I guess that's it. Any questions on your end?

—No, sir.

(sliding back of chairs)

—Thank you.

—Good luck, Grant.

(shaking of hands)

—Remember: A winner is a loser who never gave up.

(frown)

—Um . . . Wouldn't that more likely be a longtime loser?

(Lightfoot already opening the next file:)

—'Scuse me, what?

Six

*I*t didn't take long for Lee and Doug to unearth the parallel bands of steel, thick with rust in the sharp ore rubble and flatly sloping away from the natural grade of the mountainside a few hundred feet south and uphill from the buildings they'd already found. Simple geometry was in play, just as Rayna had predicted; the tracks stretched straight and parallel back into the mountain (how inefficient it would be to put a curve in it, since the whole point was to push the cart out and back taking the shortest path possible), and only a short section needed to be uncovered to enable them to sight back and find the presumed opening of the Blue Lark, a shallow hollowing almost indistinguishable from the natural terrain, but, once they saw it, clear evidence of a man-made event. They shucked their shirts and started digging, shovels clanging, strained intakes of breath, the squeak of wood handles twisting in soft hands. Doug's massive white gut undulating as he hacked at the rock and dirt, he sang at the top of his lungs a song whose words he only partially knew:

> *"Ohhhhhhhh . . .*
> *do you remember Sweet Betsy from Pike?*
> *Rode west in a wagon with her husband Ike!*
> *Duh duh duh duh dum dum dum . . .*
> *and a big yellow dawwwwg . . . !"*

Doug's pertinacious participation in what began as Lee's sin-
gular adventure was beginning to bug Lee; as he shoveled slag,
he contemplated the various ways he might be able to escape
from what he could only vaguely describe, in quantum terms
(and only to himself), as a Dougian Decoherence, in which the
gold mine was the environment, and Doug was a system that had
become irreversibly entangled with it. Of course, if he was right,
Lee knew that Doug could never be dislodged. Which would be,
Lee admitted ungenerously, a real fucking problem.

For the first time in a long time, Lee missed his brother.

Half a day's work yielded a faint progress: maybe five linear
feet, all told, into the stubborn mountain. By one o'clock, Lee was
the only one working. Doug, rosy with sunburn and exhausted,
was flopped out on a flat rock, snoring, his head wrapped in his
T-shirt to keep the sun off. At three, Lee stepped back to inspect
their—his—work, and a huge slide of dirt and rock cascaded
down and backfilled everything they'd accomplished.

So the following Saturday, a mustard-yellow backhoe on a
flatbed trailer pulled by a jeep rolled down the main street of
Basso Profundo, bringing Rayna to the stoop of her store and
rattling the doors and windows of the mostly boarded-up or
broken-down buildings between which empty lots left gaps like
pulled teeth. Minutes later, Lee at the wheel, the backhoe itself
was rolling down ramps from trailer to street, vomiting blue
exhaust, and making a godawful racket as it lurched back past
Rayna and the General Store and up the access road to the mine.
With Lee at the controls and Doug, foam earplugs stuck fast
in both ears, guiding him with hand signals, the beast quickly
clawed out a vertical crater several yards into the mountain, and
Doug was frantically signaling for Lee to stop.

"Good Lord, we've hit something!"

Lee killed the engine and hopped down as Doug eased himself
into the trench and brushed dirt away from a thick beam of wood.

"We've hit something! Crossbeam! Part of the mine's original entrance, no doubt. See? Here." Doug brushed more dirt away. "Here's the side support."

"I wonder how much farther we've got to dig?" Lee killed the diesel and swung down from the cab of the backhoe, looking around for and finally seeing what he wanted: a length of ancient, rusty pipe. He told Doug he didn't want to knock the old timbers apart with the blade of the backhoe.

"Well, lookit the slope." Doug was busy getting all technical and pedantic. "We got another ten," he guessed, "or twenty feet before we get past the caved-in part. And that's being conservative. Hopefully that timbering further in held."

"Which is what I'm talking about," Lee said.

He walked into the trench and stabbed the pipe into the wall of dirt that they presumed was the mine opening. The concussion stung his hands. Again and again, putting his weight against it and pushing and pushing, and then all of a sudden the pipe plunged right in, like a straw going through a Big Gulp go-cap.

Lee said, "Whoa."

Doug, lecturing, rambling really, talked right over Lee's worried surprise, unaware: "You know, they used to get Welshmen to come in and open these mines. Just the men, though, never the women, oddly. Your Welsh being the only ones crazy enough to risk getting buried alive. *Lle bynag y bydd pobl, bydd yno Cymry, a lle bynag y bydd Cymry, bydd yno rai o Aberdar*," Doug mangled. He said it meant: "Wherever there are people, there will be Welshmen, and wherever there are Welshmen, there will be men from Aberdare."

"It's kind of a motto of their kith and kin," Doug added. "Or one of them."

Water spat from Lee's pipe. Gurgled. Died to a drip. But there was a deeper rumbling; Lee felt it through his boots, motel Magic-Fingers on the mountainside, and Lee knew that it wasn't right.

"Doug?"

Doug, oblivious: "That's where most of your trouble is, first hundred-or-so feet—"

"Doug. Get out of—"

"Your short-statured Welshman, see, displacing a proportionately smaller quantity of rock—"

"—out of the—"

The whole wall of dirt burst on them, followed by a concussive surge of bright orange water, rock, and mire.

"—trench."

Lee leapt out of the backhoed gash, then reached back and grabbed Doug by the back of his shirt as the cascade of water coursed past him. Doug was knocked off his feet, and Lee couldn't hold him; the shirt ripped and Doug was swept cartwheeling and squealing like a javelina across the ragged apron of the mine tailings, and then he disappeared over the edge of a newly created waterfall.

"Doug!"

There was no response. And for a guilty moment Lee imagined a Doug-free dig.

Lee scrambled to the edge of the apron and did a controlled slide down the tailings beside the cascading mustard-colored water, shredding the seat of his pants, and finding Doug stuck, wedged into a broken ore trough, gasping for air. Lee dragged the big man to dry land. CPR was out of the question because Doug was already vomiting up a mustard bilge, but Lee obliged to flip Doug onto his back, and with his hands on either side of Doug's belly, pumped the water out until the coughing became dry heaves, and Doug's arms began to flop around and he moaned pitifully.

"What. You all right?"

Doug just lay there for a moment, blinking up, insensate, at Lee. Then suddenly his legs twisted, and he flipped onto his belly and began crawling back up the slope.

"Doug?"

Lee scrambled after his big fat quantum entanglement. At the top of the tailings, Doug stopped, hands to either side of his shoulders, elbows angled, like a bullfrog about to leap. Doug went still, wondering at a dark square that had seemingly been cut in the mountain with a sharp knife, the sides perfectly parallel, water continuing to drain out in surges like a bottle tipped over and emptying.

Lee and Doug just stared, amazed.

Meanwhile, down-mountain, on the main street of Basso Profundo, an enormous, rectilinear, chrome-and-ebony Cadillac CTS belonging to the township's only elected official pimp-cruised up the road at a parade gait of about five miles an hour. Rayna was out behind her store, ostensibly emptying garbage but actually smoking a furtive cigarette that she was planning to later tell herself was the last one she would smoke, ever, and she was about to stub it out and raise an arm and wave to the driver of the Caddy, when she heard a peculiar rushing sound coming down through the trees. She had only time enough to process that it was similar to but not the same sound an eddy of wind might make when it coursed through the conifer forest, and then there it was: a tsunami of liquid yellow-orange that splashed hard into the back of her building and curled back and nearly swept her off her feet and surged right through the open back door, through the storeroom, out into the store proper, surging, swirling around long enough to sweep away most of the lower shelf items before bursting out the front door where a sturdy, short-statured woman in blue jeans and Dale Evans boots, Mayor Barbara O'Brien, was climbing out from behind the wheel of her Caddy. The orange mine water came spouting out the General Store and nearly washed her right back into the front seat and filled the entire passenger compartment to the middle of the wraparound dashboard, instantly staining the ivory leatherette upholstery and premium carpets a pumpkin color that would prove to be permanent. Water crested the rear quarter-panel and sheeted across the trunk, found its way insidiously through the undercarriage, flooded the trunk, and ruined almost seven hundred dollars' worth of Amway products her Platinum upline IBO and sponsor had, just that morning, sort of shamed her into ordering. Soaked to the skin, Mayor Barb gripped the steering wheel and grimly watched as the unholy river curled downhill into the forest again, carrying corn chips, flip-flops, saltwater taffy, cereal boxes, and other sundry General Store merchandise with it to God Only Knows Where.

Up at the freshly reopened Blue Lark Mine, Doug Deere was on hands and knees, crouching on high ground above the washed-out trench in which a reduced stream of Day-Glo yellow hell-water was still drooling from the mouth of the mine. Doug aimed an uncertain flashlight back into the darkness, and his hand began to tremble.

"Oh man. Oh boy. I see gold. Lee? I see gold! Holy Toledo, Lee, I can see the gold! Can you see it? I swear, I can see it! Where's the helmets? Oh, sweet gold, I see it everywhere."

"We can't go in yet," Lee said, as he pulled on rubber boots.

Doug looked at him as if he'd lost his mind.

"Not until we've shored up the opening," Lee said.

"What?"

"C'mon. You know we've got to keep all this loose rock from crashing down and covering the entrance, Doug. Then we've got to check the original timbers for rot and foundation-creep, so that the whole nine yards doesn't cave in on us once we're inside it. We've got to muck out this sediment. Dig a trench for the water to drain—"

"No! No!" Doug shrieked like a petulant third grader. "There's gold in there, Lee! We go in! We get it! We bring it out! Happily ever after!"

"Nobody goes into my mine 'til it's safe," Lee said.

Doug just shook his head. "Don't be a dick."

"You're not going in my mine until it's safe, Doug."

"Look. A) it's not just your mine. *Partner.* And B) try to stop me."

Doug rose to his feet and hopped down into the trench with a big splash, slipped, and was deposited rudely in the soughing muck, hands and arms disappearing to the elbows and his legs stuck fast by suction. Again, Lee briefly considered the moral and legal complications that would arise if he just left Doug glued down there, and how long would it take a man of Doug's considerable size to suffer from lack of food and water, though it was more likely he'd die of exposure, but at least Lee wouldn't have to listen to any more stories.

"Darn it," Doug was saying, depressed. "I could use a little help here."

"Gentlemen?!" A woman's voice barked at them from across the hardpan, and Lee turned and squinted and then shaded his eyes to find Basso Profundo Mayor Barbara on horseback at the edge of the claim, a big, silver town marshal's badge resplendent on her chest, twin Remington rifles holstered on either side of her saddle, and a sidearm strapped to one leg. On the big mare she looked small, her eyes black, her hair salted grey, her latte skin stretched thin by a couple of modest, cut-rate face-lifts; there was a distant trace of Arapaho in the square of her shoulders and the cut of her nose, but the rest was garden gnome and lukewarm Guinness. She didn't look much amused by Doug's pratfall; the orange cast of her still-wet jeans gave Lee his first clue as to her purpose. "Are either of you aware of the Environmental Protection Agency's penalty for the unlawful release of mining effluent?"

Doug stood, his hands uprooted and sluicing mud like a creature in a *Swamp Thing* movie.

"I am, but it's his mine," Doug said.

"Are you a sheriff?" Lee found himself asking. The badge was that phony-looking.

"I'm marshal and mayor and postmistress of Basso Profundo Township, and you're up to your buttocks in EPA violations," the mayor told him. "There's a thousand gallons of toxic waste pouring down my main street, Mr. . . . "

"Garrison," Doug said helpfully. "Lee. G-A-double R-I . . . "

"Shut up," Barb told him. She wasn't a completely hardheaded woman, but when confronted with problems, she preferred a heuristic process and the fat one was harshing her mellow.

"Look," Lee explained, "I'm sorry, really. We were trying to find the opening of the mine, and it just blew out like a, I don't know, geyser or something. Doug here nearly drowned."

The Mayor looked speculatively at Doug.

"You ever hear of Nicholas Creede?" Doug asked.

Lee thought: *Oh Jesus*.

"Son of a farmer, enlistee at sixteen in the Cavalry of George Armstrong Custer as a Quartermaster's protégé, then an Army Scout—"

"Um, Doug? Time out. Maybe the Mayor doesn't want to . . . "

Undaunted, for the next half hour Doug Deere rambled about the too many close shaves with hostile Indians to recount, and how the man could have written several books about his western adventures if he'd taken the time, but how instead he'd caught gold fever and invested eight hard years with no women, hardtack, and a pickax in search of the precious yellow metal before striking the Bonanza Mine north of Central City and making his first pile. "Twenty thousand dollars in one year," Doug said. "Creede turned to silver mining in Leadville and tripled that. It was find after find, crisscrossing the Rockies: Columbia City, Nevadaville, Beaver City,

Tincup, St. Elmo, Rockdale, Winfield, Latchaw, Nederland, Ouray, Silverton, Georgetown, Midland, Ward, Fourmile, and Free Gold Hill. He fell in with a prostitute from Naches, bought her cheetah fur serapes and whalebone tea sets and midget ponies that lived indoors, built a house the size of the governor's mansion, and then had the whore disappeared by some specialists when she became addicted to laudanum because who needs to live with that noise? His income in 1892 was a thousand dollars a day, and it was said that at one point he hired a man simply to walk in front of him spraying sweet-scented waters so that Creede wouldn't have to smell the vagaries of Victorian sanitation practices."

When, however, finally the fat man was finished, Lee had a headache, but Barb's eyes were dreamy and round, her mouth slack, and her horse impatient underneath her. Doug shoved his hands in his pockets and tilted his head like a televangelist about to set his liturgical hook.

"Cut to the chase? It's a gold mine, your honor, and we were anxious to get to it," Doug said.

Mayor Barbara shifted in her saddle. You could almost see the thought bubble: *Gold mine?*

"Well," Doug wound up, "yeah, you know, lot of the original documentation says it was worked for silver, but these old rascals, they used to lie about—"

"I know," the mayor said, cutting him off.

Lee read her face. There was in it something he'd seen in Doug's, at the county records office, when the possibility of a gold mine first arose there: a shift of posture, the slight, soft-jawed confounding, eyes losing some of their near-focus, then finally narrowing, distracted, as if the world were falling away. It was a lucid dream, a promise, a prayer. That gold mine quale.

In quantum terms? Here was another system. Lee knew that different previously isolated, noninteracting systems occupy different phase spaces. And when a new system (Mayor Barb) entangled itself with the environment (the gold mine), the dimensionality of, or volume available to, the new and more complicated but possibly less litigious "joint state vector" (Lee, Doug, Barb, and the mine) increased enormously. Or, to put it more simply (as he would for any of his high school honors physics students who might be interested in pursuing quantum theory in their spare time): Each environmental degree of freedom contributed an extra dimension.

The endeavor expands.

Lee sighed.

"Hey, I've got an extra helmet in the trunk, if you'd like to join us," Lee said to the discomposed marshal, mayor, and postmistress. "We were just about to go in."

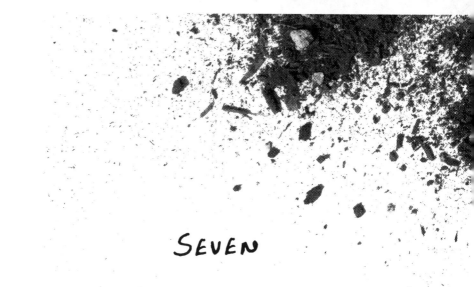

SEVEN

FROM THE DESK OF

303-PYramid 4-4031   **STANLEY BEACHUM, ESQ**   WWW.BEACHUM.COM

Office of the State Court Administrator
Division of Probation Services
101 W. Colfax Ave., Suite 500
Denver, Colorado 80202

To Whom It May Concern:

In the matter of the recently completed probation review and early release of Mr. Grant Garrison, who had been serving a five-year sentence for aggravated assault in the Territorial Prison at Cañon City, I wish to direct my extreme disappointment and utter disbelief to those charged with evaluating the record of the afore-mentioned probationer.

What have you done?

Are you out of your collective minds? Did you read the court record? Or did you choose to ignore it in some, I don't know, puddle-headed belief that releasing an un-repentant criminal into the public arena will result in anything less than further misbehavior? Gentlemen (and women), need I remind you I was the victim of

Mr. Garrison's violent, unprovoked attack? Let me take you back for a moment to the night in question, a clear night, sweet summer dawning, the patio of a local, open-air bistro here in Evergreen. As I meticulously recalled for you in my letter of dissent, I was enjoying an evening of rare bonhomie—to wit, a congenial meal with some friends—when Mr. Garrison intruded, rudely confronted me, berated me for imaginary insults, threatened my companions (who included a close friend and associate of Colorado Governor Vukovich, as I mentioned in my account of it, and who will, I am sorry to say for your sakes, surely be reporting, anecdotally, to the Governor on the next occasion of their meeting), pulled me out of my chair, and, a celebrated pugilist, proceeded to strike at me with his bare fists repeatedly, holding me up so he'd have better leverage, flattening my nose, concussing my brain, fracturing the left supraorbital foramen, my jaw, and shattering my left eardrum, rendering me forever hearing-impaired on that side.

I lost consciousness and woke up drugged and bandaged in the emergency room. I remained in the hospital for a week and still suffer aftereffects, including facial nerve damage and post-traumatic stress.

This is a dangerous man who still has largely unexamined and unmitigated anger-management issues. Two years ago, a clever defense lawyer and a boyish demeanor deceived the court into issuing a lenient punishment for this horrific assault. You have been fooled by the false geniality of a sociopath; I now fear for my very life and limb.

Cordially,
Stan Beachum

"Too direct?"

Beachum searched his wife's impassive face for some clue as to her true opinion of his letter; that she would tell him that it was fine was a given, but so was the certainty that what she told him and what she thought were usually entirely different things.

"It's fine," she said.

He waited.

The baby teetered around the table, making motor noises and grabbing at anything solid for support. Beachum worried about the kid, fourteen months and still not really walking. That couldn't be good. In the Beachum family, babies generally started walking at nine, ten months. Weaned. Talking. Reading at two wasn't uncommon, especially for the girls, who tended toward precocious, according to his mother. This failure to perambulate could only mean that some sketchy, recessive genes from his wife's protein pool had pushed to the front of the baby-building line, so to speak, and now God only knew what other developmental delays and intellectual compromises had been made in the construction of this one.

"It's brittle," she added finally.

"Brittle." Beachum frowned. Brittle?

"And whiny." She picked up the kid and absently checked the diaper and then swung the baby around to face her.

Beachum didn't know which was worse, brittle or whiny.

"And it makes you sound kind of cowardly, actually."

Beachum took the letter away from her and tucked it back into his iPad man bag.

"I mean, rehabilitation, isn't that the whole point of the correctional system, anyway?" his wife asked. "Correction. The successful return to polite society. And I would think they want people getting out early," she said. "Saves taxpayer money, etcetera. You're the big antigovernment, antitax guy."

"This is the man who crippled me."

"Mmmm. And you're expecting the Nanny State to permanently disappear him for you?"

Her tone was playful; she may have been gently teasing him, but Beachum still bit the inside of his mouth and felt the heat in his ears. These conversations never went anywhere productive and were generally better avoided.

"I hope he knows enough not to come back here," Beachum moped.

His wife got up suddenly and let the baby slip, stiff-legged, lightly to the floor with a squawk. From the sink, her back to Beachum, her hips cocked, she asked, "Why would he come back here?" The baby swayed rubbery on soft feet like a Steamboat Willie cartoon, stayed upright for a moment, then folded forward, assumed position, and crawled after her.

"You hear about Lee's gold mine?"

She hadn't, which surprised him. It seemed as if it was all any of his clients who knew Lee (from living in Evergreen, or because he'd taught their kids angles of momentum and how to change the oil in their cars) were talking about. Even in the rich, speculative tradition of Colorado fortune hunting, literally buying a gold mine felt, to the quick-kill, house-flipping, line-of-credit, bubble-chasing, credit, swap, default, and hedge crowd, unhinged.

And yet . . .

Down deep, they wondered if Lee was on to something.

Because . . .

Gold.

Gold. The ur-investment. The ultimate hedge. Gold is the thing people turn to when the world starts to fall apart, despite its impracticality, its relative uselessness. Gold is the safe haven of crackpots and conspiracy theorists, the fallback position of free-market zealots, the mythological go-to manna that speculators and commodity traders worship because of its magical vulnerability to mania.

They mocked Lee. And prayed that his was the fool's errand. Because.

If it wasn't?

They were the fools.

They'd have missed out on a sure thing.

And nothing, Beachum knew, galls the fortune hunter more than missing out on a sure thing.

"He won't come back here," his wife seemed to decide, out of nowhere, about Grant, after Beachum had done the abridged explanation of her ex-husband Lee's latest hijinks. "He's too stubborn and too proud," she said, meaning Grant. "And he never liked it here, anyway. He went to school back East," she pointed out. "There's nothing for him here except Lee, and over half the time those two want to kill each other."

The baby climbed her leg and made its noises: "Bah bah bah bah BAH?" She ignored it, busy with the dishes in the sink. Beachum made a mental note to Google intelligence-enhancing techniques for toddlers. His sister's oldest had listened to Beethoven while the fetus was still in vitro, and now the kid was at some exclusive egghead boarding school in Gstaad, studying cello and nearly fluent in three languages. Switzerland!

"I'm just saying," Beachum said.

He'd had a chance to invest in the Baby Beethoven thing, but that was back when P&Ls were supposed to make some kind of sense, so he'd backed off, and missed out. The stock had gone through the roof before science came along and debunked most of the popular myths about the benefits of prenatal stimulation with case studies and facts. If a man had invested early and got out before the whole thing crashed . . .

Beachum's wife turned to him with her Skeptical Face. She was the most attractive woman who had ever acknowledged him, and he knew she didn't love him but it didn't matter. Beachum was transactional; this wife was a good investment, confirmation of his virility, a long-term asset that you simply held and let appreciate.

"I am ready if he does choose to come back here, though," Beachum reassured her.

"What does that mean?" she asked, continuing to look skeptical, which stressed him.

"It just means I'm ready."

"Ready how?"

"Ready in every way," he said, hoping not to get backed into a corner again. He pushed up from the table. "Ready Freddy," he joked, smiling at the small, possibly developmentally challenged (*dear God*) child hugging his wife's left leg.

The baby burst into tears.

EIGHT

*L*ee had never experienced a darkness as absolute and oppressive as that first pitiless, soundless gloaming in the Blue Lark Mine. Thirty feet in, looking back, the outside world had shrunk to a rectangle of dazzling light, already strange and remote. The headlight on his surplus store miner's helmet knifed forward through the humid air, but darkness pressed in all around it and gave the illusion that what its beam captured was all that existed, shifting as his head moved, whatever it left behind lost to the darkness, no longer real.

Bent over and struggling to keep her balance, Mayor Barbara stayed close behind Lee, and Doug trailed behind them both, still talking:

" . . . four years before his death, Creede was accused of arranging the murder of the man who held the mortgage on his father's farm when the man refused to allow Creede to pay the note. The charges appeared in anonymous letters addressed to Mr. Creede care of the notorious *Rocky Mountain News* reporter E. Jarvis Cassini," Doug explained. "Creede claimed they were blackmail."

"Does he ever effing run out of juice?" Barb asked Lee.

"He's got a big tank," Lee said.

"My second husband was a talker," Barb mused. Her head-lamp futzed on and off schizophrenically. "When he died, I had them sew his mouth shut in case he got the urge to deliver his own eulogy from, you know, the box."

Lee didn't think she was kidding.

"One of the accusers surfaced sometime later." Doug's voice, bouncing brittle off the hard facets of the rock: "Found dead in a Pullman sleeping car in Wilson, Kansas. There was never a connection made to Creede."

"It's a mine for midgets," Barb complained, ignoring him now. Even the mayor had to crouch, as she followed Lee, to avoid banging her helmet on the chiseled stone. The shaft was about five feet in height.

"No, no. Historically," Doug explained to her, "this part was dug by Welshmen. And they're short."

"They are not. Sean Connery is Welsh, and look at him."

"He's a Scot," Doug said.

"Still. He was the best Bond."

"It looks like it opens up just ahead," Lee said.

He kept moving, slowly, bent-over, surprised at the sloppy wetness of the tunnel, everything dripping, boots moiling through the shin-deep mud, and making lewd sucking sounds. Sure enough, another thirty feet and they could stand up straight; a head tilted back revealed, in the light beam, a cavern now thirty feet in height, with timbers crisscrossing it every which way, a latticework of support beams that suggested this part had been mined or had collapsed.

Silt-water ribboned down from the roof shadows; the walls glowed weird and slick. Lee reached out. Doug and the Mayor were still close behind him, afraid to stray. His hand, palm flat, pressed into the wall and disappeared. Deeper, deeper, halfway to his elbow in a wall seemingly made of mud.

"Jesus," Barb said, creeped-out.

"What?"

Suddenly Lee jerked back, tried to pull it out, and screamed as if something had hold of his hand.

"It's got me! Run! Run!"

Barbara and Doug turned and collided, Keystone Kops. Doug yelled, pushed her, Barbara's boots slipped, Lee caught her. He smiled, pulled his hand and arm out of the goo.

"Kidding," he said.

"Oh boy," Doug wheezed, "shoot, oh man, oh man. Don't *do* that. Don't." They both glared at Lee, unamused.

"Sorry." Lee wandered further into the mine. Doug and Barb hung back; they didn't trust him now. For a moment, there was only the soughing of their boots in the mud, the rustle of their clothing, and the soft huff of breathing.

"There's another shaft here that intersects," Lee called back to them, but they couldn't see it, only the beam of Lee's helmet light and a faint ghost of his pink face beneath it.

"I'm going back outside," Barb said. She turned to walk out, and Doug turned to watch her, and his eyes got big.

"There it is," he exclaimed. "Didn't I tell you? Look at that pooch! Place is lined with pure gold!"

To the Mayor's right, where the mine first widened and cut taller, in the light from Doug's helmet, the sloping ceiling seemed studded with fat golden nuggets gleaming back at them. Doug sloshed impulsively forward, shoving past Barbara, falling to his hands and knees again, and crawling the last five feet, pulling himself up, clawing the rock wall to reach up to the glittering roof of the mine just over his head and discovered:

"Drops of water," Doug said with disappointment.

Drops of water that ran down Doug's hand when he touched them. Fat drops that plunked to his helmet, shorting out the light with a fizzling sound, and plunged him into a terrible twilight lit only by the distant square of egress at the end of the short, Welsh-cut mine opening.

"Water. It's just water."

"I thought mines were supposed to be bone dry." Mayor Barbara was wet and disgusted. She looked for Lee, as if it was his fault. But Lee was back at the tunnel junction, and he had his head up, assessing the overhead timbers of the big room.

"You know, before we do anything, we're really going to have to shore all these up," he said.

Clanking sounds came from deep in the mine, down in the mountain, spooking the Mayor.

"There's somebody in here."

"Tommyknockers," Doug told her.

"Tommywhat?"

"Mine ghosts. Actual sound of the mountain, shifting. Rocks groaning. In the old days the miners said they were the ghosts of buried miners, calling for help, trying to get out. Or warning us about cave-ins," he added ominously.

As abruptly as it started, the knocking stopped.

"You know way too much about this stuff," Mayor Barb told Doug. She was ready to leave.

"I know way too much about way too much," Doug confessed, somewhat immodestly. He reached up to slap one of the huge timbers right over his head, continuing, "Lee, I hate to contradict you, but these timbers have been here a hundred years, and I promise you, they ain't going nowhere."

The sodden, rough-hewn beam he slapped shifted slightly, sending a load of loose rock above it showering down on them; the sound of that rockfall mostly drowned out the sound of Doug and Barbara screaming as they hauled ass toward daylight, crouched over, duck-legged, boots sliding in the mud. Lee, no fool, was right behind them, but not screaming. At the entrance, more dust and mud and rock and wood were sliding in from outside, almost in slow motion, but creating a worrisome impediment to their exit. Lee grabbed Barbara and lifted her off her feet, under his arm, pushed past Doug (whose screaming was causing him to lose some pace), and carried the Mayor through the swiftly diminishing strait of cannonading dirt and stone, stumbled out into the blazing sunshine, and didn't stop until he was standing in the shallow ochre pond that had formed in front of the mine at the end of the trench. Lee carefully put Barbara down and steadied her. She brushed limp hair out of her eyes with a clean spot on the crook of her wrist. Doug waddled out of the mine a moment later, missing a boot, still screaming incoherently, and covered so thoroughly with mud and dust that he was primal. The topsoil had stopped caving into the mine. It was, now that they were out of it, a minor backfill, a simple settling of the new excavation that looked to be not nearly as deadly as it had seemed from inside.

The three gazed back at the mine opening in silence, as if trying to make sense of it.

Then Lee smiled. And started to laugh. He laughed loudly, relieved, exhilarated, alive.

It didn't take long for Doug and the Mayor, irreversibly entangled in the venture now, Lee knew, to join in.

Of course later, when he learned of it, Lee felt horrible about and completely responsible for the water damage to Rayna's store. He spent the next weekend helping her muck out the yellow goop and scrub the gritty residue off the floors and walls with sudsy buckets of Barb's Amway flagship multipurpose Liquid Organic Cleaner after the goop had dried. Lee was helping her in the sense that Rayna sat behind the checkout counter while he mopped and swept and cleaned and ordered supplies that Rayna tallied up on a shipping document.

"A case of ten-penny nails . . . "

"Mayor Barb says you're a high school teacher."

"Four dozen galvanized steel tie-downs . . . "

"My mom taught second grade, before she had kids."

"Twenty twelve-bys . . ."

"Thanks for helping me clean up."

"No, check that: twenty-five." He looked up at her. "Those come in sixteen-foot lengths?"

Occasionally when he looked up, he found himself meeting her level gaze; she had been staring at him, not writing. More than once when this happened, his heart juddered like a schoolboy's, and he thought: *What the fuck?* This time, however, she was studying her list.

"What's your wife have to say about your gold mine?" Rayna asked.

"We don't know it's a gold mine," Lee said, fazed. "And, anyway," he clarified, "she, my wife, doesn't say anything."

"Why not?"

"No, ex-wife, not, no, anymore."

"Ooo. Is that English?" Now of course she glanced up at him.

"Divorced, is what I'm trying to say. I mean. I'm. Me. Not married. How did you—?"

"The ring."

And, as if cued from offstage, Lee twisted his wedding band nervously. "Ah. Right."

Rayna was immediately apologetic: "Sorry. Sorry. It's just . . . my radar's up. Kind of a rebound thing."

She held up her own left hand. No ring.

"From what?"

"The new me," she said, not answering the question.

"From the new you?" Lee was confused.

"No."

"Were you married?"

"Not exactly." Then: "How many twelve-bys?"

"Mine won't come off," Lee told her. "Honest to God." Lee held up his hand, wiggling the finger. "It's stuck."

"Metaphor?"

"I teach shop," Lee said, frowning, fazed again.

Rayna waited for Lee to catch up; she chewed on the end of her pen as if she couldn't have cared less whether he was married or not. A sort of comfortable silence settled between them, and for once Lee didn't try to figure out what it meant or ruin it. He resumed sweeping.

A graphite-grey Range Rover came up the street, slowly, and inside it a couple of tawny faces turned, nearly in unison, to look into the store at Lee, their eyes preternaturally white even behind the extra-dark faux-gangsta tint of the Rover windows. Its chrome hubcaps spun past, gone.

"Five hundred feet of nine-gauge electrical wire," Lee had resumed ordering, "four dozen clip-on lights . . . "

"You could cut it off."

Stopping, mid-sweep: "What?"

"You could cut the ring off," Rayna said. "How long have you been divorced?"

There was another, but less comfortable, silence born of a strange, probing intimacy Lee hadn't felt in a long time.

The Range Rover had turned around and was coming back. This time Lee looked back at the faces of the two men staring out at him. They were, what, holy moly if they weren't Indian, as in not Native American, as in factory-direct from Mumbai, but sporting fancy cowboy-cut dress shirts that fit their narrow shoulders as if they were tailored. Framed by the windows of a Range Rover, Indians on the main street of Basso Profundo, a complete non sequitur, and then gone.

"Lee?"

"Fourteen months. Fourteen months since it was final. Look, do we have to talk about this?"

"No. Sorry."

Rayna's eyes fell, her head inclined, and she studied the or-der form. Lee looked out the window at nothing and wished he hadn't said what he just said. He did want to talk about it. He wanted to talk to Rayna about it, but now she wouldn't even look up at him.

"I should probably get some duct tape," Lee said finally.

Rayna, nodding, writing it down, agreed, observing dryly that there probably wasn't a project worth doing that didn't involve duct tape.

THE SPECTER OF
WANT AND DISASTER

Nine

THE KANSAS CITY STAR METRO SECTION, PAGE 10B, BELOW THE FOLD:

SALINA MAN FOUND HANGED IN BASEMENT
by Ainsy Farrow
Exclusive to The Star

It was a smell that Marissa Dbrovna had hoped she would someday forget. The perfume of death, a body in decay, wafting through her kitchen window on morning breezes, she was sure of it. But it took her four days to convince the Salina police to send a car and checkw it out.

Yesterday morning, Patrolmen Bob Flynn and Stuart Nelson forced entry and found an elderly man hanging from a clothesline noose in the basement of a rust-brick house in the 2200 block of Logan Street.

The Salina County Coroner estimates the victim had been dead for eight to ten days. Cause of death was strangulation. The name of the victim is being withheld until authorities can find and notify his next of kin.

Neighbors who gathered on the sidewalk in front of the crime scene spoke of a lively, gregarious septuagenarian who loved to regale them with stories of his purported adventures as a modern-day gold miner in the mountains of Colorado and Utah.

"He just recently sold a darn mine on eBay, if you can believe it," Mikey Lowell said. "Over thirty thousand bucks, I saw the darn check. Either that, or he was really good at lying."

For Dbrovna, a soft-spoken woman "well into" her forties, the smell of the ripening corpse was a chilling reminder of a 1993 massacre in Ahmici, Herzegovina, a largely Bosniak village from which Dbrovna fled more than a decade ago. Over a period of several hours, Croat soldiers murdered at least 120 villagers, including women and children, in the culmination of the Lasva Valley Ethnic Cleansing Campaign. A subsequent war crimes trial at The Hague resulted in numerous verdicts against high-ranking Croat military leaders, and even some politicians.

"Men shot at point-blank," Dbrovna remembered. "Houses set fire to with flame launchers. Much with the raping. Children, their little bodies charred.

"I hid in a smoking shed," she said. "I saw it with my eyes. Two mosques even in Donji, blown up with the explosives."

Dbrovna did not know the neighbor who hanged himself, despite living next door to him.

"We were hand-waving friends," she explained. "Taking the garbage, there he is, make to wave. You know.

Coming and going, hello, wave. But we did not talk of things, even small things, no.

"And now he is gone. It's horrible."

Police officials and scientific investigation technicians were observed going in and out of the house throughout the day and into the night. Salina Police Department Spokesperson Missy Holiman said the investigation is ongoing.

TEN

*D*owntown Evergreen was as he remembered it, just a slowed-down, two-lane stretch of Highway 74, at the confluence of the Cub and Bear Creeks, a narrow canyon lined with shops and businesses trying hard to stay rustic. The plumbing truck rolled to a stop at the single stoplight on the highway, and as it idled there, Grant slid out of the back with his nylon bag, slapped the fender, and waved goodbye to the driver, whose name he'd already forgotten, and who, grinning back at Grant from the big side mirror, stuck one hairy arm out the window, and aimed his waggling fat thumb skyward.

Grant dodged through traffic to the covered sidewalk in front of The Little Bear. He was welcomed home by a pretty discouraging, greasy blast of hot, beefalo burger barbecue smog, blown down from the kitchen vents by a swirling breeze, but he did not go inside. Through the open door he could hear what he worried was a B-side Nitty Gritty Dirt Band song, and he thought he saw, in the saloon gloom, a few familiar faces sucking the early beer and arguing about anything. He had not thought about The Little Bear during his one year, eight months, and twenty-seven days away. He hadn't thought about Evergreen at all, one way or the other. It was not in the chemistry of Grant's genome to dwell on the past or in the past; his was always forward movement, and not so much purposeful or deliberate as inevitable, like the tornado on the horizon or the drunk driver crossing into your lane. Forward, in this case, meant uphill, skirting the highway, through the new retail development designed to cater to the continuous growth of the commuter population; Evergreen had begun as a logging camp, and then a trading post so that miners from Idaho Springs and Bailey could save three days and avoid a trip to Denver or Golden. For the first half of the twentieth century, it thrived as a tourist town with cabins for rent and a man-made lake and a number of swank alpine hotel resorts. But the interstate that cut through the Front Range to the north opened up the entire area to Denver developers looking for prime mountain acreage on which to build the kind of quarter-acre-of-heaven Colorado exurbs that Denver yuppies and rednecks and ex-hippies all craved after a few years in what Lee liked to call "Omaha with a Mountain View."

Grant took the jogging path over the dam and skirted the far edge of the Evergreen Public Golf Course, Colorado's first mountain golf course, carved in 1925 out of the former ranch of pioneer cattle rustler Julius C. Dedisse, who, when he willed the mountain park to the City of Denver and named it Eden, possibly intended it to be a 420-acre utopian clothing-free zone, but Denver had more modest plans. The City built the thirty-foot dam on the frisky flooding Bear Creek, creating the lake that ate the golf balls of all future unsuspecting golfers who, unfamiliar with high-altitude and rock-hard fairways, hit straight and long between the fairway bunkers, as any sane player would, and watched their tee shots carom crazily off the hardpan fescue, and, in never more than two or three spectacular bounces, plop into the lake short of the bunkers. Lee and Grant had done a brisk business with a borrowed canoe and a couple of telescoping ball-retrieval implements one summer until the club pro chased them off.

Grant quickly found the hiking trail that had once connected course and lake and Dedisse Park to the self-proclaimed Gem of the Rockies, Troutdale-in-the-Pines. A four-story, lichen-rock–covered, three-hundred-room resort hotel on a beautiful bend in Bear Creek Canyon, Troutdale was, when Lee and Grant were growing up, the site of so many battles and skirmishes and trespasses and betrayals, they considered it their personal playground. Shut down and abandoned in 1961, locked in endless litigation and grand plans for reopening as an executive retreat or a drug rehabilitation center (depending on the county meeting you might have attended), Troutdale-in-the-Pines was their clubhouse in the summer, haunted all fall, an icy fortress in the winter, and Camelot Castle in the spring. They couldn't get to school without passing it. Their parents forbade them from going in it, but were, not surprisingly, helpless to prevent them from doing so. There was supposed to be a security presence on-site, but that would have been Sheriff Edgerly, the former Clear Creek County lawman whose fondness for fruity liquor got him un-elected and prematurely retired, and ultimately prevented him from operating a motor vehicle, which, contractually, he would have needed to get from his double-wide in Conifer to Troutdale in order to fulfill his responsibilities as court-appointed caretaker of the property. The boys were on their own, free to search for artifacts of the dignitaries and celebrities who had supposedly stayed there in its heyday: Herbert Hoover and William Jennings Bryant, Esther Williams, Ty Cobb, Lillian Gish and Groucho Marx and Lionel Barrymore; free to invent wild tales that the hotel was haunted in order to keep other kids away; free to get drunk on 3.2 beers and piss out the windows; free to make war with each other, room to room, with broomsticks and Tony the Tiger Styrofoam antennae balls and, later, Airsoft guns and frozen snowballs. It was in the ballroom of Troutdale-in-the-Pines that Grant first got laid, on a cushion of parkas, by a limber, enthusiastic Marion Gilroy, not the backseat of the Plymouth, as he later told Lee, which was the opening salvo of their civil war. Grant had, for some sentimental reason, wanted to spare the hotel from becoming their Fort Sumpter; now, coming out of the trees, he was confronted by the half-completed, riverside housing development, Troutdale Estates, and while Grant remembered everything about the old resort, all the adventures, all the mistakes, he felt no sense of its loss. Burned down by vagrants, demolished, graded, and subdivided, of the hotel only the hand-built stone retaining wall along one arc of the river remained. New asphalt curled through the trees linking fat, two-story, neo-eclectic homes with detached garages and dryscaped lots of sustainable native plants and postal boxes on rough-hewn cedar posts.

In the driveway of a hillside home, a slender, striking woman in her mid-thirties struggled to put a baby into a car seat in the back of her new white Hyundai minivan while keeping her just-past-its-sell-by-date coiffure from getting smushed by the sliding door. Successful, she disappeared into the house and returned with a Swedish jogging stroller that she folded up and threw in the back of the car.

Across the street and down the hill, Grant stood motionless, watching her, with a slightly confounded expression on his face. Just watched as the young woman slammed the car doors shut, got behind the wheel, and fired up the V6. The Korean car burned a little oil. She backed out of the driveway and drove past Grant. He turned his back to the street and looked, his hands jammed contemplatively in his jeans pockets, as if there was something really interesting about the unsold house in front of which he was standing.

After it had passed him, Grant turned again and watched the white car until it disappeared around a curve. For the next sever-al moments it seemed to flutter through the trees, appearing, dis-appearing, appearing, dappled with light like a memory he was trying to recall. Or forget. Then it was gone altogether and Grant picked up his nylon duffle and returned through the pine forest in the direction he had come.

Redolent with a pesky afterburn of patchouli from Dr. Harounian's eau de cologne, the Evergreen High School teachers' lounge was also suspiciously silent when Lee walked in to refresh his coffee. Three or four teachers were scattered around the big table trying to A) ignore the donut tray, and B) create sufficient distance between themselves and Harounian (Spanish I, II, III, and seventh grade Health), who was reading the morning paper and grading tests. The coffee smelled like burned cinnamon, which meant that Mrs. Coslet (Civics and Pep Squad) had reimposed her will on the Bunn-o-Matic. But caffeine was caffeine, and Lee was refilled and shaking the Coffee Mate into his cup when there was a rustling of papers behind him, the squeaking of a chair, and "How's that gold mine, Mr. Garrison?"

Lee turned. Vandenberg (AP Bio, Botany, and Intro to Earth Science) grinned back at him in a friendly way that was, for Vandenberg, insanely out of character.

"Terrific, Mr. V.," Lee said. "Fantastic."

Vandenberg just smiled and nodded like a bobblehead. Lee took his coffee cup and walked out. From the hallway, after the door closed behind him, Lee could hear everyone back in the lounge burst into laughter about something.

He didn't break stride.

Automotive class was a block period, almost two full hours, an elective that in many districts had been eliminated due to lack of funding, but Evergreen was flush with tax base from those upscale Denver expat commuters, who demanded a lively and varied curriculum for their gifted children, most of whom, despite sterling transcripts, would choose to stay in Colorado and wind up in middle management at a data storage or telecommunications company. Nobody seemed to mind that the future of the internal combustion engine was murky, at best, or that none of the kids crowded around Lee—worrying over the engine of a Dodge Ram truck chassis that had wheels and transmission and steering wheel and seat and no body whatsoever—would likely ever look under the hood of their cars after high school. There were fourteen boys and one girl. Lee also taught physics, but it was the practical classes, auto and wood shop, that made his day.

"The action of the pistons accomplishes two things: On the downstroke, it pulls the fuel into the firing chamber; on the upstroke, it brings oil from below to lubricate the cylinder, at the same time compressing the fuel mixed with oxygen, which is ignited by the spark, causing an explosion that drives the piston back down into the cylinder and results in what?" Lee asked.

No one spoke up. At least four students were texting on cell phones, heads down, hands pulled in. Lee's laissez-faire classroom policy toward personal peripherals and new technology was fairly scandalous among his fellow faculty.

"Something good on YouTube, Gary?"

One of the texters looked up, but not guiltily.

"Anybody?"

"Torque."

Lee knew the voice, but was momentarily disoriented by it. Not a student. Not a teacher, unless Biederman was disguising his Chicago-born Northern Cities Vowel Shift. The voice came from behind him. That Biederman knew anything about torque was questionable. Lee turned: Grant, in the doorway.

"Torque. That could be right," Lee said.

"Nothing moves without torque." Grant crossed and Lee got up and the brothers embraced in an embarrassing bear hug.

"You aren't supposed to be out for another three months."

"I was rewarded for extremely good behavior."

"You should have called me."

"Why? You know I like busses." Grant became aware of the class, gaping at them. "What are you little pissholes looking at?"

The boys who were snickering suddenly fell silent. The lone female, a gender-confused six-footer who called herself Dotty, blushed. The classroom smelled of cedar and pine and petroleum oils. There was a huge, unfinished wooden cross splayed out on sawhorses in the back of the shop. Grant knew better than to ask about it.

"We're brothers," Grant explained, finally. Then he hauled off and kissed Lee full on the mouth, startling everybody, including Lee.

"Or at least that's our story," Grant added.

ELEVEN

L̲ee's house, the house they both grew up in, was a Colorado ranch-style, the comfort food of Rocky Mountain residential architecture: L-shaped, cross-gabled, and unpretentiously trimmed in redwood-stained cedar. Its thick eyebrows of rambling, overhanging eaves sheltered dark thermopane windows bracketed by faux shutters and little concrete patios jutting out from sliding doors everywhere. A steep roof of fire-resistant cedar shake shingles stepped down smartly to the requisite three-car garage. Once it had been the center of their universe, but, after their parents were killed by a drunk driver on U.S. 285 and Lee came back from college to live with Grant as he finished high school, whatever gravity had kept them in its orbit was gone. The house needed new gutters, fresh paint, and purpose. It was a book with the pages ripped out. A shell washed up by yesterday's storm.

An over-easy sun was settling in the crook of Mount Evans as Lee's Jeep pulled into the driveway. Lee got out, carrying bags of takeout Cowboy Ming Chinese food and talking nonstop:

"The main shaft goes eight hundred feet into the mountain, and there are two branch shafts that go a hundred and twenty-two respectively, left and right, plus a downsloping shaft that's filled with water, but we sunk a fifty-foot line down it and couldn't touch bottom."

Grant dragged his single suitcase out of the back of the Jeep and glanced at the suppositorial bumps and long shadows of Lee's side lawn septic-tank installation (reminiscent of "Cadillac Ranch," a.k.a. Carhenge, the Ant Farm Art Collective's Amarillo planting of ten nose-down, half-buried cars in the Texas flatlands at angles supposedly corresponding to the Great Pyramid of Giza, although Grant was fairly certain Lee had no knowledge of it when he installed the things) before hurrying up the steps after his brother.

"Of course, we didn't go all the way in since we're still shoring up the main timbers; we used Doug's laser level to guesstimate the distances. It could be that the branch shafts take a hard turn deeper in, in which case there's no telling how far they go."

Lee stood in the middle of the empty living room, where two folding aluminum lawn chairs comprised the furniture, and faced a tiny flat-screen TV resting uncertainly on its own upended cardboard box. Grant hadn't seen his brother so excited about anything in a long time.

"And as for the downshaft, again according to Doug, they didn't go down unless there was something really valuable to be had below because of the, you know, considerable difficulty of bringing the ore up."

"The fuck is this Doug?"

"What?"

"Doug."

"Oh, he's—"

"Maybe we should eat in the kitchen."

"Ideally you'd slot another, lower shaft on an angle in from the mountain, of course, so you didn't undermine your primary ingress."

"Lee."

"Yeah?"

"We gonna eat the Chinese or what?"

"Yeah. Lemme just . . . " Lee put the bags down and went into the kitchen, where he made a lot of noise, and returned with five mutant chopsticks evidently crossbred with sporks.

"In case one breaks," Grant observed.

"What?"

"Lee."

"What?"

"I'm out."

"Yeah."

"I can't believe I'm out."

"I know. Me neither."

"Your haircut's for shit."

"I know."

"You still going to Shorty? He's blind."

"I know. But he hasn't raised his prices in twenty years."

"Because he's blind."

"True." Lee tugged at the unruly nest on his forehead with resignation. Grant just grinned at him fondly.

"So who is this Doug?"

Lee had piles of photographs of the mine, five-by-seven color snapshots, plus hundreds of jpegs on his laptop that he could put in slide-show mode to pop music that Grant didn't recognize. Lee found a snapshot of himself, Doug, and Mayor Barb, badly framed, standing, smiling, next to the entrance to the Blue Lark. Their legs were comically dripped in incandescent mustard mud. Lee thumbed the grinning image of Doug Deere, whose right hip and love handles were sliced off by the edge of the picture:

"He's the Clear Creek County Clerk."

"And then some. And who's the pony keg?"

They stood in the kitchen and ate Kung Pao chicken at the counter with Cowboy Ming chop-sporks while the jpegs faded one into the next on the luminous laptop screen. There was, Grant had noticed immediately, no refrigerator in the kitchen, just the space where one should be. That was going to be one of his next questions, but he wanted to let his brother's batteries run down a bit further.

"That's Mayor Barb."

"Holy bull dyke, Batman."

"Cut it out. She's not. And anybody ever point out you're a homophobe?"

"You. And I probably am. What's your point?"

"She's just—"

"Manly?"

"Astray."

"A stray."

"No. Astray. Off course. Amiss. She's mayor and the law and the sole postal person of Basso Profundo and she hawks Amway, in case you need some vitamins or cleaning products. It turns out I'm out-of-bounds EPA-wise with a variety of toxic effluents as a consequence of my opening the mine, so it's actually pretty fortuitous for me to have her on the team."

"Yeah, and, so, about your 'team' . . . "

"But I should caution you," Lee continued, cutting his brother off, "sometimes Barb talks of multiple ex-husband chicanery and the distinct possibility of disowned progeny, so you'll need to really watch your mouth with her, Grant, or she might shoot your balls off and mount them over her fireplace."

Grant smiled. "Next to yours?"

"I think mine are over a different fireplace."

Grant nodded, thoughtful. "Basso what?"

"Profundo."

"Oh bro. That shitty little would-be ghost town up toward Keystone? I hate that place."

"Well it's beautiful, up above."

"In an oxygen-deprived kinda way. Lee, if we strip away the romance, you know, your usual dreamy shroud of idealistic I-don't-know-what, and cut to the chase, as they say, whoever they are: Is there gold in this mine or what?"

Lee put the snapshot of Barb back in a different pile than the one he took it from and resumed showing Grant another pile of more scholarly studies of the mine proper.

"This one's from inside."

"Lee."

"We rigged up low-voltage lights down the main tunnel to where it branches out."

"Lee. I hate it when you go all parallel."

Lee opened a kitchen cabinet and reached among the books stored there for an old U.S. Geological handbook with mining claim surveys in it.

"According to the School of Mines survey, it's a drift mine, which means it goes straight into the side of the mountain rather than vertically down, with tunnels branching horizontally off from the downshaft. Although there is a downshaft *inside* my mine, but that's another story, and it's still a drift mine because of the straight-in egress." Grant yawned. "Anyway," Lee continued, "it's smallish, for a drift mine, as if they just got started, which is exciting because it could mean it never played out. There are three principal shafts and one that caved in, right here. Now, USGS says the mine is silver, zinc, and lead. But this old geologist who hiked up there told me the tailings are gold mine tailings, and Doug says a lot of times the old miners would fudge their yield reports to conceal the fact they were sitting on gold. I mean, you'd be amazed, man, these guys were always lying about yields, about locations, about assays."

"Dog eat dog," Grant said.

"Exactamente."

"Or Doug eat dog, from the looks of him." Grant waited for Lee to laugh, which he didn't. "So we're talking how much in potential value?"

Lee clammed up.

"You thought I'd forgotten my original question."

"No."

"Is there any precious metal in the mine?"

"I don't know. I don't care. That's not the point."

"Mmm. What is the point?"

Lee took a deep breath, held it, exhaled.

"I'm not judging," Grant said. "I swear. I need to know."

"Okay. Well. Yes, I guess it would be okay if there was some gold," Lee admitted.

"Was that so hard to say?"

"But it's not . . . not the goal." Lee stammered, "I mean, the goal is just the looking. You know what I'm saying? The hunt. To be honest, it will almost be disappointing to actually find anything because then inevitably it will turn into something altogether different. Not what I want. A business venture. You know? A job."

Grant said that this sounded like early justification for the possibility of not finding anything. A kind of preemptive rationalization of failure. Lee admitted it might sound that way, but insisted the mine project, as he called it, was part of a larger metaphor of exploration and self-discovery, which, Grant conceded, after pointing out how incredibly lame *that* sounded, was in Lee's case, anyway, long overdue and welcome as long as it didn't lead to ridicule and public humiliation.

"The septic field is an art installation," Lee pointed out, defensively.

"You bought the gold mine on eBay," Grant said.

"I don't care what other people are saying."

It was true; Lee never did. Grant thumbed the pictures of Doug and Barb and wondered aloud mordantly if Lee's putative partners understood that the gold wasn't the point.

"They can think what they want to think" was Lee's answer.

"Explain to me again why you need a team?"

"I don't. No, you're right. It's just, like I said, Barb is like insurance, and additionally advantageous, in a civic sense, not to mention kind of lonely and lost, and Doug . . . well, Doug is kind of like a really crappy copy of *The Great Gatsby* with the cover almost coming off and notes in the margins scribbled by some pretentious ass, but, actually, and you hate to admit this, useful sometimes, so you can't bring yourself to throw it away, even if you get a first edition for Christmas."

But Grant was more interested in another photograph, one that caught his eye when Lee shuffled past it. He took the stack from Lee and found it again.

"Who's this?"

Lee looked. "Oh," he said. "That's Rayna," he said. Then Lee continued, his finger drawing imaginary lines of intersect on the USGS map book, "So anyway my theory is that the gold, or silver, or whatever, was here, where it all caved in, which means we just have to dig laterally from here . . . to here. And we'll find it."

Grant wasn't listening. He studied the photograph of the young woman in front of the General Store. Shorts and a T-shirt. Lovely. Casting her disapproving eye and tilted smile at Lee and Doug in their Halloweenish mining getups.

"Maybe Rayna's the gold mine."

Lee stopped talking and looked at his brother and took the photo away and slipped it carefully back into the stack of snapshots in his hand.

"Local girl, Grant. Not your type."

"No?"

"Nope."

Grant considered himself a pretty good student of Lee's inflection and intonation, which rarely corresponded directly to his mood, but after years and years of close study, it could be decoded with some confidence, and, taking into account the roughly twenty-one-month absence during which time Lee might conceivably have learned to hide his signals (though Grant doubted it), the statement "not your type" carried a weight and a worry and a forceful possessiveness that Grant had not seen in Lee in, like, forever. Or maybe never.

It cheered him right up.

And Grant, being Grant, also took it as a challenge.

"Check it out." Lee held up a hideous picture from inside the mine in which the camera flash had essentially turned every surface into a tiny plane of hellfire. "Here's that vertical downshaft I was talking about. I think what they did was they tried to go down to get back to the gold, which was here."

"Is that water?"

"Yeah, I told you the mine was filled with water."

"You think of a mine, you think, I dunno, dry. Dusty. Underground desert."

"No, mostly they're wet."

"Huh."

Lee held up another photograph. "Here's looking back to the entrance," he continued. "See how low that first length of tunnel coming in is?"

"You talk to Lorraine ever?"

"What?" Lee glanced expressionlessly at Grant, but failed to convey the intended sense of I-don't-care.

"Lorraine. Talk. Do you?"

"No." Lee held his brother's stare evenly. "Why?"

"Oh, I dunno. Because."

"Uh-huh."

"Because it's been, what, almost two years, and you haven't even replaced the fucking fridge."

"I don't cook much."

"You don't cook with a fridge, bro. You put beer in it."

Lee changed subjects. "The mine's in both our names."

Grant frowned. "It's what?"

"I put the deed to the gold mine in both our names. In case something happens to me, I want you to have it, and in case we actually find something, I want you to have half."

"What would happen to you?"

"I don't know. I'm just," then he stopped. "You know."

Silence. The two brothers stared at each other. Grant smiled.

"What about your team?"

"We're just playing around, you know. Being miners. Out in the fresh air."

"They're gonna want a piece of it."

"Sure. They work hard; they're helping. We'll figure it out if it comes to that."

"You didn't give them shares, did you?"

"Of the land? No. God no. Just you and me, on the deed."

Grant shook his head. "You're an idiot."

"Yeah, well. It's in the blood."

"Not in my blood."

"Our parents were Civil War reenacters," Lee pointed out to his brother. "So. All bets are pretty much off."

"True dat," Grant laughed.

"Remember the story about when Mom tried to join the Second Colorado Volunteer Infantry for the battle of Honey Springs down in Oklahoma?"

Grant couldn't stop laughing. "As a man."

"They didn't allow women to participate."

Still laughing: "Stop."

"Before we were born. With the fake mustache," Lee said, "and a rolled-up sock down her pants and the chest binder that broke when she fell during an ill-fated flanking charge, and this medic rushed over to check for a heartbeat and got a faceful of Mom's funbag, and Dad got up and coldcocked the guy with the butt of his musket, and then they bolted away and had to hide in a thicket of chokecherry bushes until everybody else went home. Like, ten hours. With all these pissed-off Okie battlefield organizers looking for them."

"I take it back," Grant wheezed. "The gene pool. We are so doomed."

"And that was one of their more successful outings," Lee observed.

Grant laughed with his brother and felt happy, which felt stupid and weird after not feeling anything for so long. He loved Lee in the most complicated and conflicted way possible, which is to say, in the only way Grant could love anyone. He looked down at the School of Mines survey plat. Concentric free-form lines of elevation, the faint green shading, the numbers, tiny, precise.

"Here to here?" he said. "Looks easy enough. What's the big problem?"

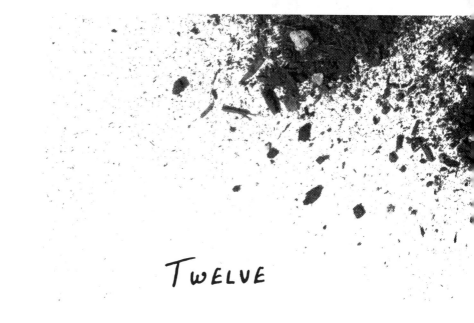

TWELVE

*P*ROBLEM #1:

The earsplitting roar of a giant rental jackhammer nearly disemboweled Grant as he and Lee drove the hellish two-man implement into a two-foot depression on one wall of the mine shaft, just past where the main tunnel split into three, spitting sparks and rock chips until Grant yelped in pain and shut it off.

"MOTHERcocksuckingsonofabitch! Fuck me!"

He staggered away, spitting grit, brushing hot rock off his bare arms, past where Mayor Barb was standing with a hose.

"Wash it down!" Lee shouted, gesturing. She opened the nozzle and directed a pulsing stream of water pumped from the bottomless downshaft at the freshly hewn rock.

Grant continued sloshing out through the viscous mud that still comprised the floor. A string of overhead lights drew a line for him to the bright daylight of the mine entrance. Halfway there, in the low tunnel Grant had dubbed "fucking Cardiff-in-a-Hole," Doug was bent over, painfully chunk-shouldered, mucking the mud into what looked to be a wheelbarrow from hell, dripping and skim-coated in evil itself. Grant squeezed past him, ripping foam plugs out of his ears.

"That is torture. No one, *no one* should voluntarily work one of those fuckers," Grant said. "No one."

He stumbled out of the mine and squinted uncomfortably in the bright sunlight, his eyes screwed up until they adjusted. He turned off his headlight, dropped his helmet on the level ground, and hunched against the shovel of the backhoe, finally going hands on knees, spitting grit again.

PROBLEM #2:

Doug soon careened out with his wheelbarrow and dumped the gelatinous Day-Glo mud from the tunnel into a little leeching pond of mine water. He sat heavily on a crate, exhausted, and looked at Grant.

"They use. Those horizontal hand-jacks at. That molybdenum mine up by Empire. I was told. A miner up there. Can go six feet. In a day. Solo."

"Don't talk when you can't breathe, Doug."

"I'm. Breathing. Fine. Winded. Thin air. Good aerobic."

"Jesus. You think this is fun, don't you?"

Doug hacked up some sediment and spat it into the leeching pond. "No. I'm dog tired," Doug admitted. "But. I'm a shareholder, and it's only fair. Pull my weight. I've got to hold up my end."

Grant stared at him and palpated a pressure point behind his ears, trying to ward off the cluster headache he could feel coming on.

"Shareholder? Lee gave you a piece of the mine?"

"Well, of any output, yes," Doug insisted. "Ten percent, just like Barb."

"Is that your reckoning or is it somewhere in writing?"

"Well—"

"Based on what?"

Doug didn't like where this conversation was headed, so he started a new one: "Lee says you just got out of jail."

"You guys didn't put up any of the money, did you?"

"What were you in prison for?"

"There's no gold in there," Grant told the fat man. "I hope you realize that. This is just like the septic tanks. It's Lee's new performance art piece. You know. He's gone all Yoko Ono and shit again."

"What?"

And Grant was about to launch into the story of Lee's front lawn found-art installation, which he had told many times, when:

PROBLEM #3:

Mayor Barb came rushing out of the mine, grinning like a lunatic. "Found some," she said.

"No way."

Grant: "Whoa, what?"

"Way." They both ignored Grant.

Doug heaved himself up. "Where?"

"You know that niche above the beams, just past the main intersection?"

Doug examined the shiny, misshapen nuggets in Barb's outstretched hand. "Fool's gold."

"It is not."

"Iron pyrite. Fool's gold."

"No, look, it's dull, it's not shiny, and—"

Doug scooped the rocks out of her hand and threw them down the mountain.

"Hey!"

In his maddeningly homespun and grandiloquent way, Doug proceeded to explain to Barb and Grant, should Grant care to listen in, that mineral pyrite is an iron sulfide with a pale- to normal-brass-yellow hue, sometimes shiny, sometimes not, with the chemical formula of FeS_2. The most common of the sulfide minerals, it is often found in quartz veins, sometimes even coupled with small quantities of gold, because gold and arsenic can occur as a coupled substitution in the pyrite structure. It took Doug about forty-six minutes to cover the topic, by the end of which time Grant was ready to take a handful of pyrite and stuff it down the plus-sized County Clerk's piehole.

"So there could of been gold in there!" Barb exclaimed.

"Well, only in Nevada, factually," Doug said, and was clearly prepared to move on to a larger-scale geological lecture involving Carson City and the eastern slope of the Sierras, but this time Barb cut him off.

"Eff you, Douglas. And the forklift that delivered you."

The argument devolved into insults. Grant's head felt like it was going to explode. Light fractured, the sky heaved away, and he sat down and let their voices break across him, incomprehensible, and watched the vast forest of slender firs rock and scissor in the wind. His eyes closed. Lurid colors splattered in the resulting darkness, his ears still ringing from the jackhammer. A veil lifted.

This was the moment Grant decided that he needed to save Lee from the mine.

"Twenty-two inches!" Lee came out of the mountain carrying the huge jackhammer over his shoulder, exhausted, his face pale with rock dust, and happy as a clam.

"Almost two feet!" Lee said, lost his balance, and toppled sideways and backward under the weight of the pneumatic drill.

Only sixty-four more to go, Grant thought.

The fancy, trailored ATVs parked outside and pulled by dualies belonged to a couple of overweight local men who loitered at the cash register of Rayna's General Store, chewing the fat. No sign of Rayna, though.

"Hear he paid about twice market value for it, too," one of the men snarked, as the bell on the door jingled and Grant came in, shedding mine dust. "And now they're working it," the man continued to explain to his incredulous friend, giving Grant the cursory look-over-and-dismissal, "with picks and shovels. He and crazy Barb and this other county payroll moron."

Grant went down the chips aisle to the back, pulled a can of Squirt from the rack in the refrigerator, then hesitated when he saw Dr Pepper stocked two racks over. Squirt had tang, but the Doctor was tempting.

"What is he, some Highland Park hedge fund a-hole who cashed in before the subprime mortgage thing?"

Equally tempting for Grant was a pint of Mountain Dew MDX. He tried to stay focused on the beverages.

"No, dude. High school teacher."

"No shit. Well, there you go. Those lazy bastards only work nine months a year."

"I know."

"Public sector union sucks."

"True dat," the paler one rapped. "It's probably a big kabuki sham he's cooked up to hook some angel investment money."

"Hi."

Both local men fell silent as Grant slipped between them and put bottles of Squirt, Dew, and Dr Pepper on the counter. He was smiling. He was Mr. Amiable.

"I'm Grant."

"Hey Grant." The two local men traded stage-frowns, wondering: *Who is this clown?*

Rayna emerged from the back room. "Guys, I can't find any Red Man. You'll just have to make do with Copennnnn . . . " Her voice trailed off as she noticed Grant. There was the faintest shift in her eyes and bearing, as if she were thinking, *Oh crap, here we go again.*

"I'm the lazy bastard's brother," Grant was telling the two men, but he was watching Rayna.

The men had fallen very quiet.

"Just got out of state prison," he said. "Can't describe for you how terrific it feels." Grant kept smiling. The feet of the men shuffled uneasily. Rayna rang up his sodas, trying to will away the faint flush that was on her cheeks. Grant watched her and waited, expecting the usual melt. But Rayna held fast at mildly distracted, and her eyes made no promises.

Interesting.

"What were you in for?" The locals looked more than a little worried now: How much had this guy overheard?

"Bad temper," Grant said, without turning to them.

The local men became very still. Rayna counted out change for Grant's twenty, and put it in his hand, her fingers brushing his. Her skin was cool and dry. Up close her features were a little lopsided in a way that didn't bother him. She asked if there was anything else he needed.

Grant looked at the change, looked up at her, and his mood lifted. *Definitely not fool's gold*, he thought, about Rayna.

"Hi. I'm Lee's brother. Grant."

Rayna had no reaction.

"Lee Garrison?" Grant added helpfully.

Still blank.

"He bought the gold mining claim, up—"

"Oh. Sure," Rayna said, as if indifferently, although she probably had already noticed the similarity in their eyes, Grant's and Lee's. "He never actually told me his name," she said casually, like an introduction. "I mean . . . or maybe I, you know, forgot it."

"He didn't tell you his name?" Lee was shy, true, but Grant suddenly sensed major female bullshit at play.

Rayna put out her hand. "Rayna."

"I know. He told me. He remembers your name. Nice to meet you. You're even prettier than the picture my brother's got of you."

Now Rayna *didn't* blush, which contradicted everything Grant had learned about women. Flattery was usually the key to the kingdom. This wrinkle was decidedly new.

"Is it the Polaroid?" Rayna asked. "I look like the bride of Frankenstein in that Polaroid, so, meh, not really a compliment, is it," Rayna added. "My skin is a calico gangrene. And my boobs appear out of level, which I'm pretty sure they aren't, 'cause I see them every day. Unless I'm just blind to it."

She likes my brother, Grant thought. *She knows his name, she just didn't want me to know she knew;* and it was bullshit that he recognized, but not the same bullshit that he thought he knew. It was new bullshit. Sweeter. *How was that possible? And, meanwhile, she's still processing the far-reaching implication of this new fact that my brother, Lee, who no doubt left her the impression that, as a consequence of his failure to sustain his marriage, he's committed to a monklike existence through the rest of eternity—my brother has got pictures of her back home that he shows to family.*

"Do you smoke?"

"What? No."

"Oh. I thought I smelled it on you." Grant shrugged. "Everybody in—" (he caught himself) "everybody where I was staying, recently, you know, smoked . . . and now that I'm away from there, I don't smell it so much, even in bars, and so when I come across it I'm like some avocationally deprived drug-sniffing dog. Maybe you were around someone. Who smoked. Recently."

"I'm around a lot of people," Rayna said.

Grant's unusually muddled thoughts resulted in another awkward pause in the proceedings, with the locals still nailed to the floor where they'd been standing, Greek Chorus, way too scared to move, as if waiting for the barroom brawl and beating they were sure an ex-con would deal them, and that they were starting to believe they deserved.

"Anything else?" Rayna asked again.

She wasn't as pretty as Grant had expected, from the photograph, but far, far lovelier; this new word that had come into his head out of nowhere to describe her, and now he thought he might not ever use it to describe anyone else.

She was lovely, and she liked his brother, Lee, indisputably. If Grant knew nothing else about her, he knew that. He was sure of it. And he was determined not to mess this up.

Which, of course, spelled disaster for everyone.

"There is," Grant said.

"Is what?"

"Something else."

"Oh. Okay."

"Would you go out to dinner sometime with me and my brother?" Grant asked.

THIRTEEN

The date itself took place four days later, on a Thursday, which is a school night, but Grant successfully argued that 1) Lee wasn't in school, 2) Lee wasn't in school, and 3) Lee wasn't in fucking school, for crying out loud, and didn't have homework and taught fucking wood shop, thank you very much, and, okay, yes, physics, but for Pete's sake, to little ignorant trilobites who could give a rat's ass about Bohr's Law. Grant arranged for them to meet Rayna more or less halfway between Evergreen and Basso Profundo, in Georgetown, a hardscrabble, Victorian mining town lovingly restored by people who loved to restore quaint old houses, an activity Grant regarded as pointless, but he didn't lose sleep over it. At twilight, Lee's Jeep rolled down Main Street and found a parking place just up the block from a supposedly refurbished nineteenth-century saloon Grant was pretty sure was never any kind of saloon until the owners, more Denver expats, refurbished the place.

"It was probably a T-shirt shop. You know. Spelled with two *p*'s and an *e*. Remember back in the day, when Georgetown was just a lot of tacky little joints selling hats and shirts and rock candy and ski posters and those postcards with jackalopes and fur-bearing fish, and the Georgetown state legislator tried to get gambling legalized, like in Central City?"

"No," Lee said. "That never happened. It went from a sad and dying Front Range mining town to a kind of low-rent Aspen, when baby-boom skiers decided to buy and build there to avoid the weekend gridlock on I-70 between Denver and Loveland Basin or Winter Park."

"Nobody in Georgetown goes to Winter Park."

"It's only half an hour."

"Over Monarch? Bullshit. That pass snows shut more than not."

"Not really, but, okay. Loveland and Arapahoe," Lee offered as a compromise.

"Or Keystone, if they're particularly impressed by size."

"Fine."

"Not to mention all those sketchy shale oil profiteers who wanted to retire somewhere they hadn't torn up and ruined."

"Whatever. You see my point."

"I see a T-shirt shoppe right there," Grant pointed out, pronouncing the *e.*

"Now," Lee said. "You see it *now.* It's *new.*"

They were nicely dressed. Anyone looking at them could tell that they were brothers because Lee had to loan Grant some clothes, which meant they were both wearing jeans, shirts, and casual cotton sport jackets. "Brothers, or gay," Grant said. Lee told him that joke wasn't funny anymore, if it ever was. "Or high school teachers, same diff," Grant added, unrepentant. Grant said it looked as if Lee had gone to the Gap one day and just bought one of everything, and Lee didn't say anything for a while, which meant Grant wasn't too far off from the truth.

"Maybe it wasn't Georgetown that wanted a casino."

Lee held the door open for Grant, so that Grant would have to go in first.

"Grant?"

"What?"

"If this is some kind of setup—"

"Don't be ridiculous."

Dark wood and red vinyl. A quaint little saloon née après-ski restaurant. Eighteen-nineties music squeezed from a lively, motorized player piano. Rayna was at the bar, waiting, in a spaghetti-strap top and a little leather skirt. *Extremely wary*, Grant thought, *but dressed to exterminate.* She stood up and both men felt their hearts skip. This was not the General Store Rayna. This was the makings of a skirmish.

"Hey," Grant said, and wondered if he could have greeted her with anything more banal.

"Hi. Hi."

"Are we late?" Lee was strangely comfortable.

"I was early. I got a ride from a rig headed into Denver from Kremmling, so . . . "

"Something smells great."

"Probably the duck. I heard this place got in trouble for shooting some ducks in Dillon Reservoir."

"Car trouble?" Lee, the auto shop instructor.

"No. I don't own a car. Grant said you could take me back over the pass after dinner."

They both looked at Grant. He just smiled and pointed toward the window. "Hey. There's a table. Let's grab it. Farthest distance from the piano, and so forth." He led them to it and pulled out a chair for Rayna.

"There's only two chairs," she said.

"You know what," gently pushing her down into the one he'd prepared, "I'm thinking I'm gonna take my supper at the bar. Do you guys mind? I've got this . . . lower back problem, from sleeping on crappy institutional bunks, you know, and, well, to be really honest with you, it's better for me if I sit on a stool."

Rayna and Lee looked at each other.

"You and I can talk on the ride back to your house," Grant added. "Lee doesn't talk when he drives; he says it's too dangerous."

"Grant."

"Lee. Sit. Sit."

Grant was already moving away, smiling, telling them he'd send the waiter right over. Again, Lee and Rayna looked at each other. They smiled slightly, almost in unison.

"Setup," they both said.

They got through small talk and ordering drinks and food without incident or embarrassment, except when Grant ordered them an expensive bottle of wine that neither of them wanted. They tried to send it back, but the waiter got bent out of shape because he'd already opened it, so Grant wound up nursing it at the end of the bar, for a while looking genuinely hurt. There was the usual where-are-you-from and my-parents-are-both-dead and oh-I'm-so-sorry that had to be done, and some biographical stories on each side that raised more questions than they answered. Then there was the ongoing mine talk, inevitably including Lee's it's-not-about-finding-gold assertion, which Rayna gamely tolerated longer than Lee thought she should have, and there were awkward pauses, but not too many.

They found a rhythm and a comfort in each other that surprised them, and was easy, and was promising.

"What did he do?" Rayna asked finally, after all the safe subjects had been exhausted. Lee had expected her to ask and had spent a good part of the evening wondering when she'd ask, which accounted for many of the awkward pauses; it was just habit. And history.

"Who?"

"Your brother. He said he was in prison."

"Yeah."

Neither one of them had eaten much. They both got more anxious, and cautious, as the evening unfolded, as if something was changing during their conversation, dynamic, an ineluctable settling seriousness. But now there was another shift, a different shift, a more familiar shift, and Lee, resigned to it, glanced over at Grant, across the room, finishing dinner, chatting with the lanky bartender, and making him laugh, and then Lee held out his hands for Rayna, palms up.

"You're probably aware that if you're a trained boxer, under the law, your hands are considered lethal weapons?"

"I thought that was just a TV crime show plot thing."

"No."

"Oh."

Lee took a sip of water and shrugged.

"He hit someone?" Rayna asked.

"He went a couple of rounds on him."

"Was he drunk?"

"Grant? I don't think so, no. Not until afterward."

"He beat up somebody and then got drunk because . . . he regretted it? Or to celebrate?" Rayna studied Lee. He didn't answer right away. "Look, if you don't want to talk about it, I understand."

"It was a one-off. Special circumstances, if that's what you're worried about; he's not a violent guy in any sense of the word, believe me." Lee got it all out in a blurt, sounding more sulky than he intended.

"Why would I be worried about it?"

"I don't know. I don't know. It's just . . . you're asking all these questions about Grant, clearly it's a topic that interests you, and I . . . "

Rayna said nothing for a moment. Her eyes sparkled, watching him, and a smile traced her lips, but Lee was too preoccupied with his own turbulent thoughts to notice.

"If you want to go over and sit with him," Lee said, "it's all right. I won't mind. Really. He's much better at this than I am. I mean, it's been this way our whole lives. He's good-looking and interesting. I know he is, and more; that's why I like him so much, don't get me wrong. We're brothers. I get it; I have to get it, right? And since I can't compete with it . . . no, no, wait, let me finish. Since I can't compete with it, I don't. I won't. This is important. I've never said this to anybody, particularly not any woman I've known, and I want to tell you so you understand that I'm not, I don't know, giving up. It's just. Well. Conservation of energy. Thermodynamics, in a sense."

Rayna reminded him to breathe, and he did before continuing: "Back when Grant was a sophomore in high school, not even seventeen, when my parents were still around and I was just his older brother going to college, I had this girl friend—woman, actually—from grad school, early childhood education—Marion Gilroy was her name. I was hopelessly gone-over-the-moon in love with her, even though I hadn't quite worked up the courage to ask her out on what could objectively be considered a date. Girl friend, not girlfriend. You know. But I was about to. I was. And I had her come over with a couple of other friends for dinner. Grant was there. And . . . yeah, Grant sleeps with her the next night. Wild monkey sex in the back of her Plymouth, for chrissakes. She couldn't stop talking about it. You know, confiding in me, because I'm her friend, and I'm his brother, and she wants some insight into him. Or something. 'He's so chill and mysterious,' she told me. I don't know. But sweet Jesus. He was sixteen; she was, like, twenty-four."

"I'm sorry," Rayna said.

Lee lowered his head, shoulders round, and took a long drink of ice water.

"And it's not like he's always on the make or anything. He's not. He's just . . . a really nice, fun guy. Clueless, rat bastard. My little brother. So."

Rayna considered Lee, then asked if Grant knew.

"Knew what?"

"That you were interested in Marion."

Lee frowned. "I don't know. Yeah. Maybe. I might have mentioned it after the dinner thing."

"Might of?"

"Yeah."

"I don't see 'might have' making much of an impression on your brother."

Lee nodded. "It wouldn't," he conceded. "But, hey, don't get me wrong, I was not upset. At all. Seriously. I mean, how could I be upset? It wasn't like I was dating her or anything. I love Grant. I do. I couldn't ask for a better brother."

Rayna pointed out that he could, but he wasn't going to get one. Lee's thoughts and emotions were so knotted he didn't have a response. Rayna asked if she ever went out with him again.

"Marion? With Grant? God no. The next week he was already onto working his way through the girls' volleyball team. It was a whole tall-chick phase he went through," Lee said. "Marion, on the other hand, turned out she was sleeping with our Whole Learning professor, who was about sixty, and they eventually shacked up in married student housing . . . I think they've got, oh, three or four kids now."

Rayna considered him with an expression Lee couldn't, or didn't want to, decode.

"I'm sorry."

"So I'm just letting you know," he concluded, "that I'm not ever surprised or disappointed when a girl, or woman, I'm sorry, tells me she's got a crush on my brother."

"I don't like this story," Rayna said.

Lee was of the opinion that it wasn't really a story she had to like or not. Rayna assured him that Lee was anticipating a problem that didn't exist. She wasn't at all interested in Lee's little brother, and, cards on the table, wasn't under the impression that this was the kind of dinner date in which she needed to make those kinds of far-reaching declarations to begin with.

"It must have ripped your heart out," she added.

"Grant?"

"No. Your ex-wife. Getting divorced."

Lee blinked. Then he looked away, as if for help, and saw that Grant was no longer sitting at the bar.

As Rayna followed Lee's look, the bartender came out and across to their table, carrying a slip of paper that Lee and Rayna both thought was a note.

"You're Lee?"

"That's right."

"Dude, your buddy had to leave? But he said you were paying his bill."

The bartender put down the check. Rayna laughed. Lee reached for his wallet.

"Yeah, I'm paying."

"Be sure to thank him for sending over the wine," Rayna teased. Lee pointed out, probably unnecessarily, that Grant didn't have any money anyway.

Troutdale Estates held the heavy canyon midnight air and a deep darkness cut only by lights that glimmered softly through the trees from the windows of the occupied houses. The sound of crickets was thick, like a sheet of brittle, one-note music, continuous; you wouldn't notice it unless you'd spent the last couple of years in a prison cellblock where night was filled only with percussion and loss.

A pickup truck rumbled up the street, and Grant rose from in the bed and pounded on the rear window of the cab, and the truck slowed long enough for him to hop down and wave his thanks to another driver; this one just flicked his lights and disappeared around the next corner. Grant stared across the street at a familiar split-level house.

A slender shadow passed across an upstairs curtain.

He stood there for a long time, until the lights in the house went dark, until nearly all the lights in all the houses were extinguished and the neighborhood slept. He stood watching, hands in his pockets, in no hurry to go anywhere.

And Lee's Jeep cornered nimbly through the curves coming up from Dillon. He and Rayna had hardly spoken on the trip through the Eisenhower Tunnel. A restful silence had settled and neither seemed anxious to break it. Tires hummed on the machine-creased asphalt of I-70. At the turnoff for Keystone they stopped for gas. Rayna got out and stood near Lee as he worked the pump. There was no moon. The canopy of stars was spectacular, and the air redolent with the bite of pine.

"Lee?"

"Yes?"

Rayna took a moment, her eyes narrowed; she was thinking, organizing her thoughts before she spoke.

"Nothing," she said.

Half an hour later the silver Jeep glided up to the door of the General Store. Rayna climbed out, came around to the driver's side, and looked in at Lee.

"A gentleman would have opened the door for me," she baited him.

"You were out so fast. I would have only been halfway there and felt pretty foolish." Rayna was smiling; Lee realized she was yanking his chain. "Oh."

"Don't worry. That whole chivalry vibe died for me when Clinton did the thing with the cigar," she told him. "I mean. President of the United States. He probably went to cotillion and everything. I mean, come on. He was a Rhodes Scholar."

"I know."

"Isn't there like a rule Rhodes Scholars have to be gentlemen?"

She looked up the street. There was nothing to see. A pool of light beneath the single street lamp. The outline of Mayor Barb's Caddy.

"I don't smoke," she said.

"Okay."

"Or if I do, it's just, like, one. Or a half. I've quit," she told him.

"That's good," he said, and let too much quiet settle.

"You going to kiss me good night?"

"I will if you want me to."

"You'll have to get out of the car."

"Spontaneity is my middle name."

She leaned her elbows on the door. "Or you can come in for a beer, but I'm not going to sleep with you," Rayna said.

Lee must have inadvertently thrown an odd, worried look at her because she added quickly, nicely, "I like to get that out of the way. It relieves a lot of tension."

"Oh." It did, somehow. And created another kind.

"I'm serious. See? We're already past it. It's all good now."

"Will you be insulted if I say I'd better get going?" Lee asked her. "I've got fifty-nine papers to grade for tomorrow." Now all he could think about was sleeping with her.

She leaned in and kissed him, lightly. Her lips were soft, dry. "No," she said, "I had a great time."

"Really?"

She kissed him again.

"Yeah."

Rayna backed away, turned, and walked happily through the headlights and up to the front steps of her store. Lee dropped the electric window on the passenger side and called out to her, "Are you saying you're not going to sleep with me now, or you're not going to sleep with me ever?"

Rayna just smiled, unlocked the door, and went inside. The door closed softly. Lee stayed there for a moment, looking at it. Then he turned his Jeep around and headed back down Main Street toward the highway and the long drive home.

FOURTEEN

*E*arly the next morning, a timid silt of wispy fog had settled in the valley, waiting for a suggestion of sun to chase it away. Grant came out of the Hiwan house in board shorts and crew socks, triggering the remote in his hand, and the garage door swung open.

The familiar smell of oil, gasoline, and wood braced him; one half of the garage was filled with things Lee couldn't bring himself to throw or give away, which meant pretty much everything. Shovels; stepladders; snow tires; a box of old unpaired basketball shoes (mostly right foot); a box of old baseball gloves (mostly lefties); ten boxes of Christmas ornaments carefully labeled and clearly unmoved for untold seasons since they supported a collection of other boxes labeled, simply, "1984 ed. World Book Encyclopedia"; power tools; hand tools; pipe wrenches; axes; a posthole digger; three ancient CRT computer monitors; an eight-track car stereo; a cassette car stereo; four Altec-Lansing floor speakers; a plaid deluxe Barcalounger; a plastic trash can filled with wire clothes hangers; some old car parts (including worn disc brake pads, a Honda clutch, one quarter of a catalytic converter, and a discharged air bag); odd scraps of metal; more surplus mining helmets; half a dozen cans of paint; a push lawn mower; a child's E-Z Bake Oven; Eddie Belasco's Mighty Morphin' Power Rangers walkie-talkies (which Lee had promised to fix when he and Eddie were twelve); a Jedi helmet; moth-eaten furniture pads; a console stereo-television circa 1953 (the Sylvania "Riviera" model); bricks; two-by-fours; sheetrock; solvents; stirrups for a saddle; deflated footballs and basketballs, including the old red-white-and-blue ABA version; a floor fan; and a giant cardboard cutout, movie theater floor promotion for *Silence of the Lambs*.

The other half of the garage was spotlessly clean. Occupied solely by a car tucked under a faded chamois cover, which Grant yanked off like a magician performing a trick to reveal a badass 1984 Chevrolet Camaro, black with silver pinstripe detailing, a T-top, and fat whitewall tires, slightly lowered. Grant ran his hand along the top of a fender where the early day's sun bent around the arc of steel and spilled its reflection across the swept, smooth concrete floor.

Already fourth period, and ten minutes into wood shop, a band saw screamed as it ripped through a four-by-four. The cut was true because Lee was guiding it, clad in oversized safety goggles that made him look only slightly more demented than his class of mostly boys, watching, wearing safety glasses of their own.

Lee had to yell to be heard over the hollering saw. "Who can give me three applications in which the band saw is superior to the table saw?"

Not surprisingly, only the two girls' hands went up.

The air-conditioning was down, so the climate in Floyd Hill Properties erred on swampy, due to the absence of functional windows and the northeastern exposure of the double-glass front doors, a Feng Shui no-no that Grant made idle note of as he got sucked inside. A big, low-ceilinged room of identical desks, with a row of enclosed offices along one side, the bullpen felt kind of sleepy and tropical, right down to the palm trees in the planter. Fittingly, one man in chinos, a short-sleeved shirt, and a pastel tie was dozing, legs propped up on a bookshelf filled with long-outdated Multiple Listing books. Grant rapped on his desk and the chino man jumped, nearly tipping out of the chair.

"Lorraine around?"

The man blinked, eyes puffy and, disoriented, told Grant (as the man emerged from his daydream) that six and a point was the best he could do.

"What?"

"Oh. Um . . . " And then with a slow-dawning and fretful recognition: "'Lo, Grant." Grant couldn't remember his name.

"What the hell-o? Is that Grant Garrison?"

Grant looked to his right for the source of a second voice and locked eyes with Stan Beachum, who stood in the doorway of one of the little private offices, power tie, blue jeans, Italian tassel loafers, and a 9mm Beretta handgun aimed directly at Grant's nose.

"Hoh boy." A shallow intake of breath, but a forced, cheerful "Stan. Hey. Whassup?"

"I still can't taste anything, thanks."

"I meant the penny stocks."

"I can't taste them, either."

Grant's lips curled up over his teeth, dry, in what he hoped to God was a smile. "You change jobs, Stan?"

"I'm trading my own account since the subprime melt, so I sublet the old place and situated my brokerage here, and now Lorraine and I can better facilitate our child-care responsibilities."

Grant pretended to be surprised.

"Whoawhoawhoawhoa—you—you and Lorraine?"

"Hey, screw you," Beachum barked. "Okay? Screw you. You're supposed to stay clear of me."

"I came to see her, not you. Had no idea you'd even be on the premises."

Beachum's fingers squeezed the grip of the gun. Grant flinched. The sleepy chino man took his coffee cup and retreated into a back room.

There was a huge board on the wall next to Beachum. Lots of house listings. Sales information. Salespersons' names. An open house flag was stuck to one of the listings, and Grant's eyes, following the chart across, found the name of the salesperson associated with the showing: Lorraine Simons.

Beachum, meanwhile, was on his slow boil. "You know, stupidly, I thought I might be *notified* before they let you out of prison. Thought I might be given an *opportunity* to maybe express *why* they should *incarcerate* your sorry ass for the full term of your sentence. Through a close personal friend," Beachum spat, "I could have gotten to the Governor himself and asked him to keep you locked up in there."

"Gee," Grant said. "I'm glad that didn't occur."

"No kidding."

"You should write to somebody and complain."

"Believe you me, I did. Heck yes, I did."

Grant was working up his courage to walk out. *What*, he wondered again, *the fuck was Lorraine doing with this git?* Beachum let the gun drop to his side, looking smug. Evidently he only wanted to scare the crap out of Grant, not actually pull the trigger, which—Grant having spent some considerable time with individuals who would have pulled the trigger already without giving it a second thought—had been Grant's assumption about Beachum's gunplay all along.

"Well. Good to see you," Grant said, staying friendly. "I don't suppose she's . . . ?"

"Stay away from her."

"Good advice. Yeah. Thank you." Grant's feet moved him back toward the door.

"Hey," Beachum called after him, following, "is employment a condition of your parole?"

"Not to worry, thanks. In fact, me and Lee, we're working together."

"The gold mine?"

"Which would make me self-employed."

"In what universe?"

Grant explained the parole rules in an abbreviated way, emphasizing that, because of the difficulty many ex-cons had finding meaningful work, said rules encouraged a certain amount of entrepreneurship.

"That mine is a goddamn joke. He went up to his eyeballs in debt to buy it, off the Internet, for Pete's sake, like some kind of moron-Ponzi-rube—and there's no upside because you can't develop the land. Your brother's the laughingstock of this whole town."

Grant stopped in the door. His shoulder twitched. He looked back at Beachum, smoldering. "What does that mean, 'laughingstock'?"

Not so bold of a sudden, Beachum took a step backward and regripped the gun.

"Listen, I don't want you around me."

"Who's laughing? You and the fucking quiche-farters in that fucking Troutdale tract home abomination upstream from where the hotel used to be? You got nothing better to do than suck down Shiraz and make fun of my brother, who, I'm just sayin', contributes more in one day at that high school, teaching your fat, Ritalin-scrubbed, YouTube-worshipping progeny to be semi-humans than you have, Stanster, in your entire greedy, pointless, subprime life."

Beachum's ears went crimson. "The terms of your release specifically prohibit you—"

"I know."

"If I call your probation officer—"

"You won't have to."

Grant pushed through the glass door, and the sultry air surged out.

"And stay clear of Lorraine!"

Lorraine. Her lively, remarkable face filling the fifty-two-inch span of a Sony flat-screen television mounted on the lichen-rock face of a massive fireplace.

"Now," she was saying, eyes smoky, lipstick *Vogue*-perfect, "if you press function key four, and then press enter, you keep the home-watch feature going while you enjoy your personal entertainment selection. TiVo, satellite, World Wide Web, and XM radio."

Lorraine. The woman Grant watched from across the street in front of her house in Troutdale Estates, here, in digital HD, suddenly squared in the upper right-hand corner of the LCD, while the rest of the screen filled with Bogart from *The Treasure of the Sierra Madre*.

"Pressing function key five, you can view all the home-watch security cameras at once."

And then Lorraine, gone. Gone from the screen, the screen subdivided into a grid of nine small boxes showing fixed surveillance camera views of various rooms, entries, and outside locations of a new house, including one, from above, angled down, of Grant at the front door. He walked in, disappeared from that view, reappeared in the foyer on another, disappeared again.

Lorraine, who stood behind her prospective buyers slumped in two of six full-feature electric recliners facing the tiny decorative gas fireplace and huge display of an in-home surround-sound screening room, lost all color in her face and needed to put a manicured hand on the sideboard to steady herself.

"Okay. Great. Let's turn off the system, using the red button, and continue our tour in the gourmet kitchen, shall we?"

She walked out, but her buyers, slow to follow her instructions since the in-home surround-sound screening room was all that really mattered to them, stayed, and continued to watch the mosaic of security monitor views because Grant had appeared in the vaulted great room, and Lorraine was with him.

Flip of a function key and this picture filled the screen. As in a movie, Lorraine leapt on Grant, happy, wrapped her legs around him, mashed her mouth against his, and appeared determined to suck his tonsils out.

"Sweet Jesus," said the male buyer.

"Turn it off, Jim," said his wife, her mouth agape.

Instead, the husband, Jim, nervously fiddled with the remote, trying to get some sound going. But when finally he did, Grant had spun out of the picture, presumably with Lorraine still affixed to him.

The buyers were spellbound.

"Like that thing from *Alien*," Jim said.

"Oh hush," his wife giggled.

"I didn't think you'd come back," the disappeared Lorraine was saying in Dolby TMX surround.

"Shit." Jim waved the remote at the screen, sequencing through the surveillance stations, unable to find them. Somewhere in the house they heard a door slam shut.

"That is so unprofessional," the wife clucked.

Jim found Bogart again, though, *The Treasure of the Sierra Madre*, on the TiVo queue in Blu-ray, and it started right up where it had been interrupted, so they settled into the soft, distressed leather of the stadium seats.

A splendorous overbuild, the master bathroom was the *Spartacus* wet dream, all gold and glass and marble and mirrors. There was even a walk-in tub with a waterfall feature. Grant disentangled himself from Lorraine and backed up.

"We can't. Lorraine, I don't . . . "

"Dear God, I've missed you."

Her smile was viral and highly contagious. The heat came off her. She reached under her skirt and pulled off her panties. Grant pretended they were just talking.

"You got married to Stan Beachum?"

"God no. We're just living together. Or, well, all right, yes, technically married, I guess—but I didn't think you'd come back. He's stable; he's a good father."

"He's arrogant and narcissistic."

"And it's kind of sad what happened to him," Lorraine continued, ignoring Grant's slur, "and pretty much my fault when you get right down to it."

"He's an asshole."

"Ooo. Honey, I really don't think you should be the one making that call."

She took his hands and backed up to the counter with the 'his' and 'hers' sinks.

"Let's do it right here. On the Vesuvian marble."

"There is no such thing. Vesuvian. That's retarded."

"It sells."

"What has happened to you?"

There was cold desperation in her bright eyes. It broke his heart. "Life happened to me," Lorraine said.

"My brother lives in a house without furniture," Grant said. "He's making a big wooden cross."

"Hello. He bought a gold mine on eBay, Grant. He plants toilets in the front yard. He went skydiving on what would have been our third anniversary and sent me a Polaroid."

"They're not toilets."

"Same difference." She moved his hands to her hips and scooted up against him.

"We created him," Grant said. "Our own personal Frankenstein.

You and me, together, separate, we cut his heart in half so we could see how it worked, we gave him the diseased brain and sent him out where the villagers could chase him with pitchforks. He deserved better. Deserves better."

"Oh shut up."

"Do you ever talk to him?" Grant asked her.

"It's a joke. The gold mine? It's pathetic. He gets all these unrealistic ideas in his head: backhoe, gold mine, Lorraine would make a swell wife for me, my little brother wants to be good but needs my help. You know I'm right. And then he's crushed when it doesn't work out. Doh. I don't feel sorry for him. I don't. He's not gonna find gold, or silver, or coal, or strike oil, or anything else of use in that mine. No, wait. He'll find unhappiness. Which is what he craves, Grant. You know I'm right. He's hardwired for failure, and I won't apologize for maybe taking advantage of it because, hey, it's what he wanted. Not Frankenstein. Humpty-Dumpty. Good luck fixing that."

"He loved you."

"He loved the idea of me. And the idea of losing me, because . . . you know."

"Jesus, that's cold."

"Yeah, well."

"Okay, but maybe he still needs you to help him get through this—"

Lorraine just shook her head.

"It's . . . I don't know. It's a wound, he keeps picking at it," Grant said, "picking at the scab and it won't heal."

"I don't love him, Grant," Lorraine said flatly.

"You loved him once."

"No, baby. I liked him. I loved you."

Grant felt short of breath. Lorraine. She put her hands on his chest and pulled her heels up to dig them into the backs of his legs.

"I love him," Grant said.

"I'm sure that's incredibly comforting for him, too. Considering."

"What about Beachum?"

"I stayed with Lee to be with you," she said, "and I moved in with Stan because he likes the idea of me with him, plus I had a baby and didn't want to wind up living under some freeway on-ramp, and maybe all this makes me a horrible person, or a selfish bitch, and maybe I'll rot in hell for it, but oh well."

She pressed hard against him again, her lips searched for his, walking up his neck, teeth sharp and scraping, while her fingers went to his belt and the zipper of his jeans.

"You're the only woman who's ever scared me."

"Heights don't make me dizzy."

They kissed for a while. He couldn't help it. He felt his pants falling.

"At least I know what I want," she added. They kissed until, as if chaste, she pushed him gently back. "I should warn you that I'm pretty sure Stan bought a gun the day he heard you got out of jail."

Grant admitted that he'd seen the Beretta and recounted his visit to the office.

"I thought he was being paranoid. But here you are."

They kissed greedily.

"How's the baby?" Grant asked her.

"Awesome. It's yours."

Grant's legs went rubbery. "What?" He tried to disentangle from her, but Lorraine kept her legs clamped around him. *What?* His mind reeled.

"Think," she said. "Count. Oh, right, you were never good at math."

Grant just gave up then. He held her, quiet.

"This is where you're supposed to engage," she said. "Ask me if it's a boy or a girl," she said. "Ask me its name."

"Mine" was all Grant could muster.

She sighed. "What do you want from me, Grant? Or are you just here on another mission of mercy for your brother before you move on?"

"What do I want?"

The bathroom door opened and the two prospective buyers poked their heads in:

"Heyoh. There you are."

Lorraine uncoupled, pulled her skirt down as if nothing had been going on, but as Grant stepped back he nearly fell over the pants snagged at his ankles, and everybody pretended not to see his boxers or the erection tenting them.

"Question," the wife spoke, all business. "There's the big screen in the living room, and the built-ins in the bedrooms, and the little one in the study, but I can't find a TV in the kitchen."

Lorraine unclipped a Sharpie from her blouse and scrawled something on her panties. The kitchen flat screen was behind a secret panel in the trompe l'oeil above the trash compactor, she told the wife, then handed the panties to Grant, as if it was all in a day's work: "There's my cell number, for future reference. If you have any other questions, Mr. Garrison, I'll be showing these people the gourmet kitchen."

She smiled, her lipstick mostly rubbed off, her eyes alive, her face flushed and beautiful, and she led the vaguely discomfited buyers away. Grant shared a blank look with the husband before he disappeared, then pulled up his jeans and saw himself in the mirror and was more than a little bit terrified.

FIFTEEN

*T*he homicide detective from Kansas had the misfortune of finding only Grant home when he rang the bell at Lee's Evergreen house. His was a polite and, he assured Grant, informal inquiry regarding property Mr. Lee Garrison had purchased on eBay from a Mr. Gordon E. (as in Elmore) Bunn, recently of Salina, specifically a mining claim in the Argentine Pass area, the "Blue Lark." The detective, who introduced himself only by his last name, Friendly, was a thick-shouldered, russet-haired man with squarish, wire-rimmed spectacles and an awkward handshake in which his fingers never got set right with Grant's. Mr. Bunn had died, he told Grant, the circumstances murky enough to warrant an investigation into it, past associates, possible motives, retracing the steps of his previous days, and so forth, resulting in the discovery of the eBay transaction and a long trip to Evergreen to ask the buyer a couple of questions on the admittedly remote chance that Lee might tell the detective something that would, quote, break the case wide open.

"How often does that happen, though, really?" Grant wondered pointedly.

Friendly wouldn't, or couldn't, commit to an answer. "You could have called ahead," Grant said.

"Uh-huh," said the cop.

"Are you staying in town? I could tell my brother when he gets home; you could come back."

Lee was at his seafaring boat club meeting, way up in north bumfuck Broomfield, but Grant was not inclined to disclose this to the cop.

Friendly murmured something about his department not having the budget for overnights, and Grant got the impression that the detective had, perhaps, come to Colorado chasing a wild hunch without his Captain's approval.

Grant invited him in. They sat in the living room, on the lawn chairs, which were not nearly as comfortable as they looked, and the chairs looked pretty disagreeable. Friendly declined the offer of a beverage and asked a series of random questions that Grant at first thought were calculated, in a Columbo-kind-of-way, but then realized were probably the detective's halfhearted attempt to buy time in the hope that Lee might come home while he waited:

"Is your brother in the habit of making large purchases on the Internet? Are the regular chairs out for upholstering? Why mining? No wife or children? Gold or silver? Did he need permits? How long does it take to drive there? How long would it take to commute to Denver in rush hour? Why are there so many ovoid septic tanks planted out in the front yard? Do you think your Rockies will ever get any decent pitchers? Is that Mount Evans? How many years did you do in Cañon City?"

That Friendly had made Grant for an ex-con was A) not surprising, and B) a hoary old chestnut that Grant irritably didn't want to let pass; was it, Grant thought acidly, the chalky pallor he'd acquired while inside the Big House and couldn't seem to shake no matter how much time he spent in the high-country sun, or (more likely) the T-shirt he was wearing, which bore the headline "CTCF RUGBY TEAM" and could only have been obtained in the small visitors' "gift" shop on-site?

"No sir, I can tell you were in the system by the way you look at me," Friendly explained, as if he could read minds. "Relaxed, I mean. Someone untroubled in the presence of law enforcement. Your normal civilian will fidget like Raskolnikov because everybody's got some damn thing chafing their ass. Except your convict, who's doing hard time for it, you see."

"How did this Gordon Bunn die, exactly?" Grant asked, changing the subject and letting the showy state school Dostoevsky footnote pass.

"Hanged," Friendly said. "A neighbor smelled him after he ripened. Bosniak," Friendly elaborated. "She grew up there; she was there during the war, saw a lot of dead people, I imagine. All that ethnic cleansing in the '90s. Ahmici. That's in Herzegovina, I am told."

A short discussion of Yugoslavian dissolution and the Balkan War ensued, short because neither man could remember much about it. Grant again offered the detective a beverage, which the cop declined.

Time passed.

Friendly asked if Grant knew where his brother had gone, and Grant, with an ex-con's reflexive circumspection, told Friendly that he didn't, no. It felt weird, lying. Especially since there was no tactical advantage to it; Grant knew that Lee would be as surprised by the news of the old miner's demise as anyone. He could answer any questions about the purchase of the land that Friendly might have, but he'd have nothing to add or offer. *Maybe*, Grant thought, *I'm saving everybody time, which is good, right?* Friendly heaved himself up out of the folding chair. He guessed that he should be getting back. Could Grant have Lee call him? Friendly handed Grant a card, embossed with a gold Salina PD badge.

"Is your brother happy with his mine?"

"Delirious."

Friendly frowned, sniffed for sarcasm, but didn't detect any. "I don't suppose he's found any gold yet? Or silver?"

"No." Grant bristled.

"Be ticked off some if he were to discover the mine was played out, you think?"

"Like ticked off enough to go to Salina and hang the guy who sold him the claim?"

They just stared at each other, expressionless. That was, yes, the target Friendly was aiming for but, exposed, he blushed slightly over the clumsiness of his question. He looked glad to be solo, no partner, so that no one would report back to his Captain about it.

"I think you'd be mischaracterizing my brother's passion for mining, if you thought it was to get rich or anything."

"What'd you do," Friendly asked, "that got you into the correctional system? I'm just curious. I mean, I could look it up."

"You could," Grant agreed, and left it at that.

He walked Detective Friendly to the front door and opened it. The smell of dust and grass rolled in thick on a dry wind. A bright, colorless pinprick of sun beat down on Friendly's unfortunate-bronze rental sedan and made the metal tick.

"Honestly? I don't think my brother ever met the man who sold him the mine," Grant said. "And I'm pretty sure he never even knew the man's name."

Friendly frowned again, thoughtful, as Grant explained what Lee had told him of the transaction: eBay, email, the firewall of a username, a wire transfer to a numbered bank account in Delaware, and the quitclaim deed transfer in Lee's name that a solicitor delivered and notarized.

"The guy didn't want my brother to know his real name," Grant said. "That's pretty obvious."

"He was scared," Friendly agreed.

"What? Why?"

"Your brother ever been to Pakistan? We found a postcard among the deceased's recent mail. Unsigned," he added.

"Pakistan?"

"Islamabad. Cryptic. Arabic writing. A Sufi saying is what we figured out finally. 'Evening becomes morning and night becomes dawn.' I think it's to throw us off scent, you know, like, terrorism and so forth."

"Scared of what?" Grant still wanted to know.

"Dying, no doubt. But . . . "

Friendly cocked his head and looked at Grant the way police officers and prison guards had been looking at him for twenty-odd months, a cheerfulness born of puissance. "Please tell your brother to call me," Friendly advised Grant. "I doubt seriously he killed anybody, but whatever killed Gordon Elmore Bunn could be catching."

The Detective backed his rental out of the driveway like a grandmother, in fits and starts, and didn't waste any gas crawling up the gentle incline, through the tree-starved neighborhood, toward Highway 74. Looking back on it later, Grant would wonder why he threw the cop's calling card away. There was no explaining it; he just went to the kitchen and took a pair of scissors from the utility drawer and cut the card into tiny triangle clips that dropped, fluttering into the wastebasket under the sink like midwinter snow.

Looking back on it, Grant would try to convince himself that he didn't want Lee to get superstitious about the mine or have his childlike joy in it compromised by the knowledge that its previous owner had met an unfortunate end. Grant would remember driving away in his Camaro, but not where he went. It might have been to the library to look at past issues of the *Kansas City Star* online and read the news stories about the man found hanged. He might have driven to town again and parked across the street from Lorraine's realty office and watched the storefront window, hating himself for waiting for her to appear.

Looking back on it later, Grant would sometimes admit to a deeper, slightly more malevolent motive for never telling

Lee about the visit from Detective Friendly or the curious hang-ing death of an old miner in Salina, Kansas. He had, when it came to his older brother, always been riven with contradic-tions: love, envy, loyalty, gratitude, jealousy, resentment, rivalry, and confusion.

Since they were little kids, some part of Grant had always wanted to destroy his brother because the alternative, saving him, would be so much harder.

SIXTEEN

"*Nor silver nor gold hath obtained my redemption,*
The guilt on my conscience too heavy had grown;
The blood of the cross is my only foundation,
The death of my Savior now maketh me whole."

A large man in suspenders, whose body did not match his high, fragile, quavering voice, stood in the Evergreen Methodist Church choir box channeling his inner Todd Rundgren to a doleful hymn while, on the other end of the church, Lee balanced on a ladder and secured the cross he made into the wall with big, countersunk lag bolts. The ratchet on his socket wrench kept triple time with the chorus:

"*I am redeemed, but not with silver,*
I am bought, but not with gold;
Bought with a price, the blood of Jesus,
Precious price of love untold."

The organ played a different song, with a kind of mid-fifties Wurlitzer feel, but in the same key, with the same notes, and the pastor—tall, shaved head, mournful features—watched, worried, among other things, that Lee would fall from the ladder and present a liability claim to a congregation that was already suffering the fiscal fealties of the previous pastor, who had gone to Ibiza with most of their annual fund and a parish elder's trophy wife. And then there were the aesthetic issues of a man who never met a Danish furniture set he didn't covet.

"I don't mean to backseat drive, but are we gonna have to see those lag bolts, Lee?"

Lee shook his head and took a round wooden plug from his pocket to show the pastor that it fit perfectly into one of the lag bolt holes.

"Beautiful. Truly."

"Thanks," Lee said.

"Jesus was a carpenter," the pastor felt inspired, in the moment, to impart.

"So was Harrison Ford," Rayna added, from behind him, unsolicited.

She came down the aisle, and both the pastor and Lee turned their heads to look at her as she stopped at the foot of the altar.

"That just popped out," she explained.

"Rayna Lincoln," Lee introduced her. "John Leonard. John's the minister—"

"Pastor. Don't hold it against me, Rayna."

"I can't." Then she glowered up at Lee and pointed out that, after a man has had an enjoyable evening with a woman, it's traditional, not to mention just plain good manners, for said man to call said woman on the telephone and let her know he had a good time and, if he did, ask her if she'd like to go out again. Isn't it?

She looked to Pastor John Leonard for support. To Lee's chagrin and dismay, the pastor seemed happy to stay and participate in the discussion. "Yes," he said, "it is."

"Unless he didn't," Rayna continued pointedly. "Enjoy the evening, I mean."

The pastor said that he was under the impression Lee had enjoyed it, even though, Lee thought, distractedly, John didn't know anything about it. They barely knew each other, and Lee seldom went to church. Nevertheless, Pastor Leonard flat out asked Lee why he hadn't called Rayna, and Lee nearly fell off the ladder as he came down.

"I was going to."

"When?"

"You made it seem like no big deal."

"Because I wouldn't sleep with you on the first date?"

Lee reddened. The pastor literally leaned into this conversation, his hands folded in front of him, his face rent by a disturbing grin.

"I had a good time," Lee said, again. "I did. I was going to call."

"Okay."

"No, not okay, I should have called."

"Okay."

Rayna looked away from him purposefully. The pastor pursed his lips, disappointed. Lee started breaking the collapsible ladder down to its portable size, and the organist accidentally bleated a long, low D-chord as she and the singer tried to find common ground between Todd and Methodist hymnody.

Moments later Rayna and Lee were outside, and the pastor was still inside, and Rayna carried some of the power tools for Lee as he balanced the ladder on his shoulder and carted his equipment back to the Jeep.

"You came all the way down here to ask me why I hadn't called you?"

"Well, I also had a dentist appointment in Arvada," Rayna admitted.

Lee hoisted the ladder up onto the roof rack of the Jeep and used bungee cords to secure it there.

"When you have to travel down from the mountains without a car," Rayna explained, "you tend to group your errands together, so you don't spend your life on a bus."

Lee didn't hear half of this because he was talking over her, recounting how she'd told him that she didn't want to sleep with him, and that he took that to mean she wasn't much interested in him, the kiss notwithstanding, and so, not to belabor it, he was led to understand and accept that Rayna "just wanted to be friends."

"Something wrong with being friends?"

"No."

"You can still call a friend. You can still go out with a friend and have fun."

"You're right. You're right."

"I mean, 'cause you make it sound like—"

"Nothing wrong with it. I'm sorry I—"

"Good. Because I'm trying to change, Lee. I need to change, do you understand that?"

"The new you."

"Yeah."

Lee nodded and looked down the long, winding driveway to the parking lot of the golf course restaurant, Keys on the Green, and beyond its tiered redwood terraces, the dark, glassy surface of Evergreen Lake. Once he and Grant had raced skateboards down that driveway through the parking lot and wiped out into the lake where the access road ran alongside it. The water was shallow there. Lee had suffered his wickedest longboard road rash on that very asphalt, a raw wound that ran from his knee to his hip and eventually got infected because the lake water was so polluted. Now, supposedly, the lake was cleaner. There were fish in it. Pale, blind, scaly talapia that came gushing out of Fish & Wildlife tanker hoses every spring like spawn of the dead.

"The old you would have slept with me?" Lee wondered.

"Oh, Lee" was all Rayna said.

"Just asking. The new me wants to know."

Rayna thought about it, then said, "I'm sorry."

"About?"

"It's all so . . . " Rayna let that thought drop and picked up a new one: "You know, this therapist I used to go to says I have a Sleeping Beauty complex."

"I don't know what that is."

"Well, it's an epidemic in women of a certain age, I'll tell you that."

The joke didn't land. Lee frowned.

"Never mind," Rayna added. She sighed. She cocked her hip and looked out in the distance to where Lee was staring. The empty parking lot, the dark water of the lake, the whitish crumbling concrete top of the dam, the thick, black forest of pine beyond the rolling fairways. Clouds roiled overhead, pooling the sunlight in restless, southward-bound blooming. Rayna sighed again, shook her head, and started to walk away.

"Where're you going?"

"I don't know," she said. She stopped, and turned back to him, sad.

"You need a ride?"

"Your brother's been calling me," she said.

"Grant?"

"Just about every day, yeah."

"Grant?"

"No," she said, "your other brother."

Then they stared at each other, quiet, for a long time, and in that comfortable silence that settled between them, Rayna smiled.

The sun was dropping behind Mount Evans when they reached the house. The sky was aflame, leaving the eastern slope all gloaming and languid in blue-darkness. After he stowed his tools and ladder, Lee helped Rayna climb onto one of the capsized septic tanks half-buried in the yard.

"Grab hold of the . . . there you go. Got it?"

Rayna pulled herself to a sitting position, then stood up, her arms out for balance, and watched as Lee hauled himself up onto the adjacent septic summit. They stayed there, not talking, separate but connected, bathed in dusty flaxen sunlight that dissolved in a growing gloom, gazing out over Lee's curious field of bumps. Finally:

"You buried all these?"

"When I first got my backhoe. City had just put in sewer service and most everybody in this development was still on septic, and I was parking this unsightly yellow creature at my house. There was a palpable grumbling about it. I thought offering to facilitate their upgrade to city sanitation by digging out the tanks might persuade the neighborhood there could be an upside to heavy equipment in the drive."

"Did it?"

"Sort of," Lee hedged. "And then not," he admitted. "I hadn't told them I was going to repurpose their tanks as installation art. The neighbors tried to get the City to intervene via public nuisance laws, but it turned out Hiwan Meadows, this whole development, had never been legally incorporated into Evergreen City proper. And the County will let you do just about anything."

"I see they don't feel the same way about motor homes," Rayna observed dryly, already defensive on Lee's behalf. There were at least half a dozen huge, rusting Winnebagos moored on parking pads within her line of sight.

They fell quiet again. There was the slow meter of crickets, and the rush of wind through the pines. Faint thumping bass notes throbbed from some kid's maxed-out car stereo. Like a lonely heartbeat.

The tops of the tanks got surreal in the twilight, lost definition, even ceased to be strange.

"What does it make you think of?" Lee asked.

Rayna thought about it carefully before she answered: "Goose bumps."

Lee looked at her. Something had softened in the way she looked back at him.

"See," she said slyly. "Start with friends, sky's the limit."

There was an ominous, low rumble, rising, and Grant's Camaro came quickly down the street and slipped into the driveway like a shark.

He shouted from the open window, "Hey you kids get down from there! Somebody could break their neck!"

Grant got out, slamming the door shut and striding toward them. There was something loose-wired about his brother's grin, so Lee hopped off his bump and made sure to get to Rayna first. He helped her dismount, hands on her waist. She let them stay there, and put her hands over his, evidently to make sure they stayed there, and that's when he noticed that his wedding ring was missing.

"Taking in the view from the metal mammaries?" Grant asked Rayna.

"Muscle car," she replied, deadpan. "Why am I not surprised?"

"Like it?"

"No."

Lee had disengaged and walked back to gaze intently down at the ground around the septic tank he'd just been atop. Rayna and Grant didn't notice at first.

"Was that you with the Tupac overcranked?"

"No. I got a vintage eight-track. Lynyrd Skynyrd and The Band."

Rayna laughed.

Lee was down on his hands and knees, searching the stubbly weeds and grass for the gold band. Rayna searched for him in the darkness, calling out, "Lee, I've gotta go, bus leaves at seven," and then, finding him, "What are you looking for?"

"Um . . ."

"I can take you," Grant offered. "Hell, I can take you all the way home. I'm not doing anything."

To which Lee answered, "No, no, no." He got back up, ringless. "No, that's not necessary. Thanks, though."

Grant looked mischievously from Lee to Rayna. Nodded, as if satisfied, as if he thought he had accomplished something. Lee didn't like it.

"Great," Grant said. "Well. Nice seeing you, Rayna." Grant walked inside.

"Everything okay here?" Rayna asked Lee.

"Oh yeah." It wasn't, but Lee knew he wouldn't be able to find the ring in the failing daylight. He needed a metal detector. Was there one in the garage? Maybe. No. A neighbor had given him one to fix, but he'd taken it to school and dissembled it for the electromagnet.

"Lee?"

"Yeah?"

"What were you doing? Hands and knees, on the ground, just now?"

"Nothing."

"Lee."

"Nothing. I thought I dropped something, but . . . didn't. It's all good."

They had to go all the way around Grant's Camaro to get to the Jeep.

The big Trailways bus was already idling, throaty, windows all lit up and cozy when Lee's Jeep pulled up in front of the tiny depot just down the street from The Little Bear. He left the engine running and got out when Rayna did.

"Okay."

"Okay."

The awkward pause they'd come to expect.

"See you."

"You know how to text?"

"I do. I don't like it."

"Okay. Well. Call me."

"I will."

"No, Lee: Call me."

To avoid another awkward pause, Lee put out his hand to shake hers. And immediately regretted it. But Rayna's smile was charmed, cautious, warming. Was it possible she actually liked that Lee didn't try to kiss her?

"I enjoy seeing you," she said, as if she was trying the concept out for herself. "It's weird."

"Friends," Lee reminded her.

"Call me."

"I will," he said. He said it again, that he would. Call.

"You better."

Lee watched until the air brakes hissed and the bus rumbled away. Rayna waved to him from a back window. She said something, her lips moving, but Lee didn't care what it was. He felt all thawed out. And his jaw ached from trying so hard not to just grin like a happy dog the whole time he'd been with her.

COLD HARBOR

SEVENTEEN

*F*lag of surrender, flag of shame.

Dawn bruised the darkness, stirring the legion of sleepy speculators milling outside storage unit 444, and the angry red tag pasted across the lock latch fluttered in a stiff wind that coursed through the long, narrow aisle. A broad-shouldered man came through the crowd politely, dressed in a tan-and-brown flannel over a filthy Drive-By Truckers T-shirt, saggy jeans that hung improbably from his hips and teased some paisley boxers, sunglasses cocked back on his crewcut, a clipboard in one fat hand.

"Okay. Make space, ladies. Ten feet back from the door."

Feet shuffling, the milling mass shifted, flowed, and Lee and Grant found themselves moving without meaning to. A woman with a garbage-bag poncho that hung to her knees crinkled awkwardly full-tilt back into them. Lee caught her and kept her upright.

"Whoopsie." She went rigid under his hands, a mongrel dog that didn't like being touched. "I'm wearing alpaca," she said somewhat apologetically, and it took Lee a moment to understand she was explaining her plastic overgarment: "I didn't want to get it all sooty," she continued, "what with the Denver dew and the dirt and the just, you know, general grime that comes of interrupted lives and long-term storage."

Lee nodded and, once he'd stabilized her, took his hands back and shoved them down in the pockets of his jeans.

"Here we go," Grant told him.

Lee had read somewhere about people who lived in storage units because of unemployment and the economy. Everyone around him this morning looked as if they could have emerged from a storage unit. And Grant had literally been in storage: Territorial Prison. He wouldn't talk about it. Everything in that hard drive has been lost, he had said, when Lee asked. You can't retrieve it, so let's move on.

The broad-shouldered man held both hands up and fluttered the clipboard. If he could have their attention, please. He could, and did, and proceeded to explain the rules: ten-minute viewing period, after which the bidding would begin; no crossing the ten-foot DMZ; no flashlights; no stools or height-enhancement devices; all sales final; the winning bidder would have forty-eight hours to empty the storage space after which the management team would load it up and haul it away and assess a ten-dollar-per-cubic-foot penalty for which said successful bidder would be required to leave a credit card imprint as assurance.

A question arose from a thin man who didn't have a credit card but brought his checkbook. No was the quick answer; unfortunately, there were no exceptions. It was a rigid formula, and the big man was sorry but the credit card imprint procedure was required. He toggled the crotch of his pants as if there might be a small animal in there, the inseam was hanging so low. He glanced at the display of his cell phone, and then he spat out something lumpen onto the pavement, and rubbed it with his boot.

"Any other questions?"

"Who are all these people?" Lee asked his brother.

"The key to this, as I understand it from some reality TV show I watched once with these OG lifers down in Cañon City," Grant said, ignoring him, "is to look for the suggestion of spaces behind what's up front. It's a geometry problem. Negative space. Pockets, cavities, where, I dunno, there could be a motorcycle hiding. Or an ATV, or a Wedgewood stove, or a pinball machine. Or some antique furniture, or, well, anything valuable, really. You want to be able to cover your bid and then some."

Lee said he wasn't planning on bidding.

Grant said he'd heard of people claiming contents of a foreclosed container with a bid of fifty dollars and finding over a hundred grand worth of pristine early Jack Kirby comic books preserved in plastic sleeves. The broad-shouldered man had produced a giant pair of red-handled bolt cutters from somewhere, and as the first glint of sun shivered over the slotted steel roofs of the Lock'n Go Self Storage lot, the padlock snapped, dropped, clattered to the pavement, and the unit's door yawned open.

Lee squinted and craned to see over the crowd in front of him. The inside of the container looked as if somebody had backed up to it a dump truck filled with clothes and broken things, emptied its load into, and then crammed the door shut. A flat basketball flopped out and wobbled down the driveway.

"Fuck a duck," barked the alpaca woman, aloud. "Criminy. They been through it and took away all the good stuff."

"Maybe not," said a goateed man next to her, who Lee guessed was some relation. "Don't be a negative Nelly."

"Why are we here, again?" Lee asked his brother, but Grant had pushed to the front of the viewing area and didn't hear him.

Ten minutes proved to be shorter than Lee thought. Half of the prospectors drifted away, grumbling like the alpaca lady, not interested. Another third just stood and speculated about shapes under bedspreads, the contents of a stack of sturdy U-Haul moving boxes, the viability of that microwave (or convection oven?) just becoming visible in the back shadows of the container as the new day brightened, and whether the curve of chrome that some thought they saw exposed in the tangle of some blue jeans and work shirts was the handlebar of a carbon fiber racing bike or just the front curl on the grip bar of some geezer's shitty walker. But there were a few quiet, purposeful doyens who sipped from steaming Dunkin' Donuts coffee cups and kept prowling, back and forth, restless but purposeful, changing angles of observation and scribbling notes and adding columns of figures that Lee guessed were attempts to guesstimate the value of everything visible to hedge their losses in the event that under all the junk in plain sight was just more junk and disappointment.

For a moment, Lee wished they'd brought Rayna, as Grant had suggested when he announced the Denver storage space excursion. But nothing good had ever come of Grant suggesting Lee bring a girlfriend anywhere, and while Rayna wasn't really a girlfriend yet, whatever Rayna was, she was not someone Lee wanted to overexpose to his brother's cheerful and relentless ruination.

"I seen you at the Centennial Swap Meet," the woman in the trash bag was asking and telling. Lee shook his head. "I think yes," she said. "I think I never misremember a face. Mmm-hmm. You'all was selling liquid cinnamon extract and stinky incense from Whereverthehellistan. You got that Ford with the TruckNutz hanging from the hitch, which is hilarious."

Lee drifted away from her. Disappointment. Right. Suddenly he'd figured out why Grant had brought him.

"I'm thinking we set a limit of no more than a hundred fifty dollars," Grant said sotto voce, moving in front of Lee. "Unless it's just pure garbage underneath." Grant estimated they could get most of their investment back by selling the blue jeans to this guy he met in prison who bundled used denim and took the bundled lots to Mexico where they hired little kids to rip the pants apart and sew them back together as distressed fashion jeans and then market them to East Coast hipsters for unholy profits.

"This is not the same as a gold mine," Lee said.

Grant stared at him blankly, as if he didn't know what Lee could be talking about.

"Time's up!"

The storage door swung shut and the broad-shouldered man angled back to the front of the gathering, holding up his pants with one hand; the crowd pressed in on him, impatient to begin their bidding. And so it began: minimum bid of $50 rising in $5 increments steadily up to $135 and then a pregnant pause as people gut-checked their credit card balances and appraisals of the contents of the unit. The lady in the trash bag and alpaca shook her head regretfully and walked away. The goatee man stayed. Maybe they weren't related.

"One forty. Do I hear one and a half? One fifty in the hat. One fifty-five. One fifty-seven? You sir, one sixty, thank you. Is that it?"

"One seventy."

"Two!"

Grant was bidding. *Oh Jesus.* Lee pushed to the front to find him.

"Two ten."

"I like where you two're going with this," said the big man. "I like your fire and conviction."

Lee found Grant locked eye-to-eye at ten paces with a rail-thin dude whose handlebar mustache had to be a disguise. It was waxed to a fine, ridiculous point and took two lazy turns from each side of the fiercely misshapen nose before pointing skyward. Grant was grinning his you-wanna-fuck-with-me? grin, and Lee tensed for the likelihood that if Grant didn't win the bidding he might want to punch the mustache man out. Or worse.

"Two twenty."

Lee nudged Grant, and Grant shook his head. "Two thirty."

"Two forty."

"It's Rollie Fingers all over again," Lee observed, whispering sidelong to his brother. "Remember what happened to the Dodgers in '74."

"Three hundred dollars," bid Grant; he had never been much interested in baseball history.

"Sold," said the broad-shouldered auctioneer with a tug of his pants.

And that was that.

Later, knee-deep in what proved to be not junk covering hidden treasure but simply junk covering more junk (as the alpaca woman had suspected), Grant banged his hand on top of an old Protontube TV and kicked halfheartedly through the piles of blue jeans, which were threadbare and worthless and riddled with mold.

"Story of my life," Grant said, but not bitterly.

"Not really."

"What?"

"The story of your life: It isn't about taking chances that don't pan out," Lee said. "If that's what you mean. That's not what you do, Grant. That's what I do."

Lee watched his brother stalk around the container without saying anything for a while. A panel van rattled down the driveway between the containers, flashed momentarily past the square opening of theirs, speakers muffled and booming. Jay-Z. Lee recognized the beat and bark from the hallways and parking lots at the high school.

"And this isn't the same as a gold mine," Lee added.

"I don't know why you keep saying that."

"We came here," Lee continued, "because you think that all I want from the gold mine is the payout. And you wanted to show me that maybe there were easier ways to get that thrill."

"We came here," Grant disagreed stubbornly, "to bid on a big box of Cracker Jack and hope there was a prize inside, that's all.

If you want to make some correlation with your as-yet-unprov-en-to-have-any-value-whatsoever   hole-in-the-fucking-ground, go ahead, Lee. It's mental masturbation. I don't do metaphors."

His foot hit something and he stopped and bent and pulled from the denim sea an old double-bore shotgun.

"Hey."

Lee considered his brother with the shotgun and thought: *Oh, great, just what he needs.*

"See what I mean," Lee said.

He walked out into the sun. Classic. The endless serendip-ity of Grant. Sometimes, uncharitably, it made Lee wonder even about the assault felony and the prison term and what golden parachute that adventure had engendered that Lee couldn't quite gauge because there had to have been an upside in it for Grant; there was always an upside for Grant.

"This baby has got to be worth three hundred bucks, huh?" But Grant wasn't looking at the shotgun with the eyes of a man intending to sell it.

The Front Range of the Rockies leaned away, panoramic against cartoon fluffy white clouds and the pristine robin's-egg sky like some cheap cardboard painted scrim for a community theater musical. The big dance number at the end of the first act. Impossibly grand and beautiful. Not to be trusted or believed. Lee didn't like Denver. It tried too hard to impress him. Turn your back to the mountains, and Denver was just Dallas with less oxygen.

"Hey," Grant called out, chipper now, from the depths of the container. "Get a loada this: complete set of Bronco bobblehead dolls, 2002 season. Sweet. Now we're talking."

And Lee was always a little unraveled down here: the thin-set spread of housing developments, the creeping foreboding he felt—he knew—without cause. But Grant was fiddling with the shotgun again. Breaking it open, checking the bore, testing the triggers, lost in some byzantine calculation that was sure to raise havoc sometime soon.

"I don't see any cartridges, do you?"

Lee wanted, needed, to get back to his high ground.

EIGHTEEN

*T*he following Friday, to the wobbly rhythm of the Junior Orchestra's wan "Pomp and Circumstance," a sea of black squares shuffled, shuffled, shuffled down the steep center aisle of the Evergreen High School football stadium grandstands, a nervous mosaic. Graduating seniors descended to the track, spilling off single file to sit in folding chairs that faced a temporary stage.

And little more than a mile away on the diagonal, Grant's black Camaro was parked across the street from Lorraine's split-level, and he leaned against the front fender, watching the house and frowning as if he was disappointed in himself for even being there. Due to the eccentric vagaries of canyon acoustics, over the shoulder of forest that separated river from lake he could hear the faint strains of the graduation march mingled with the soft bubble and hiss of the river bending behind him.

It's yours.

Lorraine finally passed in front of a bedroom window upstairs, holding her baby. She stopped when she saw Grant. She stayed there for a moment, staring back at him, almost truculent. She waved and smiled.

It's yours.

Grant jumped off the hood of the car, ran to the driver's side, got in, gunned the engine, popped the clutch, and was already halfway down the street by the time Lorraine appeared on the front porch of her house, discontented but not surprised.

Lee was at the microphone on the graduation rostrum when he saw what he was sure was Grant's Camaro speeding up Highway 74 toward Bergin Park and the interstate. A smear of black against green. He rubbed his finger where his wedding ring had always been and continued, "And so I am very happy to announce that the winner of this year's Evergreen High School Weyerhauser Paul Bunyan Woodworker of the Year Scholarship—"

A cherry bomb firecracker arced from the sea of black square hats and backward, over the howling graduates, and exploded near the boxes of diplomas with a deafening *boom.* Girls shrieked, boys laughed, the parents in the bleachers clicked tongues, and Lee forged ahead:

"The Woodworker of the Year Scholarship goes to Ben Culhein, along with a $200 gift certificate from A&A Auto Parts."

There was polite applause from the parents, and a chorus of mocking "woot-woot-woot" from a section of boys who, though they did not know it yet, would not be receiving diplomas, just a blank card that read: FAILED TO MATRICULATE, and the principal's private phone number for the parents who, because mail had been intercepted and messages erased, would discover this unfortunate fact after the ceremony was over. An awkward, large-limbed senior boy who still wore orthodontic braces, Ben Culhein rose in the back row and tried to make his way to the front through a gauntlet of jostling friends.

"Ben's senior project, in case you were curious," Lee told the audience, "was a chest of drawers on the front of which he hand-carved an original woodland scene of native Rocky Mountain wildlife." None of which, Lee neglected to add aloud, looked like any earthly organism.

The Camaro was long gone. Ben Culhein thumped up onto the stage, abashed, and Lee handed him a certificate and shook his hand. Ben had black sports antiglare patches under each eye, marked with New Testament verse numbers. He looked genuinely thrilled. There was no recipient of the Lockheed-Martin Achievement in Physics Award this year, so Lee turned away and sat down, letting the scattered applause take Ben back into the gallery of his classmates. Lee settled into his folding chair next to Mr. Harounian, who murmured:

"No Lockheed-Martin?"

"No. Not this year."

"*Estos niños no tienen ninguna ambición*," Harounian scowled.

"Micky Jacobson has the grades, but he punted the SAT II test, and Lockheed-Martin has that baseline minimum score you gotta hit or forgetaboutit."

"Cry me a river," Harounian said.

Lee just nodded and wondered where Grant was going.

Some guys just can't commit!

Rayna was behind the counter reading a fairly recent edition of *Cosmo* when Grant walked into her General Store an hour later.

And some guys will commit but don't think it means the same thing that you do. Make him talk! Make it part of your sexy-time. Communicate. But don't give ultimatums, unless you're prepared for both possible answers to the question!

"Hey."

Rayna did not look up.

"Do your pupils dilate when you're getting ready to dump a girlfriend?" she asked him.

"What?"

Rayna showed him the magazine. Some airbrush perfect and posed brunette supermodel with roiling lips gazed fiery out from the cover, the tip of her fuchsia tongue between her teeth, as if thoughtful or something.

How to Break Up without Breaking Up.

Reading His Body Language.

Ten Secret Sex Techniques to Keep Him Faithful.

Plus: Cosmetic Surgery—When Is Too Early?

"I don't know. I've never watched my eyes when I've done it. Not that I've done it all that much. I might be interested in some of those ten techniques, though," he said.

Rayna put the magazine back in the rack and looked up into his eyes coolly. Grant saw that she knew he had done it, disappointed his girlfriends and lovers, many, many times, and that it didn't scare her. Grant asked her if she knew anything about shotguns, and moments later she was sighting down the double barrels of the Remington Spartan 310 Grant had liberated from the Lock'n Go storage unit in Denver. She asked if he was going hunting.

"No."

"Skeet?"

"Easy for you to say."

Rayna didn't even smile. Grant had reached for a kind of flimsy automatic flirty wit that even he knew, the moment it came out of his mouth, was not going to fly here. It usually worked on cocktail waitresses and women on the rebound, in bars, generally, after eleven-thirty, probably in both cases because of inattention. With Rayna it was more than a waste of time; it felt like an admission of weakness. Grant wondered why he even cared.

"Do you know anything about shotguns?" Rayna asked him.

"Not really."

"Well this one's pretty nice: walnut stock, automatic ejectors, and a ventilated barrel rib. See here? It uses screw-in choke tubes. People usually buy it to hunt fowl or shoot clay targets."

"Sure. That's a good idea."

"Mostly because you don't have to be very good at aiming," Rayna added.

"Ah."

Rayna stared at him again, in a way that ordinarily would not have made Grant so uncomfortable.

"What?"

"I have to ask myself the question, though: Who sold a shotgun to a convicted felon?"

Grant told her about the trip to the storage unit foreclosure auction, the successful bid, the serendipity of finding something of value that could justify his and Lee's three-hundred-dollar wager, pointing out that as such, the shotgun could be construed to be Lee's and, furthermore, the shells Grant wanted her to sell him for it were a surprise for his brother, who, now that you mention it, had got a serious hankering for hunting skeet or whatever.

"Lee?" She looked doubtful.

"I had to bring the gun so you could sell me the right bullets," Grant said.

"Shells."

"Yeah."

For a while, Rayna just studied him again. Grant never minded women staring at him.

"What are you really up to?" she asked.

"You were lying about not liking the Camaro, weren't you?" He looked right through her. Rayna shivered. Grant thought: *Okay. Here we go.*

"Yes. A little."

"Lying a little or only liked it a little?"

Rayna shrugged, noncommittal. "I don't think I can sell you shotgun shells," she said.

"What does your magazine say about good girls and bad cars?"

"Wear a Hooters T-shirt and learn about drifting," Rayna said. "And that there's usually not enough room in the backseat for anything constructive from the feminine point of view."

"Depends on the girl, I guess," Grant said.

"Don't kid yourself," Rayna demurred. There was still the question of a felon buying ammunition for a weapon he wasn't supposed to possess, she pointed out.

"Well," Grant said, "I definitely can't buy or own a handgun, but a rifle, well, and I think the NRA would support me on this, a recreational rifle, or target shotgun, if you will, would be my God-given right as an American, albeit one who had run afoul of some liberal, penny-ass laws. And as for the shotgun shells, hell, that doesn't even factor into the Second Amendment or any federal restrictions I'm aware of. I could be buying them for some craft projects I'm doing. Or decorations on a birthday cake for my brother."

Rayna gave back the shotgun. Their hands touched. Rayna shivered again and put both her hands in her pockets.

"Can I buy singles? Or do they come in a box?"

"I really, really like your brother," Rayna said.

Grant smiled and told her that he did, too. Five minutes later, he walked out with the gun and a box of shells and a nice chamois-cloth cover that Rayna found under the counter, which Grant thought would come in handy since he only planned on using the shotgun once.

The stadium at Evergreen High School was in twilight shadow and completely empty except for the chairs, which Lee and a few of his vocational-education kids were folding and stacking on carts to be pulled back into storage until next year's commencement when, from the far side of the field, a couple of nut-brown men in cowboy-cut suits came marching toward Lee, and while he thought he recognized them, he could not say from where. They'd arrived in a gaudy red helicopter that spiraled down out through blades of sunset that broke over the jagged shoulder of Mount Evans after the ceremony ended and the last parents were clearing the stands. A couple of maintenance staff serving as parking lot ushers tried to wave them off, but the chopper landed anyway, on the grassy practice fields. Lee watched the two men step out before the blades had even settled and duckwalk with heads lowered to confer with the parking guys; money changed hands, like a tip to a valet that keeps your Mercedes at the curb of that fancy restaurant where everybody can see it, and you can just walk out after dinner and get in without waiting with the hoi polloi.

And, as anyone would, Lee thought: *Whoa.*

They looked vaguely familiar. He'd seen them before, somewhere: the dead eyes, that close-cropped black hair full of some shiny product that caught the dim gleam of the waxing gibbous moon, but when they opened their mouths to speak it was with the cut, slightly lengthened dipthongs of the Wyoming plains.

"Mr. Garrison?" The taller one extended his hand.

"That's me."

"Saul Slocumb, sir. My brother, Paul."

The smaller one smiled. Perfect teeth. His eyes aimed at a spot just off Lee's face. "Nice to meet you."

"Your names rhyme," Lee said.

"Poetry of life."

Paul glanced back at the track and worried, "Are there chemicals on this grass?"

Lee didn't know.

"We've come to discover that you're in the mining business," Saul Slocumb explained. "Coincidentally, so are we."

"Wyoming, sadly to say it." Paul frowned.

"Copper and other useful minerals."

Lee told them he owned just one mine and wondered how they knew, but the Slocumbs had a script and stuck to it.

"Our daddy started with one incursion just outside Jakarta," Paul drawled. "A mere sliver of opportunity that played out beyond his wildest expectations over the next ten years and provided him with capital and resources to explore and develop over five thousand subsequent claims worldwide with a net yield of several hundred million dollars."

"Somehow Wyoming was where we landed," Saul added. "Cold and windy. God bless it."

"Or not," Paul said.

Lee allowed a respectful moment to contemplate this, then asked how he could help them.

"Long story short, sir? We have recently procured the Silver Bell, Hawthorne, and Granny King Patent Mines and related claims directly northeast of and due east of the Blue Lark—"

"Which is my mine," Lee noted.

"Yes sir, it is indeed."

Lee told them that he thought all those other claims were just abandoned, causing Saul to shake his head gravely. "No sir, no, they are part of the Slocumbs' growing Colorado portfolio."

"The Clear Creek County Clerk," Saul said, "has hinted that you and your partners might—"

Lee cut him short. "Partners?" He thought aloud, "Doug? You were talking to Doug Deere?"

"Douglas Deere, yep, that's the gentleman," Paul said. "Long-winded to the nth. We thought of tag-teaming the listening part since he appeared capable of talking the stick out of a corn dog. Barely credible capacity for the microbrew they call Fat Tire, however."

Saul, peevish at the interruption, pressed on. "Mr. Deere said you might conceivably entertain a cash offer for the Blue Lark Mine, so that we could consolidate our Argentine Pass holdings and exploit them in the most efficient way."

"Doug doesn't own the mine."

The ensuing, awkward, and pointedly malevolent (or was it just Lee's imagination?) silence was spoiled by a clatter of folding chairs as a badly stacked group fell off the roller cart that Lee's students were maneuvering along the track. They looked sheepishly over at Lee. Saul Slocumb slid his fingers into the waistband of his pants as if holstering weapons. Paul Slocumb stared anxiously down at the grass under his feet and said, "You know, if there's DDT on this bluegrass, I'd prefer to stand over on that track composite."

"Doesn't own the mine," his brother echoed.

It was the first time Lee had seriously contemplated the possibility of a real strike rather than merely the diaphanous dream of one. The finding, the digging, the speculating, the calculating, the bonhomie of the common cause (although with Doug and Barb there was always a concomitant pall of uncertainty, as in, what-have-I-got-myself-into-with-these-people?), and now Doug had been, where, at some random bar talking it up and fielding offers from strangers? There was, again, a faint whiff of hazard to the Slocumbs. Maybe it was the aerial arrival; maybe it was just the incongruity of their appearance and their accents, Wyoming by way of Waziristan. Lee half expected them to pull out long talwars now and threaten him.

Threat. That was what he sensed, however nebulous, lurking behind the smiles and the civility.

A threat. Of what?

"Full disclosure: We had several conversations with the previous owner, Mr. G. Elmore Bunn, about selling us the property, but only the preliminaries, you understand, hopeful hypotheticals, nothing, we admit, formal or binding or in writing, but imagine our complete astonishment to discover that he had sold the mine on eBay."

Lee said he'd not known the man's name.

"It's not important," Saul agreed.

"We're happy for him," Paul chimed in. "And for you. Your good fortune, we mean. Because we think you'll find our offer generous. Can we, um . . . " He gestured away from the grass.

"You don't really believe there's any gold up there?" Lee asked as they walked toward the track.

"Why wouldn't there be?"

"Gold and silver," the other brother said. "I can tell you this, we've had the Granny King assayed, and the numbers were promising. I learned, from your Mr. Deere, the prior owner of your claim had done likewise. We've seen the paperwork. They're not, by any means, sir, played out. Oh no."

"Perhaps it's just a mix-up," Saul continued on his stubborn bearing, "but, as we said, your friend, Mr. Deere, the County Clerk, inferred that you and your partners would be open to—"

"Look," Lee interrupted. "Doug owns a share of any profit we might see from this mining operation we're playing at. But . . . 'Blue Lark.' Get it? I mean, the name says it all, as far as I'm concerned, a blue lark, and the land itself belongs to me. It's a hobby, and it wouldn't matter to me if we spent the next ten years up there hacking away at the rock for nothing. And it's not for sale, and I'm sorry if you came all this way on the word of a friend who has spoken out of turn."

Paul began violently stamping his feet on the track to shake the chemicals off them. *Bam! Bam! Bam!,* all Rumpelstiltskin.

Saul shook his head like a dog as if something had entered his ears that didn't belong there. "How can it not matter?" he asked. "How can this man go in the mountain without some expectation of reward? No, you are lying."

"I'm not. I'm sorry."

"There is nothing to be sorry about," Saul said, "unless you are lying, sir. That's the only explanation. There is a Sufi story about a man who cut down a tree. Do you know Sufism? We are not adherents, mind you."

"We're Presbyterians," Paul allowed.

"But, there is a story," Saul continued, "where this man, he cuts down a tree. And a Sufi passing by, who saw him do it, crosses to where the tree has fallen and observes how the branches and leaves still look so fresh, you know—full of sap and happy because this tree does not realize that it has been cut down. The woodsman shrugs and tells the Sufi that while this may be true, while the tree may be ignorant of the damage it has suffered, it will know enough in due time. Upon which the Sufi bursts into delighted laughter and says, 'Yes, and meanwhile you cannot reason with it!'"

Lee smiled politely and tried to figure out what Saul was getting at. Was Lee the tree? Or the woodsman?

"It's just a story," Paul told him.

Dark had dropped on the valley with its typical lack of ceremony, and the sky glowed incandescent shades of blue and purple, impossibly dark and bright. "There's another story," Paul said, "it's longer, but here, I'll ruin the ending to make my point clear: A tiger offers a man three rupees for his ham sandwich. The man refuses so the tiger eats them both."

"That's a good story," Saul said.

There was an edge to their smiles.

"So then." Saul stared at Lee intently.

"No," Lee said.

With disbelief bordering on outrage, Saul expressed his profound disappointment that Lee didn't even want to hear their offer.

"No," Lee said. "No thanks."

Rayna's eyes opened. Awakened by a subterranean *boom*. Or did she dream it?

She had a strong craving for a cigarette.

Sitting up, then, she heard a second dull *boom,* not very loud, but it thumped in her chest like a low bass note or drumbeat, and she got up and went to the window and peered out into the darkness, not so much expecting to see anything; she just needed to look.

Had it come from down-valley or on the mountain?

Then again: *boom.* That made three. Then silence.

The noise scared her. Rayna was not easily scared. Opening the window, she felt a cold breeze and heard the hushed shudder of wind sifting through the pine trees, the noise of a million needles trembling at the end of fluid, swaying branches like an ocean; it rolled in waves. She never got used to it. The moon was low, and the wash of stars across the sky was dizzying. The cold caused her to tremble. She wanted a cigarette and knew that there was a whole new carton of Kents in the storeroom, delivered yesterday, fresh sweet tobacco that she could fire up and enjoy, as long as she ignored the horrifying FDA warning pictures on the pack. She stood at the window for a long time, listening, watching, waiting, but there was no more disruption. The night held her.

Smoking made her think of Lee.

The cigarettes made her think of Grant.

Did she dream Grant? His midday visit, the shotgun and the shells? She knew she hadn't. She wished she had, but she hadn't.

Shit.

NINETEEN

A couple of Doug's hairier friends, Vick and Steve, soul patch and mutton chops respectively, were already sawing timbers on the far end of the tailings when Lee and Grant hiked up to the mine. Some glorious sunshine beat down on the Argentine Pass from a cornflower-blue, cloudless sky, taking the edge off the high-altitude chill. Grant made a dry comment about a crisis of facial hair that Lee didn't quite hear over the power saw.

Earlier that same morning, Lee had padded, sleepy, from his bedroom into the bathroom and had the shower turned on before he saw what could only have been muddy ochre footprints on the floor tiles, but they were there for only a moment before the water washed them away. The bathroom floor was unsullied; the carpet in the hallway showed nothing. Lee pushed open the door to Grant's room, found Grant awake, out of bed, standing, yawning, scratching his groin, and sniffing through a pile of clothing for a clean shirt. He looked up at Lee without focus.

"Hey."

"Hey," Lee said.

For a moment they had just stood there, looking at each other, then Lee padded back down the hallway again to take his shower.

Now Doug came out of the mine in his mud-slick waders, mud the selfsame color as the muddy footprints from the shower, yellow-ochre-incandescent-shit-viscous mud that Lee had seen so much of now it was burned into the back of his eyes. And maybe in the shower, on the tiles, when it wasn't there.

"I didn't tell them. I didn't," Doug said.

Lee remarked that if that was true, how did Doug even know that Lee would be wondering if he had told anyone anything since the only way Doug could have known Lee spoke with the Slocumbs after graduation was if Doug had talked to them himself, earlier, and sent them in Lee's direction?

"I don't know from any Slocumbs," Doug insisted. "I don't know what you're talking about."

It went on like this for a while: Lee dogging Doug and trying to engage him in a disputation while Doug pretended that he had something really, really crucial to get done outside the mine that consisted mostly of walking away from Lee while the mud on his waders dried and flaked off and the hairy friends sawed.

Grant's eyes ached and his head pounded. It wasn't a hangover. He hadn't been drinking. He'd tried the pressure points already. No luck.

"Well if you didn't tell them," Lee was saying, "who did?"

"But as long as they're interested in buying us out," Doug wondered aloud, as if just coming to the idea, "I don't see why we can't have a sit-down meeting of all the shareholders and—"

"No."

"I'm going down to get some aspirin," Grant said.

"Do you know who the Slocumbs are?" Doug asked.

Lee saw no purchase in pointing out that Doug had claimed he didn't.

"I'm going down to get some aspirin," Grant repeated.

Lee wasn't listening. Doug started edging away from him again. "Major, major players on the world mining scene," Doug alleged. "No individual actually finds gold in the modern age. You stake claims, you find a junior—a smaller exploration outfit—and sell them options to raise penny stock funds to chase the promise, and then when they get lucky, they turn around and sell to a major who has the resources to go in and get the lode. This happens to be a golden, if you'll pardon the pun, opportunity to cut out the middleman, Lee. By which I mean the junior."

"There's a world mining scene?"

"You can't mess with these guys."

Grant skated loose tailings back down into the trees, his course set for Rayna's General Store, to get his head cured.

"What about Creede? What about the triumph of the individual and—"

Doug cut him short: "Creede woulda been all over this, and you know it. Smart money's all in the royalties and the stock options."

"Doug. It's my land."

"Oh, now you're gonna get technical on me."

"No. I paid for it. I pay for all the equipment."

"There's other kinds of investment. Sweat equity."

"What you have is a share of the potential mineral rights, if we, personally, find anything. Ten percent of a wish and a prayer. If I sell the land—" Then Lee backtracked. "Never mind, I'm not interested in majors or juniors or anybody else."

"You don't have to shout."

"I'm not shouting."

"And who helped you find the mine? And who helped you dig the entrance out?"

"I acknowledge that, Doug."

"And who got his friends from the molybdenum mine to come up here and help us timber?" Doug shouted, gesturing toward Vick and Steve, who had stopped sawing and fired up a fatty to watch the argument unfold. "And who got the mine helmets?

And who knew about tommyknockers, and the Welshman, and the Coblynau?"

"I bought the mine helmets." Lee frowned. "Coblynau?"

"Mine gnomes," Doug explained. "Butt-ugly gnomes in little mine uniforms. They're about yay-high," he said, chopping just under his knees. "The Welsh think they haunt mines and quarries, working real hard, all day and night, but never finishing. They might even be the cause of rockslides."

"Never finishing what?"

"Yeah," Doug said, veering back into the mine. "Wouldn't you like to know?"

Lee chased him, ducking his helmet under the first header. The front tunnel was lit by a string of fat white Christmas tree lights connected to the gasoline generator that dully flatulated outside. Somewhere, deeper in the mine, Mayor Barb was tap tap tapping away at the rock, and tossing fragments into a metal bucket. At the intersection of the main tunnel and its tributaries, Doug stopped retreating and turned, the light blazing from his helmet hitting Lee full on so he had to shade his eyes.

"No doubt a lawyer'd have something to say about your—your—your so-called definition of ownership!" Doug hissed.

"I don't think so. You want to ask one?"

"No. I'm just offering that a legal opinion might have you whistling a different tune."

Lee sighed. "All right. What do you think is fair?"

"Let's take a vote."

"I'm the majority shareholder. I'd win."

"Majority of what?!"

"Exactly."

There was a confused pause as Doug caught up with himself and seemed worried that he'd jumped to Lee's side of the argument.

"I'm not selling the mine," Lee said again.

"Look . . . " Doug regrouped. "How about let's just . . . get a god-damn assay done then. Value the ore. And find out what the what is."

Lee said fine, and asked, since Doug seemed to be the expert on the subject, where in Denver they could take a sample to be tested. Doug backpedaled, offering that the assay might be kind of expensive, but Lee said he'd pay for it.

"Since it's my mine," Lee added.

Doug pulled a well-worn plat map out of his back pocket and spread it on the crude workbench they'd built in the cross-ing on the other side of the flooded downshaft. "We should take samples from four or five different potential deposit areas." He pointed them out: "How about here and here. Here. Here . . . "

Barb came out of the darkness, helmet ablaze, lugging a pail full of rock fragments.

"And here," she said. She dropped the pail and went back into the shadows. The voices of Doug and Lee rattled through the rocky passageways and fractured into a kind of geological patois. Her helmet light swept the deep recesses of a crevice. Tiny bits of something yellow glistened.

She sighed.

Remembering the fool's gold, she wondered if it was worth the effort to climb up into that gap and get one more sample.

Rayna was ringing up picnic items for some day-trippers and their children when the doorbell jingled and Grant strolled in. His coy-ote eyes met hers and stuck; he stood awkwardly in the main aisle, watching and waiting until the tourists ambled out the door.

"I just wanted to make sure," he said, "to be clear about, or, more to the point that you understand why even if I wanted to, I couldn't do anything . . . with you . . . because, well, you know. Lee saw you first."

Rayna didn't say anything for a moment.

"And I have a headache," Grant added.

"First. You mean like 'first dibs'?" Rayna asked him. "Like I'm a big fat cat's-eye marble or something?"

"No—no—listen—"

"How'd those shells work out?"

"Fine. I don't know. Ask Lee."

"You don't know?"

"Look, Rayna—"

"Prime piece of steak," she said, returning to her previous thought.

"All right. Okay. Let me just—you got any Naproxin?"

"I'm not. I'm not a marble, Grant. Or meat."

"The other day—"

"I'm not a trophy you win at the end of the race. Or let your brother win, for that matter, because you're trying to prove that you've got, I don't know, what? Character? Integrity? A modicum of restraint? Do either of us believe that?"

"What I'm trying to say is that what was going on the other day at the house is my brother really likes you and he was warning me off. So. Which, by the way, I think you should be flattered by. Because he's fucking picky. Not that it means anything if you're not equally interested."

Rayna just stared at him coolly.

"He just, he doesn't always make those things clear," Grant said, elaborating. "But—anyway, it's because of that, that I can't—you know—"

Rayna rolled her eyes. "No. I have no idea what you're talking about."

"Hook up."

"'Hook up.' Gee. Where'd you learn all the hip 'tween lingua franca, boyfriend, reading *Twilight* back in the Big House?"

Grant's mind balked. "Fuck you," he said. "You don't know what you're talking about," he said, harder than he wanted to.

"Oh." Rayna held her ground. Unfazed.

Grant tried sulking. It didn't play. Rayna's eyes drilled into him. "And you're telling me this why?" The room tilted, and Grant almost reached out to steady himself. He felt his pulse in his head. They just studied each other and time had no reference suddenly. A second, a minute, an hour, it was all the same. Nothing.

"Never mind."

"I know all about Marion Gilroy."

Grant affected innocence.

"You are not a nice guy," she added then, quieter.

"No, I'm not," Grant agreed.

"Could you, um, button your shirt all the way up? It's kind of distracting," Rayna said then. Grant looked—sure enough, his shirt was open at the neck down to the middle of his chest like some kind of Vegas lounge lizard. He tried to fix it and discovered two buttons were gone.

"No buttons," he said unnecessarily.

"No shit," Rayna said. "I'll sew them back on for you."

"What?"

Rayna was already walking to the front door. Her legs scissored, her hips rocked. *Jesus*, Grant thought.

"We've got buttons," she said. "We've got needles, we've got thread. It won't take but a minute." She flipped the YES, WE'RE OPEN sign over, so it read SORRY, WE'RE CLOSED. Then she turned back to Grant. "There."

Up in the mine, Doug carefully stripped a chunk of rock off the side of the wall and dropped it in his metal bucket. "Pearl de Vere," Doug called out.

"What are you on about?" Barb shot back from a darkness her helmet light momentarily cleaved.

"Beloved soiled dove of Cripple Creek, grand madame of the

Old Homestead house of ill-repute. Favorite flaxen-haired flesh-toy of the miner millionaires from Poverty Gulch. Many a good man has been ruined on the silky shores of woman."

Barb's voice barked at him to stow it.

Deeper in the mine, Lee stared at his own reflection in the bottomless water of the submerged downshaft. His headlight glinted off something, bright and gold. He leaned closer. A shotgun shell casing rested on a timber about four feet down, distorted by the clear water. Curious, Lee found a length of wire, straightened it, and plunged it into the shaft, fishing.

"Pearl eventually betrothed herself to one C. B. Flynn, a hard-working and prosperous mill owner, but the fire of '86 burned them out, and some pious Baptists blamed it on the Old Homestead," Doug waxed. "Flynn hired out to Monterrey, Mexico, where he contracted cholera and died, but Pearl had never given up on the oldest profession, so she relaunched her sexual services enterprise with great success, prancing nearly naked in French silks down Main Street every morning in an open carriage pulled by a team of fine ebony horses. Children were made to shield their eyes when Pearl rode past."

Barb's irritated response was inaudible.

Tiny particles of grit swirled in the sallow beam of Lee's helmet light as he fished for the shell. Refracted by the water, the wire missed twice, then dislodged it, and Lee slipped the wire's end delicately into the spent hollow to lift it up and out. But as he pulled, the water resisted and the wire bowed, the shell slipped off and tumbled away, down where his light finally couldn't penetrate the darkness.

"There are those who insist that abstinence is the proper course of action for a miner until he's made his strike. I'm just saying. The mountains are littered with stillborn reminders of promiscuous wildcatting," Doug concluded.

In her stub of a slant-shaft, Mayor Barb braced herself in the crevice she was mining, boots slipping on slick rock, gloved hands clutching at outcroppings, her hammer banging wildly from her belt.

Rayna squinted cross-eyed as she threaded a needle and Grant looked to sit on a flat spot atop some wooden crates in the back room of the General Store, but Rayna snapped at him without looking up: "Not there. That's dynamite."

"Jesus. Don't you have to have a license for that?"

"Technically? You do, yes. To make it, to sell it, to have it."

"And a special place for it. I mean . . . "

"What?" The needle caught light as it slid down the thread.

"Dynamite."

"It's the Wild West, Grant. Outlaws get shotguns, girls store TNT. Sit."

So Grant sat on a big can of roofing tar, and Rayna dragged another one right in front of him. Her legs got between his, her pink naked knees pressed together and lightly brushing against the insides of his thigh denim.

"Why don't I just take off the shirt?" Grant asked.

Rayna smiled, distant. "Oh, no, that's why we're putting the button on it. So it doesn't fall off," she said. She leaned into him, positioned the button, and began to sew it. The top of her head declined inches from Grant's chin, mouth, lips. Her hair smelled like surrender.

"Don't . . . move," she said.

In her slant-shaft, Mayor Barb's hammer and chisel hacked hard at the crease in the rock. A chunk fell loose, and she just managed to catch it and put it in the canvas pouch around her waist.

In the darkness, Doug sang—screamed, really—the theme song from the movie *The Man Who Would Be King*.

"Duh DUHHHHH da duh duh duh duh DA DA DA!"

In the mine, deeper, shrouded, like an astronaut at the edge of space, Lee crouched, low, near the soughing mud, running his hand over a series of dull yellow, metallic smudges in a hollow at the dead end of another stub shaft.

"Duh dee da da da dee da duh da da DAAAAHHHH!"

With his fingernail, Lee flicked a couple of gilded flakes into the palm of his hand. They didn't seem to be too friendly with the mountain rock. Just visiting.

He studied them, his breathing shallow, the light from his helmet jittery with doubt.

"Conversely, if he didn't have an interest in you," Grant was rambling, and he never rambled; it was as if some alt-Grant had leapt into his body. He was inside, looking out, but not in control of anything: his body, his mind, his mouth, and rambling on about this and that, like, well, like, okay, Lee's virtues, Lee's lofty intentions, Lee's gentleman to Grant's . . . hmm, well, what?

"Who?" Rayna was already nearly finished sewing the second button on his shirt. Intent. Committed to the task. And Grant began to mistrust his read of the whole situation. Double—no—triple-thinking it. *What did she want?*

"Who? Lee." *Lee.*

"Oh. Lee." She leaned in and bit off the thread. "Lee isn't here. I thought that was your strategy."

She sat up, and came face-to-face with Grant, her hazel eyes locked on his.

"This is, this is why I'm saying," he was stammering, and he never stammered, "you know, if you weren't, if you weren't, well, interested in him . . . "

"Am I making you uncomfortable or something?" Rayna asked.

"Yes, you are."

"Good. That makes me feel pretty." She buttoned his shirt up. "There."

"You are pretty," Grant said, a little insincerely, but, rattled now, he had to ask, "Rayna, are you interested in my brother? Or is this going in another direction?"

Rayna's hand was steady as she traced lightly down from the first button she fixed, to the next one, feeling the fabric. "Your brother," she repeated hollowly. "You say it in a way that makes me understand your love for him, without even having to question it, without having to know anything more about you. Was he a good brother? Did he share his toys, did he torture you when your parents went out to play bridge, were you always trying to measure up to him, was he the better student, did he protect you from bullies? You love him," Rayna observed drily, "but you came here to fuck me, Grant. In fact, you've taken it as a personal challenge that I didn't peel off my panties the first time you showed your face, which, by the way, the old me was mightily tempted to go ahead and do, and, believe me, has presented the new me with a personal challenge of an equal and opposite nature.

"And here we are, fourteen inches apart, and I can feel the heat from your legs and the sweetness of your breath, and in the Victorian version of this encounter, I would fairly swoon, right? Now, maybe I'm missing something, but the question of whether I am or am not interested in him seems to be beside the point, a sort of Cosmo-meets-Jane-Austen-thing, or maybe just a strategic consideration, from your perspective, as you muster your troops for another assault on my strange new resolve. Am I interested in your brother? I realize this might sound weird right now, but I believe it's none of your business."

"Like your smoking," Grant observed.

"I don't smoke," she said. The next button popped off in her hand. "Whoops."

"Guess it's not me," Grant observed quietly. He was thinking maybe this would still turn out all right; he couldn't help it. "This shirt just wants to come off."

"Think so?"

"Yeah. I do."

And so he'd made his play. Her eyes stayed locked on his; she said then, "It's lucky we've got more thread." And she leaned in with her hands on his chest and she kissed him. Long enough, but not too long.

"Yeah, I'm interested in Lee," she said finally, taking a breath and pushing back. "Very. I am. So. Yes. Sorry."

"That kiss didn't seem too interested in him."

Rayna shrugged and said, "That kiss wasn't me. It was just what my lips wanted."

Grant stood up. His head had cleared. He said, "You know what? This may be as close as I'll ever come to understanding women because I'm happy and sad at the same time."

"You ought to send that in to *Cosmo*."

"No, I'm serious. Maybe it came out wrong."

"Oh. I'm sorry, then. No, it's just me. The old me," she added, gloomy.

"You keep talking about her."

"Yeah." She sat back. She studied her hands, her chewed-down nails. "The old me was more like you than I want to admit," she said. "You wouldn't have liked her."

Grant stayed quiet.

"Nothing to lay siege to, nothing to ruin. The old me was vainglorious, Pompei during Vesuvius. Hot mud and ash raining down, too proud to run to safety, too stubborn to be scared.

"It was just dumb luck that I survived it," she said. "And still I miss her," she admitted.

Neither of them said anything for a while. There was the hum of the refrigeration units out in the store, the click and creak of the building as it caught the sun. And someone outside the store, knocking on the front door. Grant didn't have anywhere to put his hands. They felt big and clumsy, hanging at his sides like mitts.

"You gonna get that?"

"I don't think so. They'll come back."

"It sounded like Lee," Grant said.

"You can tell it's Lee from the knocking?"

"He was the best brother," Grant said. "I didn't deserve him. He did everything you said and then some. And I loved him and I hated him, and I know him and I don't understand him."

"Deserve has nothing to do with anything," Rayna scoffed. "And he's still your brother, what's with the past tense? And what in the world were you doing," she wondered aloud, "up on the mountain last night with that shotgun and my shells?"

It was Lee at the door.

His Jeep was parked across the street, behind Grant's Camaro, and he stood there at the grocery store entrance for a long time, staring at the CLOSED sign in the window, without any expression, and Rayna and Grant waited, back in the store's shadows, motionless, until Lee drew his conclusion, returned to his Jeep, fired up the engine, and spun a tight U-turn.

"Shit." Rayna watched him drive away. She asked Grant what he would tell Lee.

Grant closed his eyes. After a moment, he said, "Rayna, I did eighteen months in state prison for beating the living shit out of this stockbroker from church who Lee thought was having an affair with Lee's so-called wife, Lorraine."

There was a silence in the store. The refrigeration unit shut down, and they could hear the distant sawing from Doug's friends up at the mine.

"He was bragging about it. The stockbroker," Grant explained. "Bragging that Lee thought he was the one, I mean. Telling everybody he'd hung the horns on my brother by fucking her, fucking my brother's wife, Lorraine. Talking the shit. You know."

"What happened to him?"

"Beachum? Oh, hell, I guess he landed on all fours."

She waited.

"He married her, didn't he?" Grant said.

"Did he?"

"He did, yeah. They've got this . . . kid."

"And Lee just let you do it? Beat him up?"

"Well. It's not like he was there to stop me."

"I don't understand," Rayna said. "Did you think he—Lee wouldn't . . . "

Grant took a deep breath and talked over her: "No. No. Look, here's the deal: I did it because he's my brother and he never gets a break and I love him and because it was actually me who was fucking my brother's wife."

With that, Grant unlocked the door and walked out. And even before the door banged shut behind him, Rayna's eyes were blind with tears.

TWENTY

BROOMFIELD BOAT & YACHT CLUB
June Meeting Minutes
(7:15 PM, Winchester Avenue IHOP, Broomfield, CO)

Present: Jon White Bear; Daryl Carver; LizBeth Carver; June Etchevarria; Buddy Etchevarria; Dr. Pat Kyumoto, DDS; Jack Jackson, Esq.; Lee Garrison; Mary Grace Jackson-Rifkin, LN; Boo Buskirk; Sissy Voigt; Roy Voigt; and Raphael Zabrinski.

Absent: Melissa Johnson, Herve Johnson, and Vaslov Mrek.

Others Present: Guest speaker: Lt. Sheila Swanson (USN-ret.) and SN Susan Johnson (USN-rct.), her friend and former shipmate.

Proceedings:
· *Meeting called to order* at 7:15 PM by Boo Buskirk, President.
· May meeting minutes are amended and approved.

· *President's Report:*
- Recommends that if the Location Committee is not able to find a new meeting place by the end of this month, the club should

continue to meet in the current location through the end of the year. Mr. Carver states that if the meetings don't move he will not be able to continue with the club. He produces a doctor's note concerning allergies to chemicals comprising the maple scent of pancake syrup. Several members urge Carver to go ahead and resign. Mrs. Etchevarria suggests a painter's breathing apparatus or the sterile face mask many people wore during the H1N1 epidemic, which Ms. Jackson-Rifkin indicates she could bring home free from the hospital. After much discussion, Mr. Carver agrees to try a modified painter's mask he purchased for the club's last America's Cup celebration at the Royal Fork on Colfax Avenue, and the club unanimously confirms continuing to convene at the Winchester Avenue IHOP until next year.

- Mr. Garrison is asked if he would say a few words about his gold mine, as it is currently a topic of much speculation among club members, if the twitter and email traffic since our last meeting is any indication. Mr. Garrison says he would prefer not to talk about his gold mine, as there is no boating involved. [Secretary's note: He has some off-color opinions about tweeting and texting that are best left unrecorded.]

- Treasurer Kyumoto and Sergeant-at-Arms Mrek attended the National Boat Show in San Diego June 5–7, and Dr. Kyumoto gives a brief review, promising next month to give a longer presentation and show the short video tour Mr. Mrek shot of the new Stamas 310 Tarpon that he put a down payment on before his wife found out and froze the account. MOTION is made and seconded that the club send someone to intervene with Mrek's wife, Ishvuk, to assure her that it won't happen again, so that Mr. Mrek might rejoin the club.

- Mr. Garrison asks Dr. Kyumoto about the new Nordhavn trawlers. Dr. Kyumoto says he didn't see any trawlers at the National Boat Show. Mr. Garrison insists trawlers are always a big part of any boat show, and the Nordhavn is the Cadillac of recreational trawlers. Dr. Kyomoto opines that if Mr. Garrison wants to talk about something, why doesn't he talk about his gold mine, or is he embarrassed about it? Mr. Garrison accuses Dr. Kyumoto of not even knowing what a trawler is. Mrs. Etchevarria requests a point of order. President Buskirk has misplaced his gavel. Mr. Zabrinski says something nobody can understand on account of his accent, but Sissy Voigt, translating, although no one knew she spoke his language, says Raphael recommends tabling this discussion since no one in the club knows anything about trawlers. Sissy blushes suspiciously as she says this, and Mr. Zabrinski has one of those Continental smiles favored by the rakish rival in romance novels. Mr. Garrison wonders what the point of a boat club is if you can't ask good boat questions. Mr. White Bear offers a MOTION to censure Mr. Garrison for his "dispiriting attitude" and wonders if, perhaps, Mr. Garrison's gold mine is incompatible with Boat Club goals and guidelines. No one seconds it. Mr. Garrison expresses considerable doubt that the aforementioned Boat Club goals or guidelines even exist. President Buskirk asks Secretary Etchevarria to read the Goals and Guidelines for the record, but the Secretary admits she left her handbook at home. Mr. White Bear posits that maybe Garrison would like to just go ahead and join the Aurora Gold Mine and Ghost Town Jeeping Club and turn in his anchor pin. Mr. Garrison offers to go discuss this with Mr. White Bear out in the parking lot. Mr. White Bear would like some guarantee that Mr. Garrison's felonious little brother isn't waiting out there in the shadows. President Buskirk gavels the argument, insists that cooler heads should prevail; a MOTION to table Mr. Garrison's inquiry about Nordhavn trawlers at the National Boat Show is seconded and passed on voice vote by a clear majority.

· *Finance Committee report* provided by Treasurer Kyumoto: We have $31.19 in the treasury, not enough to buy waffle-fries or re-

freshments for everyone present. MOTION to take up a collection to do so fails by a vote.
- Mr. Jackson suggests a weekend car wash event to raise money. No discussion results.
- MOTION to accept financial report seconded and passed.

· *Water Safety Committee's report* provided by Sissy and Roy Voigt: This week's topic: Using Your Jeans as an Emergency Life Preserver. Video downloaded from YouTube won't play on anyone's laptop; MOTION to postpone Water Safety Committee's presentation seconded and passed.

· *Main Speaker:*
- Lt. Shiela Swanson, USN-ret. Multimedia PowerPoint presentation about Lt. Swanson's final tour of duty aboard the aircraft carrier *Ronald Reagan*. Highlights include a harrowing tale of night landings during Operation Enduring Freedom, a photo-tour of the "Arab Market" held aboard the USS *R.R.* while anchored off Dubai, and the King Neptune Line Crossing ritual for first-time sailors (nicknamed Pollywogs) upon crossing the International Dateline, during which SN Susan Johnson (USN-ret.) fondly recalls drinking carrier homebrew from a beer bong, stripping naked, and coating herself in cable grease to be pitched overboard where she nearly drowned. Helpful pointers on navigation in the absence of a GPS system ensue, also methods of dead reckoning, pilotage, celestial navigation, knot tying, and the use of sextants. Susan Johnson demonstrates the sextant until it breaks. Questions during the follow-up mostly center on seasickness and its remedies.

· *Other Business:*
- President Buskirk announces that he has recently hired a new secretary, Karla Quilty, and that she is selling her low-mileage, mint-condition 2003 Civic, in case anyone is interested.

· *Assessment of the Meeting:*

- Dr. Kyumoto reports that the past three meetings have run over the intended two-hour time slot by almost an hour. President Buskirk requests that members be more mindful and focused during discussions and suggests that the Club Development Chairman, Ms. Jackson-Rifkin, analyze the issue and report on it at the next meeting. Ms. Jackson-Rifkin suggests that maybe certain people (she doesn't want to name names) should just shut their mouths and open their ears. MOTION to adopt the principle "if you can't say something nice, don't say anything at all" passes with one dissent.

- Mr. Garrison offers to chair a committee to provide more information about sailing and boating at the meetings. He says it's hard enough to be in a boat club in a region that receives less than five inches of moisture in an entire year and is thousands of miles from the nearest ocean. Several members remind Mr. Garrison of the many local navigable waterways, including the Cherry Creek Dam, Chatfield and Bow Mar Lakes, plus the South Platte River and the High Line Canal. Garrison submits that tubing in the High Line does not qualify as boating "by any stretch of the imagination," and asks repeatedly whether anybody in the group actually owns a boat yet (not including Mr. Voigt's radio-controlled replica of the USS *Indianapolis*). Mr. White Bear's MOTION to censure Mr. Garrison is reintroduced, seconded, and passed unanimously. Mr. Garrison departs the meeting without further comment.

- Membership votes unanimously to thank Lt. Swanson for the stimulating talk and wishes her and Susan Johnson best of luck with their new Chick-fil-A franchise.

· Meeting adjourned at 10:47 PM.
· Minutes submitted by Secretary June Etchevarria.

TWENTY-ONE

*I*t credibly looked, for a moment, as if Lee'd been crucified backwards on the cherrywood cross he'd made. But he was only giving it a clear-coat while Grant waited outside, smoking a cigar and watching his brother through the open church doors.

There was no retreating.

Neither Grant nor Lee wanted a siege, but here it was, and they were both pinned down by their stubbornness, throwing up bulwarks and entrenching for what they knew, from their history, although if asked they would both deny it, could be a long, bloody campaign.

"The Chaos" had been in full form earlier, when Grant staggered out of his bedroom and into the kitchen of Lee's house, sleepy, in his boxer shorts and Wilco T-shirt, the morning after his supposed transgression with Rayna. A brace of cereal boxes were out on the counter along with a gallon container of 2 percent milk behind which Lee hunched, half-hidden, alternately studying the back of the Mini Swirlz Peanut Butter Blast box and absently flipping through a boating magazine.

Morning cereal mixing was a sacred ritual Lee and Grant had observed for as long as they could remember, since before they learned to hold a spoon in their tiny fists, because their father was Serial Cereal Man who introduced them to the miracle of the breakfast bricolage. Wheat Chex, Life, and Sugar Pops. Cap'n Crunch and Shredded Wheat with a dusting of Raisin Bran. Cocoa Puffs and Yummy Mummy. Frankenberry and Wheatabix Minis. Batman, Superman, and Teenage Mutant Ninja Turtles. Granola, Special K, Lucky Charms, and Grape Nuts, with honey. The novelty whore blends: Hot Wheels Sugar Blasts with Barbie Sparkles and Donkey Kong Crunch. The healthy horror mix: Wheaties, Total, Fiber One, and Nutri-Grain. Nothing but puff-based product. Nothing but fruit-based product.

Lee had invented the single letter rule: Total, Triples, and Trix; Oreo O's and Oatmeal Crisp; Frosted Flakes, Flutie Flakes, Fruit Brute, and French Toast Crunch. Grant had responded with death by sugar: Apple Jacks, Buzz Blasts, Sprinkle Spangles, and Waffle Krisp; Homer's Cinnamon Donut Cereal, Golden Grahams, and Banana Frosted Flakes. Over time craft gave way to an approximation of art: Cheerios, Marshmallow Krispies, and Maypo. Oatmeal and All-Bran with Pink Panther Flakes. And after the death of their father, the ritual finally degenerated into "The Chaos," in which you pulled out every box in the pantry and, without thinking about it, poured this and that from a random selection of cereals until your bowl was full.

Grant sat down. Lee looked up at him, but said nothing. It was not unusual or necessarily meaningful that there was no conversation at breakfast, and while Grant felt that Lee expected and, probably, that Grant needed to explain what he was doing in Rayna's store with the door shut and the closed sign turned out, there was also that part of him that resented Lee's always jumping to the most damning conclusion where Grant was concerned; although he understood that Lee had plenty of reason and history to take him directly to that dark place. But this time he hadn't, he reminded himself, done anything wrong at all.

Lee added milk to his bowl. Grant considered his cereal options. In prison, it had been Cream of Wheat or Cheerios or Corn Flakes. No mixing.

"Remember how Dad used to use orange juice instead of milk after the whole deal with his lactose intolerance? Count Chocula and o.j. Lucky Charms and o.j."

Lee's cereal had crackled with a fretful static. His spoon had stopped, poised over the gravelly surface, and he turned the page of the boating magazine and stared at the picture of a big new ocean trawler with poles flung out behind it like some water-borne insect's antennae. Grant waited for Lee to say something, but his brother had just stared at the boats and finished his cereal in silence.

Whereupon Grant had decided he wasn't all that hungry.

Now a few hours later, in the nave where Lee was on the ladder shellacking, Pastor John was taking a family through a christening rehearsal. Proud mom, Distracted dad, the Golden Newborn, of course, and a Little Hellboy of maybe seven, who kept scudding his shoes on the floor to make a *burring* sound.

"And then the godparents will recite their oath," the pastor said, "yada yada, then you'll give me the baby, and I'll ask Duncan to come with me to the font . . . "

"No."

The boy twisted away from the pastor and dodged his mom's outstretched arms.

"Duncan!" Dad slid laterally to cut off the escape route through the pews, so the boy reversed field, leapt up onto the altar, and climbed Lee's ladder until he was, literally, climbing Lee.

"Whoa, whoa—" For a moment, Lee had all he could handle juggling the clear coat and brush while remaining relatively quiet as the boy monkey-scrambled over him and perched at the very top of the ladder, looking down smugly as if Lee would protect him.

"I'm so sorry," Duncan's dad called up to Lee in a civil voice, and then, in thundered impotence, "Duncan, you come down here right now!"

The boy, of course, didn't move. His eyes were narrowed and feral. The Golden Child was mewling. Everybody was looking up at Duncan who was looking plaintively down at Lee. As if asking: What are you gonna do about it?

"Lee," the pastor said.

"Sir," the dad said, "if you could just . . . "

"I'M NEVER COMING DOWN!" Duncan announced.

Duncan's mom trembled, pale. Duncan's dad flushed a purple rage. The breeze picked up, tugged at the open doors.

"Lee?"

"Don't make me come up there!"

Out front, in the outdoor ashtray at the bottom of the chapel steps, a stubbed-out cigar smoldered. Grant had watched the front half of this family melodrama and then had gone to the car and was waiting there, not wanting to witness what he guessed would probably just be another one of Lee's fucking miracles of patience and dependability.

Lee looked up at the boy. The ladder wobbled; Duncan's dad had begun to climb it.

"Whoawhoawhoa, mister, don't do that!" Lee said.

"Get him down then."

"Well, yeah, all right, but alive would be good," Lee said. "This ladder won't hold all three of us."

"Duncan," the dad brayed, ignoring Lee, "get down here, or else!"

Yeah, that'll do it, Lee thought.

The little boy started howler monkey shrieking, and his dad shouted back at him: "Shut up shut up shut up" in a loop. Pastor John closed his eyes. Duncan's mother was sobbing.

"Hey." Lee used his teacher voice.

The shrieking ceased, and the boy gazed coolly down at Lee

like, hey, it wasn't him who'd been making all that racket. His eyes dropped to a careful half-mast.

"You remind me of my little brother."

The boy made a snarky grunting sound, and Lee climbed up to him faster than the boy thought was possible for a man with a brush and a paint can. He gripped the ladder tightly, though. Not coming down.

"This is something he would do," Lee said, close, low, confidential, and a little scary underneath because, well, teachers know how to make you squirm. "My brother. Just to fuck with me. Is that what this is?"

The boy stared at him, worried now, eyes wide, even though Lee's tone was pleasant and his face serene.

"Here," Lee said to the boy, and he held out the can of clear coat. "Can you hold this for a sec?"

Lee's eyes were open and earnest, and so, completely confused, the boy took the can.

"Thanks. And this," Lee said, holding out the brush.

The boy took it, hooking his arm through a rung of the ladder because now his hands were full.

"Okay. So, as long as you're up here and not coming down," Lee said in that low, quiet, expressively agreeable voice, "why don't you just go ahead and you fucking finish painting the cross because I'm out."

And then Lee climbed down.

Duncan's dad was hissing, "What are you doing, what the heck are you doing, mister?" But Lee just slipped past him, silent, and walked out of the church.

And Duncan's dad looked up the long ladder at his son.

And Duncan's mom blew her nose and wiped her eyes.

And Duncan's will deserted him.

And Pastor John Leonard—it just got the better of him; Pastor John prayed that his new cross wouldn't be ruined.

An argent lure sliced through the air, scattering sunlight as it spun and arced and clattered loudly into a tin bucket in the un- mowed grass. Through her store window, Rayna watched Mayor Barb give a jerk to the fishing rod she held loosely in her hand to make the lure dance back out of the bucket, and then she swiftly reeled in the twenty yards of six-pound test Rayna had sold her last week. A Subaru powered up Main Street doing about fifty and fishtailing. Barb scowled until she recognized Doug's car. He skidded into the dry gully where a gutter would be, climbed from his car, walked straight to Barb, and squeaked, "It's gold. Barb, it's gold."

"What?"

"The assay."

"What?"

"You heard me."

Then Doug and Mayor Barb were dancing like dervishes, her spinning rod whipping its quicksilver lure around their heads insanely. From inside the grocery store, though, Rayna could only make out the sharp, incoherent consonants and the ends of Doug's exclamations.

"Excuse me? Miss?" A throat cleared.

Rayna turned away from the window, to her cash register, and rang up a six-pack of cherry cola for a customer in a straw hat. By the time she turned back to look out the window again, Barb and Doug were riding up the hillside and into the trees on Barb's unhappy mare.

"You should have left that pissant ankle biter up there on the ladder."

Lee and Grant were hunkered down near the broken Blue Lark mine buildings, directly below and just slightly left, or south, of the mine itself. Lee sat on his haunches, staring at a hollow, sapling-studded depression in the mountain slope directly ahead of him. Grant was behind him, bent over, like a caddie helping a golfer read a green, busting his brother for what he assumed had happened in the church with the little prick.

"You see it?" Lee asked.

"The Darwinian solution," Grant continued.

"You see it?" Lee was ignoring him.

"No." Grant yawned. If he'd been more interested he would have been bored. "Another dozen years," he observed, continuing his rant, "and you'll have that little shit in a chem lab or something and he'll blow somebody the fuck up. I mean. Last thing we need is more useless clutter in the evolutionary pool," he added, though he didn't really believe it. "But no," Grant said, "you had to save him. Am I right? My brother the saint."

Lee ignored him and pointed. "Parallel ridges," he said. "Right there. The ghost of some mine cart tracks." Grant struggled to see what Lee saw: the faint suggestion of raised bands that extended from where Lee had positioned himself, running straight into the bottom of the rocky hillside hollow.

Grant frowned. "Another mine?"

Doug's strangled voice came up from the trees: "LEE!"

Lee ignored it. "No. A second egress," he said. "A later attempt to bore into a vertical vein they may have found the tail of up above."

"LEE!?"

Lee stood then, and he and Grant watched Doug and Mayor Barb emerge sideways from the forest on Mayor Barb's breathless and complaining and considerably overloaded horse.

"WE DID IT! WE GOT IT! WOO! WOO-HOO!!"

As if he didn't hear them, Lee looked at the hillside again and pursed his lips thoughtfully. "Could be we've found a way to drain that downshaft," he said.

"GOLD! WE FOUND GOLD!"

Grant couldn't take his eyes off them; he watched as they

arrived, ungainly, and the horse literally groaned. Grant looked from Doug and Barb arriving and then to Lee not even reacting to them, to their won-the-lottery, big shit-eating grins that Grant didn't much like but was about to let form on his own face, ready to let out a celebratory whoop with Doug and Barb, but Lee, his brother Lee, had no reaction at all.

"Lee?"

Lee wouldn't look at him. Barb's mare clopped around like an Irish clog dancer, and Barb hopped off and led it the rest of the way up the slope, and then tried to help Doug dismount the poor animal, as Doug whooped, hoarse: "WE'RE RICH!"

So Grant yelled too—WHOOPED—but there was nothing behind it. It was just loud noise trying to find a reason.

"Assay shows gold in the mine, Lee," Barb said, breathless. "Doug picked the report up this morning. A considerable effing amount of gold, too, if Doug got the numbers right." Then, to Doug: "Careful getting down, cowboy, careful."

"Yeah, like I'm not gonna be." Doug fussed, "Is my foot in the stirrup?"

"Which part of the mine?" Lee asked.

Barb talked about a couple of places in the mine shaft corresponding to samples they had tested. "It's not like a big vein or anything," she admitted. "But gold is definitely there, in the rock. And the OPT is encouraging."

"It's our Holy Moses," Doug crowed. "Creede's lode."

"Creede's up north," Grant said, frowning.

"Don't get him started," Barb advised.

"Not literally," Doug said. "Lemme just," Doug stuttered, trying to dismount, "lemme just, lemme just—"

Lee processed what he'd just heard from them and still had no reaction. None. They might as well have been telling him the time of day. Grant shook his head.

"What is wrong with you? You did it. We did it."

Lee spun away from him as Doug began screaming, "I'M STUCK! MY FOOT'S STUCK!"

Sure enough, Doug's double-E boot was jammed in the stirrup and the horse was moving again. Doug hopped. Barb tried to grab the reins. Lee turned his attention back to the slope of the mountain and seemed to settle on an excavation strategy.

"We could bring the backhoe down here," he mused, "and dig that thing out. This mine might be even bigger."

"The GOLD," Doug barked, still hopping, "the GOLD . . . the GOLD is IN the mine we GOT—we don't need to dig another foot, time for the big boys to bring their toys—"

"We should try and control the effluent this time, though, huh?" Lee was talking to Barb but not looking at her. Grant wanted to scream. He walked away. Doug finally fell over onto the ground; his foot was still hung up in the stirrup, but the horse quickly lost interest in dragging him, so Doug rolled over on his back and waved his arms.

"Could somebody give me a hand here?"

Grant scudded down the tailings away from them, stormy, down into the trees, his shoulders round, his head low. Lee could tell that his brother was mad at him, but he wondered if he should care.

"Lee." Barb put her hand on his shoulder and repositioned him so he had to look at her. She said: "Lee, honey, we've struck gold. Could you just stop for one second and get a pulse and, gosh, I don't know, savor the effing moment or something?"

TWENTY-TWO

*P*yrotechnic sparks cartwheeled from one explosion into other, smaller explosions blossoming red, white, and blue, and a fiery glitter cascading down onto a three-masted Yankee Clipper ship. Old Ironsides?

The crowd: "Ooooo. Ahhhhh."

Fireworks splayed majestically against an indigo sky.

Another concussion that, oddly, made no sound. A spray of pink-ribboned needles of fire and the collective intake of spectators' breaths and the lake crickets ululating and the glistening reflection off the water and the murmuring of the voices, and more skyrockets flashed, but with no report. Majestic fireworks from New York City, broadcast wirelessly on a delayed satellite feed to several big-screen TVs scaffolded variously on the manicured lakeside fairway, near the bunkers, and decorated with fluttering festive crepe paper streamers.

"The proof is in the pudding," Beachum lectured to a captive audience, "they know how to celebrate our country's birthday back East. Don't they pull out all the stops? No state laws prohibiting the use-or-sale nonsense . . . " He sat beside Lorraine and the baby on a plaid picnic blanket among a patchwork of other families on other blankets watching the video fireworks and eating off paper plates.

" . . . if you think about it, our forefathers fought a revolution to get away from rules and regs, and look at us now, so messed up we can't even set off a Ladyfinger. Nanny State at its absolute worst. Where are we, Sweden? Fireworks are our American legacy—rockets, red glare, bursting, they're in our marrow. Truly."

When some wise guy pointed out that fireworks were Chinese, that just got Beachum going again. Down by the lake, a giant-size barbecue flamed up in the weedy rough, where meat was being seared, corn baked, sausage roasted, and Lee's forearms dehaired and toasted every time he tried to turn something on the grill with the wimpy tongs someone had provided him. A long line of buffet diners snaked past him, patient, the idle shout-outs of his neighbors floating on the darkness, disembodied from their faces.

"Hey there, Lee, I hear your gold mine came through."

"Yes it did," he said, rote.

"Hit the jackpot. Tapped into the mother lode. Wrangled the Big Miyuma. Gooooold-fingah . . . " Vandenberg's fat face, leering.

"You want a strip steak or the turkey sausage?" Lee asked the bio teacher, forcing a smile.

"Time to talk about your tithe, brother Lee." This was the other, older pastor. Not John. What was his name?

"I don't go to church. I just made the one cross—"

"Jesus was a carpenter."

"—as a favor . . . "

"Pick me a winner, Goldfinger." Vandenberg had circled back. Lee stabbed a sausage. "Turkey. There you go."

"Hey. Goldfinger! Rock and rollllll!" Now Harounian, the Spanish teacher, had picked up the 007 thread.

Jesus. "That's witty," Lee said, still rote.

"Tapped into the mother lode. *La veta de la madre.*"

"Sausage or steak, H-man?"

"I guess you ain't gonna keep teaching."

A tall kid loped past with a football, his voice cracking, "Mr. G.! Dude. Minerfortyniner! Tight. Fuckin' A, man. Fuckin' A!"

And then Lorraine, Lorraine was in front of him, looking right at him, into him, holding her baby in one arm, her squirming toddler in the unisex jumper not so much a baby anymore, and a drooping paper plate with potato salad and baked beans in the other.

"Hi."

"Sauce or steakage?" Lee asked her, scrambled.

"What?"

"I mean steak. Steak or sausage."

"Where's Grant?"

Lee didn't know. Grant took a drive somewhere; he had left early that morning. "Steak or sausage?"

"Both. There's two of us," she said. "We're sharing a plate."

At first, he didn't understand what she was talking about. Something happened to his head when Lorraine was around; he got all thick and sodden, his thoughts slowed, stupid, dull, and derailed. Sorting it out: two of them, Lorraine and the baby, oh. Lee looked away from her, down, concentrated on the red-hot grill as he deliberately stabbed first a sausage, then a big slab of sizzling beef, and held them up, but Lorraine was gone.

"We were all so worried about you, Lee." Another woman's face was there instead, with pale, fat Botox lips smeared with gloss, purple eye shadow, hair piled up and permed like Miss America in, oh, 1983. He thought he should know her.

"Steak or sausage?"

Faces, smiling, kind, convivial, filed past in a blur. Mouths all moving. In the glow of the grill, parents, neighbors, students, strangers. Nothing. Tongues. He didn't speak this language. A bright, key-groping burst of trumpets and trombones as the high school band began to play what must have been a Sousa march, up on the grassy berm behind the green. All the cool wind from the canyon came up off the still water of the lake. And in the lake's shallows, a bunch of little kids stood in knee-deep water waiting, with dour Earl Dollar, the Fire Marshal, hovering grimly nearby holding a silver extinguisher. Lee came down from the barbecue pit with a glowing stick of punk. He trudged out into the water to the waiting kids, pulled two dozen sparklers from his back pocket, and began to light and distribute them.

"Technically you're still in violation," Earl said.

The sparklers cast their magical, rippling diamond light across the lake. Lee splashed back up onshore, his pants soaked and dripping, his shoes full of silt.

"Write me a ticket. Earl, we go through this drill every year."

"Hey. It's not the money from the fines; it's the principle, F.Y.I. But? Am I looking the other way? Yes. I'm looking the other way; don't blow a gasket."

"Thank you."

"Lee?"

Lee jumped, startled by Beachum, who was suddenly behind him in the darkness. And Beachum jumped backward, startled by Lee's jumping.

"Sorry."

"No—it's okay."

The Slocumbs were behind Beachum, eating Klondike bars and apple pie from Styrofoam bowls. "You meet the Slocumb brothers? Saul and Paul?"

Lee admitted that he had.

"Good fortune, sir! Congratulations are in order!" the twins said, variously. Lee couldn't remember which was which.

"Ditto from me, but I already said that," said Beachum and advised, in a stage whisper to the Slocumbs, "just don't call him Goldfinger."

Saul Slocumb promised that he wouldn't. "I might add," he said, "and this will not certainly surprise you, that consequently our interest in your claim is, more than ever before, now truly piqued."

Lee only wanted to know how they found out.

"Gold speaks. Screams, in fact," Paul said. Lee glanced suspiciously at Beachum.

"Now, Lee, I tend to keep close counsel with my financial advice, but as I am aware of your current debt situation, let me just offer you some friendly—"

"What current debt situation?" And, to the Slocumbs, in case they had any doubts, "I'm still not selling. I'm sorry. The mine's not for sale."

"Excuse me?"

"Whoa. Don't paint yourself into a corner, yet." Beachum pulled Lee aside, his airy smile evaporating. "Lee, now I know you think I may hold a grudge against you," he said rapidly, "but I want you to know, I'm not like other people, I don't consider you accountable for your brother's crimes."

Lee wondered: *What other people?*

The Slocumbs were staring at them. Well, staring hard at Lee. Beachum turned ever so slightly, so his back was to the twins.

"Maybe now's not a good time," Saul Slocumb observed.

"And," Beachum continued at a pace, "quite bluntly, this development, this opportunity, this small gift of serendipity is, I believe, the very stroke of luck that can help you get back on track. You know what I mean? A man-made whole. I think you should hear them out."

Lee looked blankly at him. Then past him at the Slocumbs, who just continued to stare back, smoldering. "You want a piece of this action, Stan?"

Beachum, to his credit, didn't blink and shot back, low and intense, "You bet your ass." And then even lower, "I can swim with these sharks for you, Lee. I can. I can kill 'em and grill 'em."

"Is that a murse?" he asked Beachum, about the satchel that hung somewhat rakishly off Beachum's shoulder.

"No. It's what I carry my tablet in."

"Like Moses?"

"iPad," Beachum said.

"Oh. Same concept. You carry it everywhere?"

"It's got some kind of G," Beachum explained.

A raucous thump turned them all around.

"Hey!"

The Fire Marshal, Earl, held his extinguisher at arm's length while sparks showered down behind him and the kids fled, screaming with laughter as the Roman candle one of them had stuck in the deep back pocket of Earl's cargo shorts thumped out more pink and yellow balls of sparks that arced out crazily across the lake.

"Help!" Earl dropped the silver cannister and ran slipsliding up onto the muddy bank. "Criminy! Little bastards!"

Beachum sloshed into the lake water, fished for the extinguisher, found it, and ran back to shore with it aimed at Earl's double-wide backside. "Stand clear!"

"NOO!" Earl screamed as the caustic flame suppressant chemicals bit into him. "Stan—STOP!"

Paul Slocumb stepped over and shoved Beachum's aim off. Foam dusted the water roiling in the wake of the kids' retreat. Saul casually plucked the offending firework out of Earl's pocket and sidearmed it out into the lake where it spit a couple more feeble sparkballs and died with a whistling sizzle.

Earl was apoplectic. "What the hell? What the hell? What the hell?"

Lee saw his chance and ran away with the kids into the inky shadows of the golf course.

Beachum's voice chased him: "Lee?"

Lee ran uphill. Away from the Slocumbs, from Beachum, from Lorraine. Away from the hot coals of the grill and the cold algae waters of the lake; the soaked legs of his jeans stuck to his calves, and he ran, and he ran, stumbling through the high cut of a rough, then plummeting and nearly falling into a dark green-side bunker, running across the sand, up the other side, running, pushing hard, out of breath, running, struggling, up a steeper slope, up the last few strides to the top of a hill where eternity opened up in front of him in the form of billions of cold white stars and galaxies, the bright sprawl of the Milky Way, framed by sawtooth mountains on all sides, and, through a broken gap to the east, the millions more soft, warm lights of Denver. Lee stood there, breathless, bent over, his hands on his knees, his heart pounding. He could hear the band still playing (badly), and Beachum calling his name, and the sharp outbursts of laughter, and the closing of doors and crunching of tires as cars left the parking lot, and the murmur of voices, and the distant whistle and fizzle and pop of the fireworks, and he remembered when he and Grant and his parents would come to past Fourth of July barbecues with his mom's deviled eggs and his dad's brown Sherman cigarettes, and the softball game, and the flashlight tag, and the air thick with pollen, and the burned hot dogs, and the sickly-sweet tropical fruit drink from a rented fast food franchise dispenser, and the Eskimo Pies, and the girls, and the girls Grant claimed he felt up behind the storm shelter at the tenth tee, and the hush of the conifers, and the innocence, the certainty that life would unfold, that all mysteries would be revealed, and the future was scary in a good way, infinite, impossible, unknowable like all those stars and all those lights that had always been there and would always be there, promising, and your parents didn't die, and your marriage lasted, and your brother never went to jail, and what you found in the darkness of a forgotten mine shaft would be priceless and inextractable and never negotiable because the magic of the dusk and the dreams and the skyrockets mattered.

He wouldn't sell the mine.

Lee couldn't sell the mine, especially now that it had been ruined.

On the morning of July 5, Grant emerged from the wilderness of his dreamless sleep to discover that Whistle Stop waitresses are better imagined than unwrapped, and the stupid dull ache of desire that had chased him from bar to bar to the Hide-a-Way Motel, room 16, complimentary continental breakfast, was not assuaged. If he thought he could fuck Lorraine out of his system, he was wrong, and subsequently the added entanglement of a dewy-eyed small-town gal and her pear-perfect ass had proved cold harbor for his ever-growing miscellany of regret. He stumbled into the bathroom and drowned himself under a shower that stunk of motel soap, pipe rust, and propane until it started to run cold.

The previous afternoon, among the families, friends, and incarcerated in the visiting area at the Colorado Territorial Correctional Facility in Cañon City, Grant had sought counsel with his former cellmate, Bronco, a scruffy Jamaican whose gentle eyes belied consecutive life sentences for killing the two Gunnison cowboys responsible for raping his sister when Bronco was seventeen. Bronco's sister, Bobbi, Colorado College summa cum laude tragically gaff-hooked on vodka and pharmaceutical cocaine, was a willing witness for the prosecution and never spoke to her brother again.

"Gonna tell him the truth?" Bronco had wondered about Lee after Grant told him all that had happened. The outside world, for Bronco, was a long-running entertainment that didn't require him arguing with other convicts to get the opportunity to enjoy. But, like any melodrama, its banality ultimately disappointed him. Grant slid a cigarette pack across the table, and Bronco split the cellophane seal.

"What would you do?" Grant asked.

"Lie. But I'm a good liar."

"You've never lied to me."

"See?" Bronco shook out a slender cigarette. Smelled it. Then peeled the paper wrapping off what turned out to be a stick of yellow bubble gum. "Yo. This is the shit," he said.

"I don't get it," Grant said, frustrated. "Lee should be happy. He should be out-of-his-mind happy."

"Uh-huh. Let's see. You fucked his wife. Back in the day. Now you fucked with his girlfriend. You fucked with his mine. And you ain't been out of the Big House but sixty days, brother. Yeah, I bet he's giddy."

Grant pointed out that Rayna wasn't technically Lee's girlfriend, and, besides, nothing had happened there. Bronco considered the disclaimer. "And," Grant added, "Lee doesn't know I did the rest."

"Right. Man, you are so bad at it."

"What?"

"Lying."

"I'm not lying."

"Who you lying to? That's my immediate question. Me, him, or your own self?" Bronco blew a bubble. Grant closed his eyes, put his head in his hands.

"I just want to . . . do something for him."

"Yeah. Or to him. Uh-huh. Lemme know how that turns out." Bronco said, "The difference between you and me is I enjoyed capping those rapist motherfuckers, and you go crazy with the poor decision-making but then get all tore-up guilty when it don't work out, which it never does, by the way, because, like I said, the decision-making is poor right up top, so. What do you expect?"

"I don't know what I expect."

"Well, whatever it is, man, do not tell him the truth."

"About which?"

"Take your pick. Me, I've been having these thoughts," Bronco said. "Angels and shit."

"What?" This was how conversations with Bronco generally played out.

"Nothing." Bronco blew another bubble.

"Some kind of religious thing?"

"Nah. It's just, you know."

They sat for a while in silence. They'd been cellmates for twenty months, and the silences just grew out of habit. Bronco would never be released from jail, would never meet Lee, would never have his chance at a one-night stand with a Whistle Stop waitress who, for one moment, during the night, had allowed herself to believe that Grant was her white knight and the man she would marry. By the cold light of a street lamp, cast through the slit-gap in the curtain, Grant had seen the softness in her eyes when she squeaked "I love you" so quietly that she could later deny it if she needed to, and then her eyes closed and her head angled back and the bed frame complained and her hands flexed, and lightly traced, with the stiff heel of her palms, the narrow crease of his back as she dreamed of a dream.

"You're right," Grant had said, finally, in the visiting room. "I've got to tell him, don't I?"

"You what?" Bronco frowned.

"Sometimes the truth is a lie," Grant thought aloud.

Bronco looked down at him, frowning.

"And sometimes it's hard to tell the difference," Grant concluded.

"Ai'ight" was Bronco's final word on the subject.

Allie was pounding on the bathroom door and calling out to Grant that she had to pee something fierce. The door was unlocked, but Grant didn't tell her. He shut off the shower and pushed the vinyl curtain back and rubbed himself with a scratchy motel towel.

"Come on come on come on come on."

Grant opened the door and the waitress shoved through and fell on the toilet and voided herself in a grateful torrent, and suddenly it was way more intimacy than Grant cared to experience with any woman, or almost any woman, he conceded to himself reluctantly, so he went out into the room and started pulling on his clothes.

"What are you doing?"

Grant told her that he had to drive back today, and he watched the subtle shift in her shoulders and the cant of her head, like a slow-motion slap to the face, and her eyes darkened, and her mouth tightened. Grant knew it like he knew himself and could guess what came next.

"I can come with you. I got all this vacation time saved up." The toilet flushed and she was in the doorway, naked, pink, and hoping. Grant thought, *I'm an asshole.* And the moment passed.

Allie picked up his towel and started to wrap and rewrap it around herself, getting self-conscious. There was color in her cheeks as if she was blushing. Or ashamed.

"I was too easy. Damn."

"No."

"Damn! Dammit!" She brushed the tears out of her eyes. "I was. I am," she said. "I'm not crying," she told him. "Oh hell," she sighed and dropped the towel. "Shit. I'm taking a shower. Did you use all the hot water?"

"I did," Grant admitted.

"Fuck you."

"Yeah," Grant said, melancholy.

Twenty-Three

The heavens were streaked with nervous gestures of mares' tails. The forest below the mine stood ragged and black-green in the flat light, lifeless, brooding, and ill-omened. Doug reclined, propped against the grill of his Subaru, arms folded, self-satisfied, and immovable, and watched as Mayor Barb took mud-stained boots and overalls from her saddlebag to put them on.

"It's stupid. We don't have the manpower, facility, technology, or know-how to take the gold from this mine," Doug was telling her.

"I did some figuring, Mr. Pessimist," Barb shot back at him. "If the assay says out of every metric ton of rock we can yield gold worth a hundred grand, I got a half-ton pickup. One truckload and we're taking home about sixteen large each."

"Large?"

"Thousand. Dollars," she said. "Sixteen thousand dollars. For crying out loud, Doug, don't you watch TV?"

"Do you know how tough that is? To hardrock mine and move a half ton of ore?"

"There's a 'can' in every 'can't.'"

"We sell to the cowboy Talibanis," Doug insisted. "Negotiate a hefty royalty. Let them do the hard part and pay us for the privilege to do it."

"Ho. If you don't pull your weight, round man, why should you get anything?"

"Fine, equal work for equal pay. Go there. How come Lee gets to decide what our cut's going to be?"

"Didn't he put up all the money?" Rayna interjected. She'd come hiking up from the access road, and they only noticed her now. She was breathing hard. And still smoking. They watched her, suspicious, as she took one last drag on the cigarette and then flicked it into the leeching pond, where it hissed, flared, and died.

"You are not an impartial jury," Doug decided.

"Lee in his office?"

"Utterly," Mayor Barb said.

Rayna walked into the mine shaft and became a silhouette, the overhead string of lights rocking back and forth above her as Doug and the Mayor continued their complaints outside.

"Listen to me. Almost all of the great gold strikes played out and left their owners penniless. Tabor, Brown, Creede, and Jackson. Gregory, Russell, Wee Bobby Womack, and W. S. Stratton. Why why why?" Doug said petulantly. "Why do you think?"

"Crazy wives."

"No. No. Greed? Also no. Ambition. Pigheaded ambition," Doug said. "They wanted to do it all themselves."

Their catfight was finally drowned out by the sloshing of Rayna's boots through the intractable diarrhetic muck. She pushed down the Welsh tunnel, crouched, then the mine shaft opened up, and Rayna could straighten her back, and, at the main intersection, she found Lee. He was sitting on a rusty, ancient stool, hunched over an improvised workbench a few feet from the glassy gape of water that filled the submerged downshaft. Lee flipped through a yachting magazine and pretended he hadn't noticed Rayna's arrival, determined not to be the butt of one more pathetic joke as invented by Grant.

"Ahoy," she said.

Lee didn't react. He ripped out a half-page ad for a seagoing fishing trawler and punched it onto an exposed nail in the beam in front of his head. A couple of other boat ads were already pegged there, curling as stray overhead drips of drainage and the ever-present humidity of the mine leached into them.

"Spending your jackpot already?"

She moved around him, skirting the edge of the watery square, and Lee swiveled and braced her waist protectively. "Careful, that shaft goes down eighty feet." Then he realized he was holding her, and he let go as if she was radioactive.

"I'd float," Rayna said, the steadiness of his hands lingering on her hips.

"You'd float."

"It's full of water, Lee. If I fell in, I'd float. I'd swim to the edge and climb out. Not that I don't appreciate your concern."

Lee stared at her, feeling a little foolish. He couldn't sustain any anger toward her. It came and went; he didn't know why. They committed to an uncomfortable pause and studied the boat advertisement.

"Trawler?"

"They're very dependable, even in rough seas."

"I'll smoke," Rayna said, "if that's all right."

"You decided not to quit?"

Rayna dug out her new cigarettes, Kools, and a translucent blue lighter she had taken from the card display next to her cash register.

"I have a new theory," she explained. "So basically I've been chipping, okay? Parsing my cigarettes and, well, telling myself that each one is the last one, which only makes each one that much more incredible. The last one! And then, after: remorse.

And the memory of that last one. And, I don't know, the yearning. And then, why not? Quit. Grieve. Yearn. Again. It's bullshit.
So. Now I'm just going to smoke myself sick, and maybe I'll get
it out of my system."

"I didn't want a gold mine," Lee said. "I just wanted a mine
that might have gold in it."

Rayna lit her cigarette. The smoke curled through the dim
mine light and hung in sheets like torn ghosts and made their
eyes water. She didn't say anything. She didn't need to.

"And I never smoked," Lee added after a while, sounding almost regretful about it.

"Of course you didn't." Rayna exhaled a visible sigh. "You're a
nice guy, Lee. A little in the clouds, but a nice guy."

Lee observed coolly that quite possibly she wouldn't know a
nice guy if she fell over one. Rayna replied that, in fact, she had.

"You," she said. "I had my heart set on you."

Lee's anger flared again; he cut her off quickly, "Right, yeah,
you know what? A nice guy is somebody to whom people feel
comfortable saying, 'You're a nice guy, Lee, now excuse me
while I go over here and have sex with the donkey.' And that's
just plain arrogant."

Rayna took a couple of thoughtful pulls on her cigarette—
full-time smoking already beginning to annoy her—and measured her response. It was important to her to get it right. She
was sorry for what Lee thought had occurred with Grant, but she
was not willing to surrender with no quarter.

"No," she said, "a nice guy is a man who can say 'I love you'
and sort of mean it. Or a guy who might even say, 'I respect you,'
and believe it. Or, 'What do you think, Rayna?'"

There followed a silence that they both expected. And out of
it, shouting, distant, arose outside. Doug and Mayor Barb.

"I don't want to know what you think," Lee said without conviction and less than truthfully.

"Nothing happened," Rayna told him. And in spite of everything he'd known to be true from his long, tangled, and ineluctable journey to this moment, he believed her.

The overhead lights flickered. The shouting, which they'd both just assumed was more Doug and Barb argument, had taken on a quality of panic. There was the rumble of an engine that Lee recognized as his backhoe. Nobody but Lee had keys to the backhoe. He stood up from the stool, frowning, and began running out of the mine.

"Lee, what is it?"

Moving from mine to world was a kind of rebirth every time Lee experienced it. The womb of darkness. The distant square of daylight that grew and grew to an unimaginable brilliance, the sound of the wind, voices, engines, stray movement—all resurrected, all for that one moment of emerging into the world brand new again. This time was different. This was Bizarro Blue Lark, some crazy alternative universe in which Doug was screaming through the deep drone of the backhoe's overcranked engine, and Barb was screaming something unintelligible from the other side of the claim, and, as Lee emerged, the huge, serrated backhoe shovel blade swung violently past, just missing his head, clipped the front edge of the mine opening, and knocked the timbers loose. Dirt and rock cascaded down around Lee. He skated to keep his balance.

Doug stood on the edge of the leaching pond, mouth gaped, a life-sized garden gnome watching as Mayor Barb, hunkered defensively into an upright armadillo ball, tried to ward off the blows of a short board gripped in the fat hand of a mean motherfucker with a buzz cut and patchy sunburn. Mayor Barb reeled, spin-staggering, dazed, and retching, to the edge of the tailings where a second man in a backward baseball cap just extended his arms and flattened his hands and shoved her off into the void.

The men didn't seem to have any interest in Doug.

The backhoe thundered past Lee, blocking his view of the

leaching pond assault and revealing, beyond it, a third interloper carrying two red plastic gas cans toward the mine, but Lee had already clambered up onto his backhoe, and now he stood on the running board trying to yank open the door or smash the plastic window, anything, to get inside the cab and stop the fourth man, who was driving. The cab door swung out unexpectedly, sweeping Lee off the step, followed directly by the driver, in camo pants and steel-toed boots, who, while the backhoe kept going, unmanned, launched himself at Lee like some kind of professional wrestler.

Now, while it may be true that force is mass times acceleration, and the driver was both bigger than Lee and moving toward him at a rate equivalent to the acceleration of his jump plus the speed of the backhoe plus a gravitational factor as he fell toward the earth—or ground—where Lee had sprawled, it is also true that the tabletop formed by the Blue Lark Mine excavation was largely paved with sharp chunks of rock and tailings, and this surface, though adequate for walking and working while wearing suitable footwear, was wholly inappropriate for gymnastic wrestling maneuvers such as the Atomic Drop, the Gorilla Press Slam, the Emerald Flowsion, or, on this particular occasion, a variation on the Simple Frog Splash, popularized by Art "Love Machine" Barr in the early 1990s, in which the attacker, after leaping, stretches out to a horizontal position, and then brings his feet and hands inward and outward before landing on his intended target in a belly-flop. The drawback of any wrestling move, of course, is that it typically requires the cooperation of the target. Lee, not particularly a fan of *La Luche* (or *Luche Libre,* which was what his father called it), nor of full contact sports in general, rolled away from the incoming driver, and consequently the man face-planted on the rocks with correspondingly unfortunate results. This was opportune because Barb's attacker, confident she wasn't coming back up the slag anytime soon, had turned his attention to Lee and, as Lee tried to get up, came powering into him and began to swing wildly.

Rayna, exiting the mine as the man with the gas cans walked past her, saw Lee under attack, Doug frozen with a look of shame-faced horror, no sign of Barbara, and the last of the backhoe as it careened off the far edge of the mine tailings and plunged downward, flipping, rolling, crashing thunderously into the trees. Rayna picked up a two-by-four, moved to where Lee was getting mauled, and hit the aggressor as hard as she could across the back. He reeled up, throwing his arms out, yelling in pain, turning, catching her broadside, and knocking her onto the ground.

"What do you want?" Rayna shouted at him. "What do you want?"

The guy in the backward cap joined the free-for-all on Lee and Rayna, and it quickly became a rout. The belly-flopping *luchador* was up on his feet but merely a woozy spectator as Rayna went down again and didn't get up. They were all breathing hard. Eventually Lee fell next to her, bloodied and beaten. The assailants kicked at him a few more times, halfheartedly, exhausted, and then their associate came sprinting out of the mine and shouted something and there was a weird sucking sound and the air stiffened and boils of smoke and flames came vomiting violently out of the mine shaft.

The men ran down the road. No more than three minutes had passed.

Doug was missing.

Barb was upside down on the steep slope of the tailings, arms turtling, scraped raw, trying to get herself righted.

At the crest of the mine road was a big blue pickup truck with a dusty logo of a graphic mountain crested by a cartoon crown and the word EMPIRE in B-movie script just below it. Three men were already in the cab, backing down the road, turning around while the backward cap guy sat behind the wheel of Lee's Jeep, the door swinging open, jacking the transmission into neutral and popping the emergency brake. The Jeep started rolling backward. The man leapt out, chased the pickup, and dove into the bed of the truck as it followed the Jeep downhill. Finally, the Jeep bounced over the huge road ruts, picked up speed, continued straight where the road bent, jumped the embankment, smashed through the aspen for a hundred yards, and then, almost in slow motion, just tipped over.

The blue pickup drifted around one hairpin corner, tires spinning, catching, throwing it into the next curve, and it sped thus down the mountain, the whine of its engine audible long after Lee and Rayna saw the last of it.

Wild, agitated cloud structures were ripping and re-forming above the ragged peaks of the Divide, playing havoc with the sun. Lee got to his feet, unsteady, his face swollen and smeared with blood, the mine timbers burning behind him, spitting flames and acrid smoke as if from the mouth of some dying dragon. He knelt next to Rayna, and his heart was pounding, and his hands stung as he brushed the grit off her face and helped her up.

Evergreen Volunteer Fire Department trucks surrounded Lee's house as Grant's Camaro slowed on the road and nosed awkwardly into the shoulder short of where two police cars were parked, parallel, across the pavement. Then Grant was out of the car and walking, unable to fathom what he was seeing: The house was on fire. Crisscrossing streams of water from the trucks blasted the flames, gilded by dusklight. Lee's giant suppository garden was slick with the sheen of overspray.

"That's far enough, son!" Earl, the imperious Fire Marshal, by day merely a Walmart optician, but here, truly a god, Grant thought. Earl intercepted Grant before he could get too close. The optician wore a fireman's coat of his own design with epaulettes, suggesting a third world general or a character from *Fahrenheit 451*. And safety glasses.

"Where's Lee?"

"House is empty. We been calling him, no answer. What can I tell you? I'm so sorry."

Wind caught the mist from the surging water and made rainbows in the dying light. Grant just stared.

"Blue flames suggest an accelerant."

"Blue what?"

"Some fool lit the darn house on fire," Earl said. "Betcha anything."

Barb's eyes darted wildly about, a fish in too little water, lids held open and unblinking by tiny metal *Clockwork Orange* retractors as the Summit County Emergency room resident used saline and a delicate swab to coax debris out before he stitched up the laceration that stretched from the bridge of the Mayor's nose to the end of what was, earlier in the day, her eyebrow. Barb's face was a swollen mass, and IV tubes snaked from bruised arms calicoed with bandages to bags on bedside hangers. She tugged on the thin cotton blanket covering her, and exposed her feet and their ochre-mud-stained socks. A crewcut sheriff's deputy with problem acne questioned her when the resident sat back:

"Did they say anything at all?"

"No."

"Names, any identifying, peculiar comments?"

"No."

"And you didn't recognize them?"

"No."

The Deputy took careful notes.

"Do you have any idea why they—"

"No."

Rayna, on a gurney directly across from the Mayor, was lying flat but was not seriously hurt. Just tired. Her hands folded on her stomach, her eyes open, aimed emptily at the ceiling tiles.

In the far corner, slumped in a chair, Lee drank water from a paper cup. His shirt was off and his chest was wrapped and taped and both his hands bandaged from the wrist to the first knuckle of his fingers. He watched Rayna, Mayor Barb, the doctors, the staff. He felt nothing. He closed his eyes and imagined a bone-white fiberglass fishing trawler slicing through the crest of a huge wave, then free-falling into the trough of foam-whisked, green-grey seawater, its propeller screws keening. The boat shuddered when it hit the surface, the rigging shivering, and its stern twisting violently starboard; on the flying bridge, Lee gripped the tiller and spun it as water washed over him, another huge wave looming in front of his little ship like a mountainside, except this mountain was moving into him, and the trawler was picked up by the ocean swell, rising, vertical on the wave, impossibly vertical and likely to fall away backward, but then the sea moved through the boat, dark water parting as the prow cut a passageway, and then the boat was on the other side, planing, exploding through the crest of the wave and starting to surf down onto a rocky decline, near Argentine Pass, free-falling down the steep slope, over rocks that punched into the fiberglass and split the hull, screws turning meaninglessly in the air, beam planing, skidding, shredding, scraping bottom on the moun-tainside and starting to come apart, the glass ripping, splitting, fold-ing in on itself, fragments of teak superstructure flying everywhere, and on the bridge Lee steered, expressionless, riding out the impos-sible disintegration of his craft with a crazy élan, as if he expected nothing less than this and could, somehow, still avert it and—

"Mr. Garrison?"

His ribs ached. Lee blinked open his eyes to the emergency room nurse looking down at him through square, sensible eye-glasses, curiously.

"You have a telephone call," the nurse said.

There was an ancient pay phone out in the lobby, and the receiver lay on the little shelf where a phone book had once been

bolted. Lee answered and said his name and asked who was calling and listened for a long time to the cold, reasoned proposal
being offered on the other end of the line with the same dead
expression he'd had on the bridge of his imagined trawler.

If they'd wanted to kill me, they would have, he thought.

"How many men were there, ma'am?" The Deputy was asking Barb.

"Six, seven. Hell, I don't know."

Rayna, sitting up, watching Lee through the glass windows of
the automatic doorway into the ER, met his gaze as he listened at-
tentively to his caller. The nurse pulled the curtain around Barb's
station, cutting off Lee's sightline to Rayna. Triple beams of the sur-
gical lights burned through the milky drapery like St. Elmo's fire.

Headlights slowly came forward, slowly defined themselves,
and slowly allowed the darkness to ease back in around them;
ghostly shapes resolved into the buildings on Main Street in
Basso Profundo, and the headlights from Barb's Cadillac turned
finally into her driveway and came to rest in two angry pools on
the aluminum siding of her house.

Rayna got out from the driver's side of the Caddy and hurried
around to help the Mayor, who hadn't spoken since the Deputy had
finished questioning her in the ER. Footsteps on gravel told of someone coming up the road from Rayna's store, a lean figure, a man.

Grant.

"Rayna, where's Lee?" And when he got close enough to see
them: "Jesus, what—?"

"We got bushwhacked." Mayor Barb spat something reddish
through the light to the ground. Rayna kept her moving, supporting the older woman, walking her into the house.

"The mine?"

"Yes."

"Fuck."

"Lee got a call at the hospital and left without saying where he was going," Rayna said. "Where have you been?"

"Somebody torched the house," Grant told her. The words sounded absurd. "Our house. Lee's house, somebody—Jesus, what—" and he looked to Mayor Barb again, and then at Rayna, unable to concentrate on anything. "Was Lee at the mine with you?"

"He was," Rayna said.

"Where's Lee?" Barb asked, suddenly aware that Lee wasn't with them now.

"You were at the mine?" Grant asked Rayna.

Rayna asked him again: "Where were you?"

Grant closed the door behind them. Barb's house was crowded, filled with a compendium of strange objects, collections, unused Amway products still in their shipping boxes—Nutrilite, Dish Drops, and eSpring bottled water. There were slender, carefully considered aisles to walk down, and everything felt disciplined, curated: butterflies pinned in antique glass display boxes, several dozen taxidermied grey squirrels mounted on polished marble bases, a clothing rack hung with fancy leather fringe vests, and the dining room table covered with freshly bleached cow skulls, numbered and dated on tiny tags tied to the desiccated horns with colored yarn.

And dreamcatchers. They hung from the ceiling and window casings, were tacked to the doorway headers, leaving barely enough room to pass, hundreds of willow hoops and teardrops woven with geometric spiderwebs of yarn or string, or sinew or nettle, in the older ones; some of them were so dry and desiccated that the surviving feathers hung like melancholy from the beaded dangles.

"I want to watch *Letterman*," the Mayor said.

Rayna asked if Barb wanted to watch the show in her bedroom or out in the living room, though Rayna couldn't seem to locate a television in the latter room's vast menagerie of miscellany.

"I was in Denver," Grant said. "I got a job."

"I need to watch *Letterman*."

Rayna asked Grant if he could see a TV anywhere.

"I said I got a job."

"Television's in the bedroom," Barb advised them. "I'm feeling kind of whirly," she added, pale.

A voice called out from the dark bedroom doorway: "I'm in here."

Doug. He waxed half-moon into the light of the living room, his face a mask of wounded ignominy. He said: "Well, I'm sorry."

For what? Grant wondered, but then Rayna was on Doug with a fueled rage, hitting him with her arms and fists and screaming, "You asshole. You asshole." Grant, completely confused now, intervened, pulled her away, and she turned on him and caught him twice with roundhouse smacks before he could grab her wrists and pin them and walk her back against an unsteady tower of *Popular Mechanics* from the mid-seventies. "Rayna, stop."

"I'm sorry," Doug kept repeating. He was so sorry.

"He set us up," Rayna said. "How much did they offer you, Doug? You get your thirty pieces of silver?"

"It's a gold mine," Doug said. "I just wanted my share."

Now Grant was catching up with what had happened. Rayna struggled to get out of his grasp, but without a lot of conviction, and Grant held her still. He watched the fat man's chest heave as Doug struggled with what was left of his self-respect.

"You may judge me," Doug declared, voice quaking. "You may think I'm a worthless piece of shit, but I never intended for anyone to get hurt, and I only wanted what I thought was my fair share. Listen: Between that time he was run out of the town of Creede and the day he packed his kit for Skagway in the Alaska Territory, Jefferson Randolph 'Soapy' Smith took one more shot at a mining claim in Tarryall, down in South Park, with his longtime accomplice and friend, the Reverend Thomas Uzzel of Denver. Now many considered Soapy a no-good bunko swindler, but the fact of it is he was largely misunderstood; the man was a romantic, a philanthropist, a Renaissance man, a dreamer whose marvelous imagination often just put him at odds with popular notions of legality and ethical behavior. And Uzzel tried to screw him."

"*Letterman*," Barb reminded them. She pushed past Doug and into her bedroom. A light came on.

"Jefferson Smith died alone and penniless," Doug told them, racing through it. "He was shot by a man with whom he'd had an argument over the outcome of a day's adventure in Skagway. But when Soapy was run out of Tarryall by the Reverend and a cabal of miners who had staked more claims than they could work, Soapy and some other misjudged unfortunates settled a new town, and they called it Fairplay, a place where every man would have an equal chance to stake a claim. And as you know, Fairplay stuck, and thrived, and remains today, while Tarryall is not even dust on the shoulder of Highway 9. So you can draw your own conclusion."

Barb made a noise in her bedroom. The bedsprings sighed. "Creede can kiss my chapped butt," she barked.

"Not the man, the town," Doug protested.

"Go," Grant told Doug.

"All I'm saying, people have their reasons," Doug insisted. "Soapy Smith wasn't a bad person. I'm not a bad person."

"No," Grant agreed, "you're a piece of shit. Go."

"And I'm sorry."

"Don't say that again."

"Well I don't have my car," Doug pointed out as a reason he might be lingering. "Lee took it," he complained.

"Go, before I change my mind," Grant said.

Doug blinked. He gauged whether Grant, after changing his mind, would be real trouble for him and, yes, Doug decided, Grant would.

So Doug left. The screen door shuddered when it whapped shut behind him, and the front door didn't catch so the wind blew in, cold. Grant stayed pressed against Rayna, just in case, but there was no softness in her and no heat. For a while they could hear Doug's heavy scuffing footsteps growing distant on the road. Grant relaxed his grip on Rayna's wrists and stepped back. And her tears came freely. And Grant didn't try to stop them, or take her in his arms, because she was his brother's girl.

TWENTY-FOUR

*T*he late-night host's gap-toothed elastic face loomed large and smiley on the sixty-five-inch flat-screen TV mounted above the fireplace in Beachum's living room. The sound was off, and someone was knocking at the door. Beachum, splayed out and snoring on the floor in front of the sectional sofa, didn't move. The baby was crying, somewhere deeper in the house, as Lorraine went to the front door and opened it.

Lee stood outside. It was raining, and he was pretty wet. Lorraine was stunned to see him.

"I need to talk to Stan."

Barb reclined on a pile of pillows, rigid, wired, unable to sleep. Classic *Letterman* blared from her TV, Rayna slept curled in a big chair under the window, and Grant was on the floor against a wall, between a bookshelf stuffed with *Farmer's Almanac*s and a stack of translucent storage bins containing what looked like McDonald's Happy Meal toys, wondering when he could safely leave, but Barb's restlessness kept him there.

"Funny," Barb said, agitated. "I want a funny one. This isn't a funny one." She picked up the remote and muted the sound.

"There's old episodes I taped in that cabinet," she told Grant, so he got up and opened the doors of a waxed pine armoire in the opposite corner and peered in at dozens of aging VHS cassette tapes, haphazardly stacked but all carefully hand-labeled with dates stretching back more than a decade and key words and running times and the single word "DAVE."

"I guess nobody tapes things anymore," Barb said apologetically.

"They do, they just don't call it taping," Grant told her.

"April 2004 there was a real funny one," Barb said.

"Hell, didn't I warn you not to mess with those curry-eaters?"

Beachum looked like he still hadn't fully awakened. His hair on one side of his head had been squashed by sleep, giving him a lopsided, Ronald Reagan mien. Lee sat across from his presumed rival, shivering and drinking tea. He lifted the cup with both hands because his fingers were stiff and cold and scraped and swollen.

"As a matter of record," Lee said, "no, you didn't."

"Well. Let's take stock, Lee. They could have killed you, but didn't. Which I take to mean we've still got some leverage."

"I just want a fair price."

"These things are a delicate balancing act," Beachum said, starting to dredge up all the old chestnuts he had squirreled away for a situation like this one. Adrenalin was coursing through him, sending shivery spikes of contradiction skittering through his thawing brain: the impossibility of this sudden detente with Lee abrogated by the promise of a sweet, sweet piece of business in the offing.

"I want Barbara and Doug to get equal shares," Lee said, "after we take the cost of the land out, and I want the Slocumbs to pay all fees. Including yours."

Lorraine came into the kitchen carrying two empty baby bottles, which she put in the sink and started to wash.

"You can't just roll over and give them what they want. They won't respect you," Beachum cautioned him.

"They tried to kill me."

"You got their attention, all right."

"I don't care what they think of me," Lee said.

"Do you want me to handle this transaction or not?"

"I don't think there's anyone better qualified to negotiate my surrender," Lee deadpanned. Lorraine shot him a look, but Lee pretended not to notice.

"Surrender?"

"Yes."

"All right. Well. I don't know what the hell-o you're on about now, Lee, but listen to me," Beachum lectured him. "Listen. Your problem is you don't understand business. They kicked the shit out of you to get you to sell. But now you've still got to play hardball or they're gonna feel silly for going to all that trouble."

"Whose car is that in the driveway?" Lorraine asked.

Lee said it was Doug's.

"Well there's no windshield."

"Really? Gee, I hadn't noticed. Guess that explains the bugs in my teeth."

He fell so easily back into the old bitter rhythms. Lorraine stared at him, stung and unamused.

"You gotta let me handle this solo, Lee. I should wrangle with the Slocumbs by myself."

"Fine," Lee told him. He looked at Lorraine again and asked if he could sleep on the sofa. Lorraine said nothing, but her husband was doing all the talking anyway.

"Sure. Absolutely. Good Lord, that's right—man, your house." Beachum turned to Lorraine, and realized that he'd forgotten to tell her. "They burned down Lee's home."

Canned laughter.

Letterman had his audience in stitches. Letterman was laughing. His guest was laughing. Paul Shaffer was laughing. Mayor Barb was asleep. Grant lifted the TV remote from her hand and pulled the comforter up over her. He put the quilt from the foot of the bed around Rayna and walked out.

A summer chill had set in the thin air. There were huge black holes in the sky where clouds blocked the stars, and a stillness, no wind, nagged at Grant all the way to his car.

Lorraine's house held a softer darkness and a prepossessing smell of her that Lee had never forgotten. On the sofa, covered by a blanket, he rested, wide awake, unable or unwilling to sleep. Somewhere in the house, the baby was crying again.

He got up, suddenly, and followed the sound up the stairs to the baby's room, where a streetlight cast fragments of white across the floor and a skeletal mobile danced above the crib. Lee looked down at Lorraine's cranky child; his big face startled the baby, and it cried even louder.

"Shhhhh."

Not so small anymore. *Boy or girl?* he wondered; the wispy, short-cut brown hair offered no clues; *girl*, he decided, and he realized sadly that he didn't know her name and had never asked.

Lorraine woke up when the crying stopped, and by the time she came into the room, Lee was in the crib, one leg hanging awkwardly over the lowered side railing, her child lying limp across his chest, quiet and content.

"Are you going to sing?"

Startled, Lee turned his head and saw Lorraine in the doorway in a baggy pair of what had to be Beachum's pajamas and sensed she'd been there, watching him, for a while.

"It looked like you were about to," she said.

"I don't sing."

"I know," she said. "That's why I waited. I couldn't believe it myself." She came into the room and stood off to one side, arms folded, as if she was not surprised to find him in the crib at all.

"When Grant was a baby I remember he cried at night," Lee said. "And I used to sneak into his room and stare into his crib and try to figure out ways to get rid of him." He read Lorraine's look of skepticism. "Not kill him, you know, just . . . make him go away. In a fundamental sense. Never to have existed. Complicated assassination plots involving helium balloons and radio-controlled cars and those model space rockets we used to shoot off into the sky—they had plastic parachutes that melted before the payload opened and never worked. I couldn't understand why my parents would let him cry like that."

"It's so they can learn to go to sleep by themselves," Lorraine said. "Your brother still has an issue with that," she added, mostly to herself.

The baby stirred and began to squall. It might have been their voices or it might have been baby-dreaming. Lorraine picked her child up as Lee struggled unsuccessfully to extract himself from the crib.

"The hitch was getting rid of him without Mom and Dad missing him," Lee said. He had a big wet spot on his shirt from where the little rug rat had sweated through its onesie.

Lorraine couldn't hide her smile, watching him peel the shirt off his chest.

"I was like, if they were going to miss him, then what'd be the point? Might as well have him around, you know, see if he'd grow up into something I could play with. Which he did," Lee reflected.

After a moment, Lorraine asked softly if Lee still hated her, and Lee said no, but admitted he didn't like her very much, which Lorraine conceded was, in light of everything that had happened between them, fair. Then there was a useless pause that only made it all feel much sadder and more pointless than either one of them was willing to admit. Then Lorraine turned away, brushed something out of her eye with her sleeve, and started to leave the room with the baby.

"Lorraine?"

She didn't stop. The ghost of her white pajamas trailed in the darkness for an instant after she was gone.

"Lorraine."

Her footsteps fell away in the hallway.

"Lorraine, I'm stuck."

APPOMATTOX

TWENTY-FIVE

There were no trees, no vegetation. Literally an entire mountain had been sliced in half, gutted, and reduced to artless mounds and slag piles by trucks the size of houses, and everything was covered with grime and rust and desolation.

A second mountain evidently awaited the same cruel surrender.

Hard, cold rain from a slate-grey dawn pressed steadily down on a massive strip-mining operation that looked like God forgot to finish this part of the earth.

Sporty but sensible, Beachum's Lexus coupe splashed along the rutted main road in, slowed slightly at a guard station where he was waved through by a man of such girth he could have been Doug Deere's long-lost twin, and continued on to a collection of trailers with a sign that proclaimed:

> *THE EMPIRE*
> *WORLD'S LARGEST MOLYBDENUM MINE*
> *SLOCUMB & SLOCUMB, INC.*

Beachum hopped from the car, ran into the main office, ran back out a moment later, and got back into the Lexus, winded, already soaked and shivering.

"They're under the ground," he chided himself as though he'd missed some essential clue.

The Lexus took off again, heading up a sawtooth, muddy road of whiplash switchbacks that climbed and climbed and climbed, then crested and disappeared into the man-made crater where a mountain once stood.

In the same rain, Lee's burned house bled black.

Rain sluiced soot into runoff that spiderwebbed the driveway concrete around and under Grant's Camaro. Grant stood outside the car in the downpour, facing the ruined house. Its structure was mostly intact, but it was brutally charred, the windows shattered, portions of the shingle roof burned through.

Grant disappeared inside, then reemerged a moment later having remembered something; he crossed the driveway and waded into the glistening field of septic tank goose bumps, circling until he found the right place, then stood, bent over, studying the ground, hands on his knees, rainwater running down his face and arms and soaking through his shirt and jeans until he saw, in the mud, a spot of gold. Cold hands clawed it out.

A wedding ring.

Grant's knees flexed and he rocked back, rested on his heels, and rolled Lee's not-so-long-lost wedding band between his fingers. There was an inscription on the inside: "ever and forever." *Lorraine or Lee?* he wondered. It was an epigram worthy of Lorraine's unfettered optimism, but read more like Lee's clueless determination.

The rain eased. Fog or low clouds hung over the Evergreen valley, reaching nearly to the ground. There was no wind, and the sound of water dripping from the trees in the forests and from the eaves of the house and from the chassis of the Camaro and running down the gutter crackled like cellophane.

Grant put the ring down on the ground and began to dig in the soft soil, scooping a hole nearly wrist deep before he stopped, dropped the ring in, and buried it completely. It took him eight minutes to drive to the public phone outside the gas station mini-mart in Bergen Park. The rain picked up and pounded down on him as he paid his quarter and dialed the number scrawled on Lorraine's underwear. He waited for the voice-mail message and, at the prompt, pressed the pound key to leave a callback number, then hung up and hurried back to the warm, dry refuge of his car.

The industrial elevator thrummed sonorously as it descended through solid rock. Its operator handed Beachum a yellow hard hat from a box behind him at the control panel. The hat was too small and rode on Beachum's head like a push button, but it didn't bother him.

Beachum had always fancied himself a warrior. He'd been one of those boys who was fascinated by war, weapons, Batman (the Frank Miller *Dark Knight* incarnation), Tom Clancy and Vince Flynn, hard heroes with unwavering values whose righteous violence was directed only toward bad men (and, but less commonly, bad women) whose single goal in life was destroying the American way of life. As he got closer to the age at which he could actually enlist in the armed services, actually become one of those hard men, it became more difficult to reconcile the love he had for the idea of armed conflict with the anxiety he experienced whenever he tried to picture himself in a firefight. He hoped this didn't mean he was a coward, and his increasingly hawkish political and social posturing was directly proportional to the intensity of his craven fears.

The elevator doors split wide to a subterranean cavern startlingly illuminated by banks of hanging fluorescent lights, a gigantic man-made cavity carved from solid rock, perhaps five hundred feet long and a hundred feet in height. More huge Empire Mining machinery moved through it on connect-the-dot roadways, fantastic steel drilling equipment more buglike than Lee's backhoe. Long mine cars carrying oar snaked and rattled down railroad tracks past Beachum, powered by unmanned drone locomotives.

The Slocumbs were waiting for Beachum outside a sleek, modern, glassed-in office area slanting right out from the rock walls of the cavern, all *North by Northwest*. Both Slocumbs wore suits with white shirts and bolo ties.

"'Lo," Beachum drawled, squaring his shoulders and falling into what he hoped was a character not to be trifled with.

"Hello then, Mr. Beachum. That's a pretty swanky murse. Pleather?"

Beachum bristled at the double-disparagement. "No, my friend. Pure cow."

They stood awkwardly, like boys at a freshman dance.

"How 'bout this weather?" Beachum offered.

"Where's Mr. Garrison, sir?"

"Busy. He's had a run of unfortunate luck."

Saul pushed the corners of his mouth down as if sympathetic.

"But," Beachum continued, lively, "I have his proxy, his power of attorney, and his blessing."

"Oh yes," Paul Slocumb said. "And I bet that blessing is a real bonus."

Rain was leaking into the Basso Profundo General Store from an overhead light fixture. Rayna noticed the puddle on the floor as she started restocking peach Snapple in the glass-door display refrigerator. A quick study of the ceiling tiles revealed a faint discoloration running along a seam from the light across the store to the wall separating the main floor from the storage room, so the roof leak was probably along the gutters on the mountain-facing side of the building, gutters that were endlessly clogging up with pine needles and subsequently overflowing. Rayna picked up the empty cartons and carried them into the back room where, sure enough, the discoloration split the ceiling and spread, in a corner, on the outside wall where, she knew too well, the gutter met the downspout.

"Dammit."

Frustrated and tired, Rayna dropped the empties on a stack of other cartons for recycling. Then she looked to the wall again, frowning; looked to the wall where it wasn't so much what she saw as what she didn't see that startled her. There was that stupid parachute, on the floor, perfectly centered inside a rectilinear outline of dust on the concrete where there once had been a couple of small wooden crates of Austin Powder Company dynamite and assorted blasting supplies that Rayna kept handy for impatient fishermen and the occasional uncooperative tree stump that Mayor Barb liked to punch out of her lot.

All the dynamite, detonator wire, and an ERNA-3 handcranked blasting machine had vanished.

In fact, Rayna's dynamite was cradled in a wheelbarrow that Lee was at that same moment negotiating through the obstinate mud of the Blue Lark Mine with increasing difficulty as the barrow's wheel became fouled with grit. The light from his helmet lanced a humid darkness and strobed across the rock.

He stopped. He took five sticks of the explosives from one of the crates and duct-taped them together and tried to wedge them up into a fissure, using some sculpting putty he'd borrowed from what Ms. Davis liked to call her "atelier" at the high school.

The clay and explosives fell loose from the wet rock. Lee tried it again. No luck. Finally, he just balanced the sticks on an outcropping and used putty to stabilize the detonator wire while he spooled it back down the tunnel in retreat.

Through the glass wall of the Slocumbs' subterranean office, Beachum could watch the impressive workings in the mine's great room. His man bag was emptied on the big oak table, tablet glowing with Excel spreadsheets and documents neatly tiled around it. Paul and Saul perused them—standing, not sitting—as Beachum nervously filled the silence with his prattle.

"One million dollars' American money up front. Nonrefundable. Four hundred and forty-nine thousand dollars for the land itself on closing. Plus all fees—"

"Can part of the fee be in stock?"

Beachum bristled at the interruption. "You know what? Lee's not all that interested in being your partners."

"This assay is unacceptable."

"Five percent of adjusted gross profits from mineral exploitation of gold deposits," Beachum continued, ignoring Paul. "Two percent of any other mineral exploitation—"

"This assay is unacceptable."

"Okay. Let's get a new assay. Meantime I'll just shop the deal around to some other major mining concerns." Beachum loved to play the bluff; it always worked, even when they knew you were bluffing.

Saul Slocumb said, "No. That won't be necessary."

"Twenty percent of any other mineral exploitation and . . . " Beachum, back to the most important part, his terms and conditions: "my fifteen percent commission. On signing. And I want some stock."

Both Slocumbs looked up at Beachum at the same time.

"I'm the only one he trusts."

A Chevy Suburban pulled into the driveway next to Grant's car, and Lorraine got out, wearing a yellow rain slicker, and she ran in high heels through the sooty puddles to the front porch.

Inside Lee's house it was charred and spooky, and the rain dripped and sweated through gaps in the roof where fire axes had worked at hot spots. A huge hole in the living room wall was covered with milky plastic that breathed in and out with the wind.

"Grant?"

Lorraine moved cautiously through the house, watching her step.

"Grant?"

At the second sound of his name, a string of multicolored Christmas tree lights flickered on, strange and beautiful. A dotted line leading her through the ruined kitchen, down a murky hallway, and into Lee's bedroom where soot and smoke were the primary damage, and Grant waited in a crèche of twinkle lights and votive candles and plastic light-up Christmas lawn ornaments, some partially melted into strangely elegant abstractions.

"The power's still on in the garage," Grant said. "I ran an extension cord. Which, hmmm, I mean, isn't that, like, rule number one or two in the firefighting manual, i.e., 'turn off the electricity,' probably right up there after 'turn off the gas'?"

"They're only volunteers," Lorraine said. "They saved your house."

"Lee's house," Grant corrected her. "And not entirely."

"They saved part of it."

"And the bed." Grant threw back the blackened duvet cover to reveal bright white sheets, damp but undamaged. Ashes swirled in the air.

"I dreamed you called," Lorraine said. "The other night? But I can't remember what you said."

"Maybe I told you about how I keep trying to help my brother and how I keep fucking everything up."

Lorraine took her coat off. She hung it on the cedar antlers of a beautifully lacquered, high school wood shop reindeer nailed to the wall.

"No. That wasn't it."

She kicked off her shoes, crossed the room, put her arms

around him, and kissed him, hard. Her lips were cold. The bottoms of her feet were stained black. Lace ashes and soot swirled in phantasms of loneliness and guilt around them. Lorraine felt feverish, despite the damp.

"Not everything is your fault, baby," she told him. "Some of us are perfectly capable of fucking things up entirely on our own."

A big flashlight in one hand like a relay baton, Rayna ran up the mine road, dodging deep puddles and sliding on slicks of hardpan. Rain poured down from black clouds. The broken mine buildings took on a spectral quality as the wood became soaked. Mist webbed the forest and the hiss of the rain on the trees and the rock followed her up to the clearing, and the flat pad of tailings where an ERNA-3 hand-cranked detonating machine sat prominently under a makeshift awning of plywood, water nonetheless beading on the plastic housing and dripping from its poised handle, wire snaking away from it, and Rayna, following this unlikely track, ran wet and scared, lungs burning and legs aching, toward the mine opening and into it ("Lee?"), sloshing through the dark tunnel ("Lee!") where only a couple of the overhead lights were still intact and lit, highlighting charred timbers that had half-collapsed from the walls, and followed the uncoiled wires that dipped in and out of the muddy precipitate on the floor like a serpentine swamp monster; then her gaze leapt to the ceiling where sticks of dynamite were wedged in with putty and bits of wood and steel nails, or nothing at all, just balanced, and her heart kind of flopped, or skipped, with a foreboding, and she floated past the planted charges, zigzagging to the main intersection of the mine shafts, where suddenly the wires coiled and tangled and seemed to take off in several directions, and she found Lee straddling an overhead beam above the flooded downshaft, hammering another charge in place.

"Stop."

He did. He looked the same, which is to say he looked as he always did, nothing of the mad scientist or mad bomber or whatever she might have expected. His eyes were clear and kind, looking at her curiously, as if placing dynamite and running detonation wire was something he did every day.

She put her hands on her knees and tried to fill her lungs with air, and she couldn't talk, and then she could, and she looked up and aimed her flashlight at him. He shaded his eyes.

"What are you doing?"

"Nothing."

"That's my dynamite."

Lee looked at the sticks of explosive he'd been positioning up in the niche and made a passable attempt to pretend he'd never seen them before. "Is it?" He finished hammering the spike into the rock, then wound some wire around the spike and the dynamite, securing it. "Hand me that wire, will you? I'm glad you're not smoking."

Rayna's flashlight beam dipped to the dynamite crate in the wheelbarrow next to her and found the detonating wire. She shook her head. "Lee."

"Yeah."

"What are you doing?"

"You already asked that."

"You said 'Nothing.'"

Lee conceded this, then admitted he was, yes, doing something.

"With my dynamite."

"Maybe. Yes."

She waited. No further explanation was forthcoming. Lee pushed his wet hair back and exhaled. She could see his breath.

"What are you blowing up?" she asked.

"Everything," he said.

TWENTY-SIX

In the ruined bedroom of Lee's ruined house, Lorraine finally grew tired of kissing and rolled up on top of Grant, pulling her knees under her, and hitching up her dress. They didn't say anything to each other. Clothes came off, but not many of them, because of the cold and their impatience and an economy of purpose that came as naturally as the rain splashing on the windowsills and through the fractured windowpanes.

Their breath was visible in diaphanous gasps.

The heat from their bodies generated a sifting, transparent brume that eddied and swirled as they shifted and stretched on the sheets of the bed she had once shared with Lee.

And Lorraine, softly, a stone skipping, a meadowlark's refrain, said, "Oh oh oh oh oh oh oh."

"They can have the land," Lee explained to Rayna. "They can have the mineral rights," Lee said. "But that's all."

He was struggling to control the wheelbarrow, scribing a deep arc in the mud with the front tire while negotiating a creosote-slicked support beam that had collapsed in the middle of the main intersection. Rayna was close behind him.

"That sounds like everything. What's left?" she asked.

Lee stopped and considered her blankly. Water poured down into the mine from above them. Rayna looked up into a rocky void.

"Where's that coming from?"

"There's a vent," Lee said. "Or maybe it was a partial cave-in—don't worry—years ago. It goes up about a hundred feet to a sinkhole on the ridge. Doug almost fell in it."

Then, continuing, "They can have the gold. But they can't have the space, between the rocks, the shafts, the passageways, this, where we're standing, what we've excavated, where I— where I dreamed that—"

"Dreamed that what?" Rayna pressed him, impatient for him to finish after he just stopped mid-sentence, overwhelmed.

"What?"

"Where you dreamed what?"

Lee eased the handles of the wheelbarrow down until the skids stopped it. His arms ached, and he shook them out and looked at Rayna, eyes narrowing, suddenly bemused. "Wait. You didn't think I was going to blow myself up in here?"

Before Rayna could answer, the mine shaft in front of them collapsed with a dull thundering rumble of rock, dropping un-impressively inward, a wave breaking in on them. Outside, the mountainside rolled in on itself in a straight line back from what used to be the mine opening: a crude, soggy, granite soufflé losing air, settling with a subaural thump.

On the other side of the cave-in, Lee pivoted, grabbed Rayna, lifted her off her feet, and carried her away, stumbling, as charred timbers buckled around them and rock splintered and the mine shafts lost shape. She dropped her flashlight. He pushed her ahead of him and yelled something about putting her arms over her head. Lee's helmet rocked off, and the light on it shattered, and everything went completely dark.

Ash from black-dusted bedcovers snowed upward into the muggy thermals that had gathered in Lee's bedroom as Lorraine climaxed, loudly, joyously, and the bed shook; she held nothing back and then melted into delighted laughter. Grant was too spent to make any noise, but his brain screamed *God Almighty*.

"That was worth it," Lorraine said. "That was so worth any wait. Holy shit." She kissed him and collapsed on him, shivering.

"You're going to leave me again, aren't you?" she asked, after a while.

Grant made the cogent observation that she was married to Stan Beachum.

"Only technically," she said. "I'm fond of him, I guess, but, oh, mostly? I felt sorry about what you did to him, and, well, you know how it is, Grant; guilt just rules me."

"Not really," he said.

"Until I see you," she added, ignoring what she knew he meant. "If you asked me, I'd go away with you right now."

Grant did not doubt it.

"But you won't," she said. "*You* won't."

Why didn't you tell me about the baby? Grant wanted to ask her. *Why didn't you write to me and tell me, and why was it only after I came back here that you did tell me?* Would she have kept it a secret if he hadn't come back? In his entire life he'd never had so many fucking questions. But instead he just breathed her name, "Lorraine."

She put her fingers against his lips, tenderly, shushing him. "Well answer me this, Batman, if you can get your cape out of your ass: Your brother came to my, our, me and Stan, *our* goddamn doorstep last night—"

"Lee?"

"No, your other brother. And he asked Stan to help him sell the gold mine—"

Grant's interrogation overlapped her: "Lee was at your house? Sell the mine to who?"

"—all wound up, middle of the night, crawling into the baby's crib, if you can believe it, and sat in there going on about you. What?"

Grant lifted her off him, swung his legs over the edge of the bed, and started to get up. "He can't sell the mine."

"And it came to me. In a kind of flash. You've got to let him go," Lorraine said. "You."

"I've committed some fraud," Grant said. "Sort of."

"Oh God. Again?"

"This time they'll blame it on him. I gotta, I gotta, I gotta," Grant was pulling on his pants and had an agitated, forward-looking frown on his face that she knew was his tell for the worried thinking of an overprotective and restive younger brother. She'd seen it once before. That hadn't turned out so well.

"Where is he?"

"Lee needs to fight his own battles," she said.

"Lorraine. You have no idea what the fuck you're talking about, so—"

"You need to get out of his way."

Grant grabbed her and shook her and frightened her with the intensity of his need to know: "Lorraine, where is he?"

For a long time it wasn't darkness; it was absence of light. Utterly and completely.

With a drip, drip, dripping of rainwater bleeding through rock, muck was washed from Rayna's abandoned flashlight, which had stuck fast in the crush of rock facing up, miraculously, the pooling water on the lens giving birth to a sallow light, primal, a dull molten glow that became brighter and brighter as the muck sluiced from the glass.

The freed beam of light cut the humid midnight of the collapsed mine and pinned Lee's ghost face against a glistening wall of rock. He put his hand up to shade his eyes, and the beam split into trapezoidal fragments.

"Rayna? Where are you?"

A sound in the darkness. Watery and scared. "I don't know."

Lee followed the line of light and dug the flashlight from the muck and cast it around, searching what remained of the mine. It found Rayna under a crisscross of broken timber, trapped like a cricket in a cage on the edge of the downshaft. She was moving. Somehow she'd been saved.

"Are you hurt?" she asked him.

"No."

"I'm pretty scared, Lee," she said.

"Me too."

He swung the flashlight back in the other direction, and it was as if Rayna no longer existed. As if nothing existed except what he caught in the beam of the flashlight. And what he saw was tumbled rock where once there was a passageway out.

"Are you afraid of the dark, Rayna?"

"I don't think so. Not usually. It's sort of comforting sometimes."

"Good."

He turned off the light, plunging them again into oblivion.

"We've got plenty of comfort then."

No light, and silence.

The eastern grade of I-70, approaching the Eisenhower Tunnel, was slick with rain. Traffic crawled cautiously in both directions, tires hissing. Weird, low, torn-off clouds hung in the valley below Loveland Pass.

Grant's Camaro powered up the hill doing about 100. He blew past a turtle-slow semi and was sucked into the tunnel.

The flashlight pulsed, and for a moment there was a freeze-frame of Lee crawling carefully across fallen rock and broken beams on his way to Rayna, and then it was pitch-black again.

"What are you doing?"

"Did you put new batteries in your flashlight today?"

Another burst of light. He had nearly reached her.

"No. But they were new when I put them in, and I never use that flashlight."

"So they could be—the batteries—two years old? Three?"

"Lee, I really don't—"

"Let's think this through," Lee said, as if for a Thursday lab in his Honors Physics class. "You used the flashlight and batteries to come and find me. We don't know how long we've been in here since the mine collapsed. Or how long your flashlight was under the mud before it got washed clean."

The flashlight came on, and he was right on the other side of her cricket cage, looking in at her. Then off.

"It's my experience that people never have flashlights with batteries that last for more than fifteen minutes unless they put the batteries in today from a new blister pack."

The flashlight came on again, light busting down hard on Rayna from above where Lee was lying across the fallen beams, looking at her. She squinted and blinked unhappily. He reached in and brushed some mud from her temple.

"They were new when I put them in," she said.

"You want to test my theory or trust me?"

The flashlight started to dim noticeably, the beam waning from white, to yellow, to orange.

"Could you repeat the options, please?"

The world went pitch-black again. But her fingers found his hand and held it with all she had.

Down on Main Street, Grant's Camaro raced into Basso Profundo, shedding mud and mist. He sprung out of the car and up onto the porch of the General Store, calling for Rayna. No answer.

Back to the idling car, he lurched off again.

At the end of the road, the Camaro went into a controlled drift, found the upslope of the Blue Lark access road, and fishtailed through the trees. All the washboard ruts in the road had gone viscous soft in the rain, and the low-slung muscle car sank further and further, finally stopping altogether on a hairpin curve, nose buried in a micro–rock slide, headlights bloodshot with mud, and tires chirring uselessly.

Grant got out and started to run up the hill.

"Now grab my hand again."

Rayna was moving, albeit blindly. Grasping at slick timbers and jabbing her hands out to keep from cracking her head on something. Dripping sounds. Rustling sounds. Lee's voice, calm, soothing:

"Grab my hand. There. Now I'm going to—see?—put it on this beam, and you just . . . curl around it . . . there. Good. There's another beam about eight inches above you—"

"That better be your other hand on my ass, and not some huge wet spider."

"There you go."

Rustling sounds, bodies falling together.

"Is that really you? Oh, shit, oh my, hold me. Hold me."

There was silence then. Dripping of water, and Rayna's choppy breathing. Now and then there were the usual, creepy, deep-groaning ghostly grievances expressed from deep inside the mountain.

Coblynau or whatever, Lee thought.

"We're dying in here, aren't we?" she said.

Lee didn't answer.

"I'm just asking because the new me asks."

There was no comforting response from Lee.

Grant climbed up onto the platform of tailings, exhausted, soaked with rain and wheezing from the run. He passed Doug Deere's broken, molested Subaru. When he saw the collapse where the adit once was, he stumbled, stopped, his mouth opened, and a single, disbelieving, mournful sound came out.

He blinked the rain from his eyes and let his gaze travel the length of wire from the fallen mountainside to the yellow detonation device at his feet. Then his gaze swept south to the generator off to the far side of the mine.

He ran to it. Put his palm flat against the flat metal of the engine housing. Still warm.

Darkness.

The dripping of water. The mountain's complaints.

"Somebody's out there."

"It's ghosts."

More despondent rock-rattling.

"Lee, somebody's out there, trying to call to us—"

She pulled away from him, out of his arms. He could hear her move away, awkward on the loose footing. He switched the flashlight on and caught her, surprised, looking back into the blinding beam.

"It's the mountain, Rayna. Walking in its sleep."

"Don't you go Doug on me," Rayna said. She picked up a big rock, crawled into the upsloping collapse, and began to hammer on the wall of the mine shaft, screaming, "WE'RE IN HERE!!"

Nothing.

"WE'RE IN HERE!!" she yelled. "WE'RE IN HERE!!"

Lee killed the light. In the black void Rayna drummed on the wall for as long as she could, as hard as she could, until her arms got tired and she could no longer lift the rock. When she stopped, Lee used the flashlight again to locate her, and crawled to her, pulled her back from the wall, and wrapped her in his arms. She wasn't crying. Her eyes were wide, an animal trapped.

"I'm so sorry."

He turned her, held her, and kissed her tenderly and turned the flashlight off.

And at almost the same instant, the unbroken bulbs of the fallen mine lights flickered on.

What—

And off.

"Ghosts?" Rayna whispered.

And on again, fluttering—off, on, off, on—a slow smile spread across Lee's face—off.

"No," he said. "It's Grant."

The mine lights stuttered and popped and after a while stopped, but it was a few moments before Lee and Rayna realized it because the light-dark pulsing rhythm had imprinted itself stubbornly in their heads.

"Grant," Lee repeated.

"Your ghost," Rayna said.

Wet, cold fingers struggling to loosen a wing nut on the contact terminals of the rattling, gas-powered generator, Grant knelt in the muddy tailings, rain dripping from his nose. Soaked through. One wire of the mine lights finally came free of its terminal, and Grant pinched it between his fingers and tapped it against the copper post three times, quickly.

And Lee and Rayna's darkness was split by light, three times, strobing Lee's quick movement across to the fallen string of lightbulbs on the shaft's muddy floor.

Now the lights flashed again, twice.

Then three times.

Lee recognized the pattern as Morse code, except, he noted, barking at the rocks that separated him from his brother, "You're sending *us* the SOS, moron." He asked Rayna to give him some light over there, and she turned on the flashlight and crossed to find Lee with a Swiss Army knife, trying to slice through one of the strands of wire from the mine lights.

"I'm gonna let him know we're here," Lee said.

Outside the collapsed mine, the next time Grant put bare wire to the terminal, he got a spark so unexpected and angry it scared him.

He frowned, tried again, and got another backfiring spark.

Then nothing. He didn't have to think about it; he sat back and left the wire loose.

Three sparks.

Grant smiled, his heart unclenched. "Hey bro."

Then he was up and running across the slag to Doug's Subaru, picking up a rock to cave in the headlight glass, jacking open the hood to dive in, half-swallowed by the engine compartment, legs flailing, hands fumbling on both sides of the broken headlight, ripping at cables, pounding on the plastic parts, finally extracting what he wanted: a bulb with some wires.

He ran back to the generator and twisted the stripped wires of the headlight bulb in position roughly between the terminal and the exposed copper wire of the mine lights.

After a moment, the headlight blinked on and off. Again. Again. Long and short. Grant laughed and sprinted away again to the car. Thunder rolled overhead, high on the mountain, but the rain had eased. Stray white baby clouds skiffed past under a sky of slate. In the glove compartment of Doug's Subaru, Grant found a pen and a camping brochure.

The rhythmic patterns of sparks from the wires in Lee's hand revealed, in splintering glimpses, his face and Rayna's expressionless, as if mesmerized.

Outside, where Grant hunched over the camping brochure, tenting it from the rain and pressing hard because the paper was wet and the ink wasn't flowing. The headlight bulb flicked on and off. On and off.

Grant wrote: B L O

His fingers were cold, cramping.

W F S

He shook the pen. Ink beaded on the paper.

F

The last letter, no ink, just the faint impression in the paper: P.

He rocked back on his heels, staring at the message.

"What the hell is that?"

In the mine, Rayna asked Lee what he had spelled out to Grant.

"His Morse code is spotty, by the way," Lee remembered, after a moment's consideration, not exactly answering the question. "About on par with his math skills," Lee said. "He never worked at it. It was always he could receive but he couldn't send, or vice versa . . . there's no guarantee he'll even get this right."

"That's positive thinking."

Lee shrugged. "Realistic."

"He'll get it," Rayna insisted.

Lee told her she only believed that because she'd fucked him. The words just came out, and shocked even him.

Rayna rocked back on her heels. Blinked. But held her ground.

"I didn't, by the way," she said simply. And she said she only believed in Grant because she didn't want to die to prove Lee's stupid point.

Lee fell quiet and wouldn't meet her steady gaze.

But, sure enough, outside the mine, Grant stared at the message he'd transcribed, dumbfounded. *Blowfsfp?* He knew that couldn't be right, but he remembered that Lee was all thumbs when it came to sending messages and was too fucking proud to admit it. Grant wracked his brain for what he'd learned from his brother twenty years ago or more. The two *F*'s were wrong. But they were the same letter, just wrong. *Blowfsfp*. *F* was two shorts, a long, a short. "Dit dit dah dit." A *U* was "dit dit dah."

He changed two letters.

The message read: BLOW US UP.

Oh shit.

Grant looked over at the detonator.

Oh shit.

Into the darkness of the mine came Grant's urgent, agitated response, flashes of light, jittery Morse code patterns that Lee translated without trouble.

"Tell him to go for help," Rayna was saying to Lee. "They can dig us out, can't they? Somebody can dig us out."

Lee watched the lights' flashing suddenly cease and scowled, "What do you mean you can't do it?"

Grant's message had ended.

"Do what?" Rayna asked.

"I was talking to Grant."

"Lee." Rayna had a worry in her voice. "What did you ask him to do?"

In that darkness, wires clicked and sparked together again, as Lee tapped a response to his brother.

"Rayna," he said finally, answering her question, but in a way she couldn't understand, "how long do you think you can hold your breath?"

Outside, the sky was darker and the rain had worsened and Grant was pacing, unhappy, the headlight bulb on the generator flashing at him, spitting letters and mocking him as he paced and translated the longs and shorts into language and argued with his brother:

"You can't ask me to do that," he said. "What you're asking me to do—"

T.

"I don't know, but. I mean, well. What are you asking me to do? Help you finish the kamikaze mission so some greedy Pakistani cowboys can't get your precious gold, or—"

T - O - R.

"which, by the way, isn't in there—"

Dah dah dit dah: Q?

He screamed it: "THERE'S NO GOLD IN THERE!" But Lee couldn't hear him.

Q - U - E.

"THERE'S NO GOLD IN THERE, LEE!! JUST MORE OF MY SHIT!!"

And then the word came together for him: *Torque?*

Torque.

Nothing moves without it.

The yellow beam of the dying flashlight plumbed the watery darkness of the flooded downshaft, and Lee looked into the depths of it with a growing uncertainty.

"Long," he said. "Short, long, short." Behind him, Rayna tapped the sparking wires together. "Two shorts and a long," he told her. "Then three shorts . . . "

Outside, Grant was writing the letters as they flashed again; he so didn't want to get this wrong: T R U S T . . .

"Two long. One short," Lee said to Rayna. "And that's it."

Rayna finished. "What did I just tell him?"

"You told him to trust me."

"Trust you?"

"Yeah."

Rayna thought: *Shit.*

Grant stared dully at the letters he'd written, the words TRUST ME, not an order, a plea; he put the brochure down on the ground and stood up. His knees cracked, his chest ached. An act of will. Every movement had to be deliberate; he was a man learning to walk again.

"Trust and torque," Grant said out loud. T-words. Trust and torque. Trust, and torque.

TWENTY-SEVEN

"**I**t's actually, technically, not torque," Lee was explaining to Rayna. "But Grant's working knowledge of physics is whimsical at best," he continued. "For all my little brother knows, Darcy's Law could be the odds of getting the head cheerleader pregnant if she's using a spermicidal sponge.

"Anyway. It doesn't matter whether he understands it; that's the beauty of science: It's there, whether we understand it or not. And it's gonna help us here. How? Well . . . Water being an incompressible solution, according to Darcy's Law, and the conservation of mass—" Lee hesitated, and then, ever the teacher, asked, "What do we know about it?" Rayna knew nothing about physics, so she stayed quiet. Lee answered his own question: "We know, A) standing water is in a hydrostatic condition; B) if there's a pressure gradient, flow will occur from high pressure to low pressure; and C) the greater the pressure gradient, the greater the discharge rate."

"I'm not going to remember this if there's a test." She knew he was talking just to keep her mind off what was coming, this thing that was about to happen that he still wouldn't tell her about.

"Remember those toy rockets you could fire by filling a bladder with water and then jumping on it?"

"No."

Rayna dipped her hand into the water of the downshaft. It was ice-cube cold. Lee loomed, a murky reflection, over her shoulder, fragmenting as she stirred the surface trailing her fingers.

"It's painfully cold," she offered, unnecessarily.

"We played this game when we were little," Lee told her. "Me and Grant. Our house, before we moved to Hiwan Meadows, was on a hill, two-story with a garden level. I was downstairs, Grant's room was right above mine. I ran a wire up, and we could pass messages back and forth by Morse code after bedtime."

Outside the mine, Grant dropped to his knees in front of the detonator, hands shaking just a bit as he carefully stripped the protective sheathing off the detonation wires and fastened them to terminals on the side. He'd never done this before, but it seemed logical. Inevitable.

Just like in all the movies, he thought.

Except, he noted, it's not torque, it's more like, well, pressure. Lee probably said "torque" because he didn't think I'd know Darcy's Law. But, he thought, is it Darcy, really? Changes in hydraulic head are the driving force that makes water move from one place to another. In this case, velocity head resulting from the explosive energy of the dynamite in the confined space of the mine on the surface of the water. Darcy's Law must be at play here, he conceded. The incompressibility of water.

But fuck physics, this was going to be all blind luck and desperation.

Two conditions, Grant told himself, that Lee knew he understood implicitly.

Inside, Lee continued telling Rayna: "So, on my signal, which was my bedroom light clicked just once, on and off, Grant had exactly ten seconds to go to his window, open it, and drop his sleepy thing—it was a stuffed killer whale he called, in a moment of little-kid inspiration, 'Whalie'—he'd drop Whalie down to me, in the window below.

"I'd put my hands out for exactly two seconds, which was the time it took for a plush stuffed whale to fall from the second floor. We'd timed it.

"A second too early or a second too late and Whalie went into the evergreen bush—I think it was one of those prickly junipers—which was a sonofabitch to get anything out of, and anyway, he'd have to wait until it was light out again, so he'd be sleepy thingless if we failed."

Rayna turned and studied Lee as he finished strapping two big rocks together with multiple turns of duct tape, in a kind of drooping dumbbell. There was a rope tied around Lee's chest, under his arms. He bent down to Rayna and tied the other end around her, tethering the two of them together.

"How old was Grant?" she asked.

"Five or six."

Lee tested the weight of his rock assemblage and adjusted his grip until he seemed comfortable with it.

"How did he know you wouldn't just let his sleepy thing fall?"

Lee's puzzled look told her he'd never even considered it.

The mine lights flashed on behind them, just once.

"Oh Jesus."

Rayna, freaking, "What? What is that?"

Outside, Grant was running across the wet slag to the detonator, counting aloud: " . . . Two Mississippi. Three Mississippi. Four . . . "

Wrapping one arm around her, Lee faced Rayna, gripped the stone barbell weight in his other hand, and said, with as much calm as he could muster, "When I say 'jump,' we're going to hop into the water. It'll be cold. The cold will probably rip the air right out of your lungs, but you've got to hold your breath, Rayna, okay? And the flashlight—hold on to the flashlight, and keep it aimed downward for me as best you can."

"Lee—"

"Shhhhhhh," Lee said.

"Do you love your brother?"

"Shhhh."

"Do you love me?"

He held her tightly against his chest, felt the trembling heat of her body and the fear in her heart. He closed his eyes, counting: "Five, six, seven . . . "

" . . . Eight Mississippi. Nine Mississippi . . . " Grant's fingers were wrapped around the detonator's plunger switch. He looked up at the collapsed mine.

"Ten."

Lee said: "Now."

They made a synchronized hop and gravity tugged them, knifing, feet-first into the flooded downshaft with hardly a splash.

Grant pushed the plunger down. The ground beneath him jumped. There was a savage, visceral, muffled thump, and a gentle spill of rocks down the scar of the mine.

Underwater in the mine's inky downshaft, Lee and Rayna sank in a frozen liquid silence like some weird primordial bathys-thing;

they couldn't breathe if they'd wanted; they thought their hearts would stop; the heat between their bodies was all that sustained them; Rayna's flashlight beam cut across dark, rotted, crisscrossing timbers from which Lee kicked them free with his boots—and above them was the hellfire of the mine explosion, the shaft suddenly lit up with a carnival of colors from the rocks, the sediment, the inferno, and the timbers.

And gold.

Impossibly: a jagged vein as wide as a man's hand, twenty or more feet in length, Lee guessed as they free-fell past it, but reaching who knows how far further back into the mountain, lode gold deposits being part and parcel of orogeny and other plate collisions, sourced from the crazy metamorphics of basalt dehydration, then shot through rock faults by hydrothermal events and left behind when the water cools and can't hold the gold in solution, and this lode all crazy dull-glowing-yellow in the expiring light from the fireball above them. Lee let go of their stone ballast, slowing their descent; he clawed at the slick rock walls of the shaft, to slow them further, to touch the gold, his fingers finding the smooth, impossibly pure metal scar in the rock and trailing along it . . . just touching it.

The concussion wave from the explosion above arrived along with a suffocating silence and turned Lee and Rayna into human pinwheels and Rayna was torn away from him, connected only by the vinculum of rope he twined around them both, air fizzing from her lungs in a stream of silver bubbles. She went limp and dropped the flashlight, and it trailed behind, uselessly sweeping its beam across them as they surged downward into darkness.

The vein was just a hallucination Lee may have had.

Then the water-dead roar of the blast found him, weird and distorted, a droopy thunder that made his ears hurt, and Lee no longer could tell up from down and as he reached for Rayna, his lungs burning, his oxygen spent, he blacked out, the current shifted violently, and then a cold grey light traced the outlines of two bodies hurtling toward a pinprick of salvation that grew quickly larger, and larger and larger because Lee and Rayna were cartwheeling toward a pinprick of day, life, part of the detritus riding spontaneous rapids that had blown out of the side of the mountain.

Water being incompressible, and energy always conserved, the force of the explosion put stress on that part of the geophysical equation that *could* give way, specifically a second adit some hopeful prospectors had punched into the mountain down below the initial strike, long since buried but with only a relatively superficial amalgam of loose rock and soil blocking it that, subjected to an outward force presented by a contiguous fluid, caused the landfill to give way, and brackish water geysered out from the steep slope of tailings below the Blue Lark Mine, throwing rock and soil a hundred yards into the trees. Grant ran to the edge of the drop and looked down as Lee and Rayna were ejected in the cascade of water and rock and muck, adrift, disappearing for a moment, and then, by some miracle, they were free of it, and Lee was crawling up out of the channel the water had gouged in the mountainside, hauling on the rope to pull Rayna with him.

She looked dead. Lovely, pale, and dead.

Grant, skiing down the loose rock from above, cried out to his brother; he was so reckless in his descent down the hardscrabble of discarded ore, he tumbled past where Lee cradled Rayna and more or less face-planted in a thicket of juniper. Oblivious, Lee looked at Rayna in desolation, angled his head to her chest, listening for her breathing. Or a heartbeat. He pushed the hair off her face. She seemed almost translucent. On the verge of disappearing.

"Lee," Grant called out to him from the bottom of the tailings.

Lee's focus was Rayna. "We're out," he said to her softly. "We're out, Rayna. We're saved."

"Lee." Grant clawed his from of the underbrush.

Lee bent over her and put his mouth over hers.

"We're out."

Grant found his feet again. Looking upslope for a moment, what he saw in front of him was, he thought, a fucking fairy tale: a sleeping princess and the prince whose kiss will awaken her. Then it was just Rayna, coughing up brackish water, jerking, pulling away, pulling away from Lee, and turning on her side as his mouth-to-mouth revived her.

"Oh God," she gasped.

Lee cradled her head in his lap. Grant scrambled up behind them, on his hands and knees, out of breath. Lee threw an arm around him.

"Hey, bro."

"Hey."

"All that practice."

Grant nodded. "Whalie. And Darcy," he added, just to show Lee he knew.

"Physics is overrated," Lee said. "Brothers, not so much. Thanks for getting us out of there."

There was an ease to Lee that Grant couldn't reconcile with what they'd just been through. It spun him around; he felt small and vulnerable. Eight years old. "There's no gold in the mine." Grant just blurted it out. "No gold except what I put in there with the shotgun from the storage unit. I salted the rock, man. I melted down some of Mom's old jewelry and shredded it up and jammed it into some 20-gauge cartridges. I'm sorry. I didn't mean to fuck this all up. I'm sorry," Grant said. "I was just tired of listening to everyone make fun of you, and feeling that kind of sorry for you that comes mostly from feeling superior, and pretending to pity you, so I thought if I just salted the rock with—"

"I don't care," Lee said. And he meant it.

"Well, the Slocumbs will care." Grant thumbed sudden tears

out of his eyes, determined not to break down and cry in front of his brother. Lee didn't seem to notice.

"Slocumbs? The Slocumbs, yeah, will do their own independent assay and maybe it'll show no gold, just like all the other assays that've ever been made on this mine, and then maybe they'll suspect I may have defrauded them, spiked my own results to cut a richer deal, and, yeah, okay, will probably want to really kill me this time, but . . . "

"But?"

Rayna moaned and shivered and Lee's attention never left her. Her eyes were closed and her mouth fixed in a straight line.

"I mean, gee Lee, wow, it's great that you've got it all so worked out," Grant was saying. "But—"

"But if I offer to buy it back," Lee thought out loud, "get this: They'll be convinced I'm scamming them *again*, and, Q.E.D., that I know something they don't . . . which, I do, by the way . . . but . . . never mind . . . " he stared at Rayna, "and . . . and the end result will be they'll just keep the mine and work it and, who knows, worst case, they might, you know, actually find some gold." He shook his head. "No."

"No?"

"No, I wouldn't like that."

"Lee, there is no gold."

Lee looked at Grant, and something in the look told Grant that Lee was using a higher math. "They can't have the mine, Grant. Ever. Promise me."

"There is no gold," Grant said again, but less sure of it now.

"Promise me."

Rayna, from another planet, said, "I'm freezing." Her face was dusted with a weird glitter and there was a high blush in her cheeks and her dazed eyes were shining. Lee tried to pick her up and stand, but he couldn't do either. He was too exhausted. "You've got to carry her," he told his brother.

Grant took Rayna in his arms and stood up. Lee rose stiffly and looked into the dun sky.

"There's no gold in there, Lee." But now Grant had lost all certainty in his voice. Lee wasn't ignoring him; he knew something Grant didn't.

"It's snowing," Lee said and smiled slightly.

Sure enough, the rain had turned to soft, wet snowflakes. And the mountain fell silent. The trees in still life. Even the water pouring from the mine had calmed to a fluttering trickle. Lee started walking away.

"Wow," Lee was saying, all conversational now, as if they were coming back from a picnic. "Holy moly. Colorado. When was the last time it snowed in the middle of summer?"

"When was the last time it didn't? Um, Lee?"

"Let's go."

Grant shifted Rayna's weight. "Lee, there's something else I've got to tell you—"

Without turning Lee said, "I don't think so."

"Lee." Grant wanted it all out. All of it. Lee deserved to know what his brother was, what he'd been, what he'd done. What he should have admitted to a long time ago.

"We have to get Rayna out of this weather," Lee said stubbornly, and kept going.

"Will you just stop and listen to me? I've got to say this."

Lee did stop; he turned, looked back at his brother, and shook his head: "No. No, you don't. Grant, I'm tired," he said. "Let's just go," Lee said, but didn't move. "Listen. Listen to me," he said. "*You're* gonna buy the mine back from the Slocumbs, but at a discount. You. After I'm long gone, and they're convinced I've cheated them, you'll take the money from Mom and Dad's trust and buy it back, okay? They won't want it because—we just went through this—they'll have decided there's no gold in it because of how I've cheated them. You'll say you're buying it back because you feel guilty about your big brother the fraud. You want to make things right. And they'll understand that because they're from Wyoming. They'll admire it. They'll think it's something you got from being in prison.

"Or, if you don't want to tap the trust, you can use some of the fire insurance money from our house."

"Why would I want to do that, Lee?"

"For me. You'd do it for me."

They stared at each other, and Grant understood that Lee knew everything.

Everything.

"Where will you be?" Grant asked.

"Gone."

"Where?"

"*Gone.* Don't ask."

They stared at each other, and Grant understood what his brother meant.

"What about the traitorous Doug Deere?"

Lee made a vague, dismissive gesture. "Nothing. He's his own punishment," Lee said.

"Can we go dry out somewhere?" Rayna asked, woozy. Her voice was small and dry and weak. "Now." She sneezed. "Please?"

Lee brushed frosted hair away from her eyes again. "Yes," he said. "We're almost there."

"How was my timing?" Grant asked his brother as they hurried down the muddy road. "I'm just curious."

"Not bad," Lee admitted. "You good with her?"

"Don't worry," Grant said. "I'm just doing the carrying; she's all yours."

"We were about half a Mississippi early, though," Lee observed.

Much later, above the General Store, as the summer snow flurried outside, in Rayna's bedroom because the bathroom itself was too small for it there was a big old porcelain clawfoot tub filled with soapsuds and bath oil and steaming water, and Rayna was in it. Her body ached, and her ears continued to ring. She took a cigarette from a freshly opened pack of Kools. Ignored the warning. Tore one in half. She lit the shorter half and smoked, floating in deep, hot, fragrant water, eyes closed.

Much later, headlights cut through the storefront windows of a doc-in-a-box emergency clinic north of Idaho Springs, revealing the lacy swirl of snow in two parallel beams. Men came stomping in from outside, brothers, young, white, respectable. The younger one, glasses and a Rockies cap, smiled at Jenny Simms, the nurse practitioner behind the front desk. It was a great smile.

"My brother here wants to give some blood," she would remember the dreamy one saying. The older one, unsmiling, tired, his face presenting some odd bruises and abrasions Jenny would have cleaned up, if he asked, his hands filthy when he pulled off his coat, just nodded. She never got a really good look at him.

Jenny led them back into an examining room and told the donor brother to lie on the examination table, and she quickly had him hooked up, tube snaking from his arm to a plastic pouch filling with blood. The younger man sat in a plastic chair across the room, holding his brother's coat, friendly.

"It came out of the blue. I don't know what's going on with him."

"It's a very selfless thing to do," Jenny said, all business.

"That's him all right."

Jenny had handed the cute one a clipboard and pen, to fill out the donor forms, but he just held the pen and watched the pouch fill.

"I'll need one of you to fill that out," Jenny reminded him.

"Does he get orange juice or something?"

"Absolutely," Jenny said.

Then, that smile again. "How about me? Do I get some?"

Jenny flirted. "Show me a vein," she said.

She never heard them leave. In the storeroom, with the noise from the condenser fan and the big refrigerator door opening, closing, the bite of the o.j. carton as she tugged the plastic seal open, set out two paper cups on the counter, and filled them to the brim, she never heard the brothers leave the clinic.

She smoothed her dress, checked her reflection in the glass-front cabinet, and took an extra moment to refresh her lip gloss. She fluffed her hair inconclusively. She walked back into the examining room, but her patient and his brother were gone. Along with the pouch of blood. It was, Jenny decided later, all such *weirdness*.

Only Grant was at the front door when Lorraine opened it, and she was surprised how she was momentarily disappointed. Grant didn't say anything about Lee, but she understood, when he didn't, that there was nothing she needed to be worried about, and when he stomped the slush off his feet and stepped inside, and he touched the back of her leg as he brushed past her, her heart skipped, and she knew that her marriage was over.

"You got any orange juice?" Grant asked, without looking at her. "I've got this craving."

"Want to see your kid?" She said it softly, almost tenderly, which, for Lorraine, was almost unprecedented.

Time stopped. Grant stayed, motionless, paralyzed, look-ing up the staircase toward the bedrooms. Lorraine pointed out, again, that Grant hadn't even asked what her name was. And then she told him: "Sam."

"It's a good name for a boy," Grant said. Caught himself: *her*. Right. A girl. He had a daughter.

"It's your middle name," Lorraine said.

"I know what my middle name is, Lorraine. Samuel, not Sa-
mantha," he argued somewhat pointlessly. Lorraine just waited,
smiling, far away until he sorted through his hurricane of emotions,
and finally he admitted, low, "I can't look at her now. I'm sorry."

Lorraine walked back into the house, leaving Grant to close
the front door himself.

Beachum held court in the kitchen. He was practically giddy.

"I owned them. I was the grandmaster flash of mercantila.
Lord of lulz. You shoulda seen me. See, truly, the beautiful part
of capitalism, and the free-market system, left unfettered to do
its glorious thing, is its ability to bring together disparate, even
highly antagonistic elements—"

"How much coffee have you had today?" Grant asked him.

"—and achieve," Beachum rattled onward, unfazed by the interruption, "and achieve a kind of harmony that would be impos-
sible under any other auspice. The invisible hand! I mean, heck:
you, me, our difficult past. Lee's mistaken hostility toward me for,
what? I say: Cupid's capricious aim, *in re* me and Lorraine. The
Slocumb Brothers' alleged acts of violence. Doug Deere's perfidy.
These things all pale when compared with the prospect of getting
some serious green stuff."

Grant couldn't follow any of it. "Where is the money?" he
asked while Lorraine, working at the sink, kept shooting signifi-
cant smoky looks at him, and he appeared just about ready to flee
at any instant.

Beachum was oblivious. He said, "They promised they'll put
it in Lee's bank tomorrow morning before they go inspect the
mine. We're taking the helio-copter, can you beat that? Lee was
totally right about them.

"Oh, and. My commission is payable upon closing. You might
remind your brother it's contractual. Not that I don't, you know,
trust him."

"They're going to inspect the mine in this snow?" Lorraine wondered.

"Well, Lorraine, honey, it's just a flyover, but they're pretty darn anxious for Lee to give them some general idea where the gold is, because what with aerial magnetic-resonance surveys and so forth, these boys have got it down to a science."

Grant said, "I'll bet."

"Man oh man, what a day, what a windfall. Hot damn! Oh, and get this, they gave him a coat. Gave us both coats." He hustled out of the kitchen on a mission, as Grant threw his "Why?" at Beachum's back.

Lorraine turned from the dishes she was pretending to wash, started to say something to Grant, but Beachum was already hurrying back in carrying an enormous arctic coat with a fur-lined hood.

"I guess they get special weather reports from the CIA or Interpol or someplace, and they even knew this freak norther was coming. Can you beat that?"

"No, I can't," Grant said, and he avoided looking at Lorraine. He took the coat from Beachum and walked out without another word.

Much later, the Evergreen High School wood shop trembled with the angry scream of the band saw, at which Lee, stripped down to his T-shirt, was making a series of straight cuts in strips of thin plywood. He lifted his goggles and inspected his work. Then he took it across to a bench where, using a power drill, he swiftly attached tiny hinges to one of a puzzle of plywood pieces laid out in the shape of two snowshoes.

When he finished with this, he picked the shoe up and tested the hinges for sturdiness and finally, for his own edification, folded the hinged piece of shoe up like origami into a small, storable square.

It fit perfectly into the briefcase opened on the adjacent bench, and then Lee started to hinge the other one.

Much later, in her bedroom over the General Store, Rayna slept fitfully, restless, tossed on the seas of her dreams. She was trapped. She was dying. She was dead. Her hands fluttered, her eyes flickered open, and she stared for one desolate moment blindly at the ceiling, scared, even though she was sure now she was alive. She turned her head to one side and found Lee, turtled in a huge fur-lined coat, sitting in the easy chair in the corner shadows, facing the bed. He had what looked like her parachute in his lap, but that made no sense.

The hood of the coat was pulled up over his head. She couldn't see his eyes. But she smiled at him anyway, and the tenterhooks, or whatever it was, fell away from her and her expression eased and she relaxed and rolled away and closed her eyes and fell asleep.

For only an instant. Or so it seemed. Then her eyes were open again, and she was rolling back to look at him and to ask him about her parachute, if that's what it was, and then to say the thing she remembered she wanted to say to him, something sweet and important that she'd thought of, but the chair was empty and Lee was gone.

Or had never been there.

Outside, the snow had stopped, and the sky bled the first raw light of another day.

STRIKE THE TENT

Twenty-Eight

And then Lee, falling.

Wind on his face, roaring in his ears.

The crimson slur of the whirlybird slicked away, above him, lost in the clouds.

Tugging off a glove with his teeth. Wind banging at his clothes as, with the frozen fingers of one hand, he tried to work the zipper of his fur-hood coat.

Falling.

Below him, a ragged glimpse of forest. High steppe. Suddenly the zipper gave. Wind caught inside the coat, blew it up huge and tore it away from Lee's body, down feathers exploding like snow flurries. Lee dropped so fast he might have been made of lead. The coat remained, soared on crosswinds, feather-down flaying everywhere, and then nowhere, a scrap of shapeless Gore-Tex gently somersaulting among the false winter clouds, for a long time.

There was pandemonium in the cockpit of the Bell Longranger, everyone shouting at once, the Slocumbs more outraged by the seemingly personal insult of his rude departure than they were concerned about Lee's fate, the pilot corkscrewing down into the cloud cover as if they might be able to catch up with Lee and pull him back aboard. Abruptly, the shouting ceased; there was silence, just the roar of the rotors and the flexing of steel and the drag and the soft percussion of the pilot's gloves on the controls and instruments as the crimson helicopter hung in a white limbo, moisture beading on the cowl, slickering to either side. The sour stink of Beachum's breakfast sluiced from the floor and made them all queasy.

Hoary clouds furled, gave away nothing.

No Lee.

And when they finally dropped through the pannus and scud and saw below them the vast sprawling, snowy brown Colorado high plains, the Slocumbs, at least, understood the futility of their descent. Lee was gone. Their pilot rode his cyclic and trimmed the collective to zigzag over the scabrous terrain until the fuel ran low and they could tell themselves that they had made an effort to find him.

Twins of a single mind, the Slocumb brothers wondered if the deal would hold and decided, each of them, that it should and would.

No one spoke on the flight back.

Beachum looked lifeless.

The pilot opened an air vent and frigid wind whistled through, serenading the three men with a tuneless dirge.

Of course, initially it was all over the local evening news and the Internet, how an Evergreen high school teacher had died in a terrifying fall from a helicopter while flying with business associates to a gold-mining claim on the western slope of Argentine Pass. There was no reason given, and nothing about preflight hyperventilation or Pakistani twins, or Beachum's regurgitated *Moons Over My Hammy*, not yet; nothing about fleece-lined boots clomping across a snow-dusted tarmac, late for their meeting, and catching up finally with three parka-clad men who greeted him cordially and made no comment with regard to the cuts and scrapes and Band-Aids on his colorless face and boarded the red helicopter that rose into a dreamy fog.

And nothing about dark gray nimbostratus clouds, out of which a tiny paper doll of a man appeared, spreadeagled, falling, falling.

Coatless.

A parachute strapped to his chest.

He pulled the ripcord and silk played out in a silvery flame. He never worried whether it had been properly packed—somehow he knew it had—and the white canopy opened, and the man was yanked out of free fall, floating down, down, down where suddenly the clouds were pulled apart, leaving wispy cottony threads of moisture through which Lee drifted, down toward a shredded white and dark undulating surface that might be a tree-less, snow-swept high-country mesa, or a whitecapped ocean, or both.

It was never a big story, though.

The lack of high stakes or verifiable treasure doomed it quickly to the "strange news" cycle, a tale of failure leading to a flamboyant suicide; it got no national play, cycled and done in less than a week.

Later-breaking updates and Internet rumor snarked with cynical claims that the victim, Lee Garrison of Evergreen, was trying to sell a worthless mining operation to some Wyoming investors who would, several days later, find themselves under indictment and facing extradition to Kansas for possible felony charges involving extortion and maybe even murder, and denying allegations that the forty-year-old physics teacher fell after a brief cockpit struggle, or potentially was even pushed from the helicopter, until official sources announced, no, it was suicide, a sad consequence of the aforementioned Lee Garrison's elaborate gold-mining Ponzi scheme that was about to be exposed.

But the felony murder rap in Kansas stuck. And the Slocumbs were undone. They never recovered from it. Already leveraged to the hilt in their mining operations, the Wyoming-bred Pakistani-American twins racked up unrecoupable legal fees that eventually forced them to liquidate their businesses, one by one, to sundry deep-pocket, mostly Chinese mining consortiums at bottom-feeder prices. A last-ditch stock offering to shore up the Empire went south when Saul was rumored to have flunked a lie detector test his attorney had arranged to refute Salina Police Detective Friendly's claims that Paul had flown to Kansas by private aircraft the day before the prospector Gordon Bunn's mysterious hanging. Eventually the twins would turn on each other, perjure themselves, and begin constructing intricate, contradictory indictments that would never be reconciled or verified. A group of Wyoming Tea Party conservatives began a letter-writing campaign demanding the immediate deportation of the Slocumbs, calling them domestic terrorists and Islamic extremists despite the fact that both men were baptized and confirmed and had accepted Jesus as their Savior in the Holy Laramie Presbyterian Church.

Those stories went viral.

The facts became unimportant.

The gesture, the fetish, the show was the sum and the endgame.

Around timberline, rocky hillocks rose from tenuous pure-white dunes of summer snow, and the icy flakes were blowing, blurring the sharp shadows and rising up startled like Don King's hair. A briefcase had tumbled down from above and hit some hardscape and broken apart, throwing papers and plywood snowshoe parts and hardware in all directions.

A lone figure clomped over a ridge: Grant, all bundled up with store-bought snowshoes and a backpack. He arrived at the busted briefcase, stared at it for a moment, then kicked off his snowshoes and shrugged off his pack and removed a plastic medical pouch of freshly drawn blood.

He punctured the blood bag with a car key. Once. Twice. Then squeezed blood wildly from the bag to the ground and snow around his feet.

A KOA reporter broke the story that a point of impact had been discovered by the victim's brother, days later, after an exhaustive search. The Denver Fox affiliate said traces of blood, a shattered briefcase, false identification, airline tickets for South America, and a pair of fold-up snowshoes the victim planned to use in his escape had been found. Mr. Garrison, one Fox wag noted, had been a registered Democrat and once signed his name to a petition supporting doctor-assisted suicide.

DNA analysis matched the blood on the scene to the victim.

But no one could confirm a body.

If anyone had thought of it, a careful canvassing of Colorado blood banks and blood donation facilities might have led to a modest doc-in-a-box just north of Idaho Springs, where a graveyard-shift RN named Jenny could have been coaxed to remember two young men, brothers, who came to give blood and left with it.

But no one followed that line of reasoning.

And Jenny got her news from Twitter and TMZ.

And a body was never found.

It was vast, unforgiving, untraveled terrain. There were limited resources available for a prolonged search. Wild animals were likely to have scattered the evidence. Or digested it.

After he finished spreading Lee's blood, Grant had folded up the empty blood-bank pouch and sealed it in a plastic bag and put it back in his pack. Wind carried the sound of his whistling away. Grant squinted up into the midsummer sun. The snow would melt fast. It would be a green August, buggy and strange.

Good for fishing, but Grant didn't fish.

He turned and walked back over the ridge.

Labor Day found Rayna's Basso Profundo General Store boarded up and for sale, and Mayor Barb was putting a currycomb to her horse in her side yard and paying pretty much no attention whatsoever to the mine road where Lorraine's Chevy Suburban zagged and bounced upward on the switchbacks to where the Blue Lark Mine waited, reconfigured, with the conspicuous new and improved lower-level adit from which Grant emerged, slick with sweat, squinting in the daylight and struggling to control his wheelbarrow full of rust-red muck and upend it in a leeching pond; he watched as the Suburban arrived with Lorraine and his daughter, and when they spilled, both laughing, from the car, the smile that broke across his face was worth whatever price had been paid to unearth it.

This was the truce, the reunion, Lee's triumph, everything finally on the same side of the Divide: friends, family, future, even collapsed hopes, dreams, mines, digs long forgotten, Creede's folly, broken promises, abandoned claims.

But it would be six, or eight, or ten more months later, in the aftermath of a tropical squall, blades of sun fanned fantastical through a teal silk sky of popcorn clouds, in a watery trough, in the storm-tossed Sea of Cham, where a fine old Nordhavn trawler moved steadily through the mountainous waves, that Lee would be found in the pilothouse, at the helm, with beard and battered baseball cap, and made to answer for his crimes.

A swell caught his boat and lifted it and suddenly there was a big bright white coastal cutter, not very far away at all, as close as it could get under the circumstances, with Chinese naval markings and a man in uniform at a megaphone yelling something that got lost in the wind and waves.

Not only couldn't Lee find words in the squalling of the megaphone, the guy was speaking Cantonese. So Lee just waved.

The man yelled and pointed to the back of the Chinese cutter.

At Rayna, in a slicker and life vest, clutching a railing for all she was worth, her hair wet and dark and straggly and her lips raw and her eyes tired.

She waved back, queasy.

Lee's boat disappeared into the trough of another monstrous swell.

The Chinese crew expertly fired a line across the water to Lee when his boat came up again; he retrieved it and secured it and the tethered boats went up and down, up and down, up and down like a carnival ride, and Rayna was sick again.

A rubber dinghy tumbled off the side of Lee's boat and into the water, two lines attached to it, one that he played out, the other the Chinese sailors used to pull the dinghy toward them.

The sailors lowered Rayna into the tiny craft. They tossed some soft bags down to her, and Lee began to haul her back across.

But the cutter crew threw their rope off and pulled away, leaving Lee and Rayna to fend for themselves.

"Wait! Wait'll she gets over here!"

The cutter disappeared over a wave. Now there was just Lee in his trawler and Rayna in her dinghy, connected by the hopeful miracle of a single nylon line on a tumult of sun-dappled water that could vanish them both on a whim.

She rose on a wave to a height of ten feet above him.

She was shouting down at him.

"What?"

She was shouting.

"You've got to help me," he yelled to her.

But as he pulled the line he realized she was adding to the slack, preventing him from hauling her to safety.

"Say it!" she shouted. He could barely hear her. She disappeared behind a whitecap.

"What?!"

"Say . . ."

A wave clipped her. She fell back into the dinghy, and the dinghy slid over a tent of green water and was gone. The nylon umbilical unspooled and burned through his hands. Gone.

"Say what? Rayna?!"

Lee jumped to the bridge, throttled up, gunned the engine, and came around as the wave broke over his starboard. The screws churned, exposed by the slope of the water.

The dinghy was tossed up on the next swell. Rayna's hands appeared first, clutching the side of the rubber boat, then her face rose behind them, smiling crazily, happy, scared, looking right at him, no more than five feet away, clothes soaked and plastered against her.

She was the most beautiful thing he had ever seen.

"Say it," she said, over the wind and the water, conversationally, no big deal. "Say it to me."

It took him only half a beat to remember. "I love you," he said. "I love you like crazy. I respect you. But . . . what do you think, Rayna?"

Rayna floated up on that carpet of emerald-green sea-swell, and somehow stayed there, defying every law of fluids and gravity, above him, looking down at him.

"I think this is perfect," she said.

The wave fell away. The dinghy capsized. Rayna spread her arms wide and leapt for the bridge of the trawler. And Lee.

And somewhat later, naked under a roiling cataclysm of storm-tossed bedclothing, she fell away from him, out of his arms, radiant. The boat swayed violently, light going every which way.

"Perfect?" Lee said, shaking his head. "Boy are you ever wrong."

Then, energized, he was up, out of the bed, down the short hallway, into the main salon, and by the time Rayna caught up with him, Lee was emerging from an overflowing galley storage bin, flashlight clenched in his mouth, aimed down, eyes intent, clutching long fat rolls of yellow paper—parchment maps—which he hurried over to the table, where Rayna waited in his plaid flannel bathrobe.

"Brace yourself."

Happy but drily she said, "Amaze me."

He unfurled an intricate antiquarian cartographer's map. Seaways of an ancient mariner, vaguely Catalan, hand-inked, with spiderweb trade routes, unpronounceable names, and nonexistent islands.

"I found these in Jakarta," he said.

"Isn't that a Target price tag?" Rayna noticed, trying not to be too critical, but already too wise to Lee's dreamy float.

"Third world can't enjoy discount pricing?"

Rayna laughed.

Another mariner's map covered the first. This one looked even older, a *mappa mundi*, with overtones of Marco Polo's

Book of Marvels and the mid-millennium *orbis terrarum* T and O style: Jerusalem in the center of the world, Garden of Eden fast on the elbow of Africa, and the sideways T comprised by the Mediterranean, the Nile, and the Don rivers. It was torn, leathered, beverage-stained, with French writing scrawled up and across one margin and Italian down the other. Lee reached for and took Rayna's hand from the edge of the table where she'd braced herself to look closer. She folded into him, warm.

"Point," he said.

She did, and he guided her hand across the treasure map, using her extended index finger to indicate: "We're here. We're right here, in the South China Sea," Lee told her, "just shy of the Scarborough Shoal. And it seems perfect here, doesn't it? It does. Perfect. Like you said. But."

"Lee?"

"Keep pointing."

She did.

He traced with her finger . . . slowly . . . lightly . . . navigating across boundaries and crisscrossing rhumb and ley lines and latitudes; secrets and sorrows; strange markings; oyster bays and lobster cays; spice fields; dead calm; corsairs; hundred-year wars; brothers' betrayals and brothers' absolution; warnings of whirlpools, tsunamis, and mad typhoons; sea monsters; magic islands; sirens; banshees; white whales and metaphors; skirting to the edge of the known observable world where the impassable torrid clime separated the saved from the damned of the antipodes. And dreams, miners' dreams, mariners' dreams, dreamers' dreams, and yes, finally, drifting to a queer, wiggly notation made somewhere, anywhere, on this strange explorer's map that Rayna suspected Lee had probably drawn himself—their hands together drifting to the middle of some vast undiscovered ocean, where there was more worried writing, so small and exotic as to be indecipherable.

"Over here," he said, looking up at her, "I guess somebody once thought there was gold."

He'd drawn the map of their world, with all its disappointment, danger, and uncertainty, an impossible, wondrously skewed Mercator projection, hoping (or knowing?) she'd come.

"People think a lot of things," she said, quiet.

Lost and found, he let the current take him, a steadfast flowing monsoon surface drift. His strong, soft, sure, carpenter's hand resting lightly over Rayna's, her body safe against his; together their hands sailed off the map.

And he kissed her neck behind her ear where it began its perfect curve.

"That's true," he said.

Author's Note

The saying "A mine is a hole in the ground owned by a liar," or, alternately, "A mine is a hole in the ground with a liar on top," has been commonly attributed, over the years, to Mark Twain. There is, however, some disagreement among modern Twain scholars on its origin and legitimacy. It may in fact have been coined by Edgar Wilson (a.k.a. "Bill") Nye, a nineteenth-century editor and wag Twain was occasionally known to quote, or by Eli Perkins, pen name of Melville Landon, another humorist and contemporary of Twain's. Whoever said it understood that mining for gold, like falling in love, involves not just a suspension of disbelief, but also purposive action, which makes it dangerous, and transports you to the strangest places, lies and all.

AcKNOWLEDGMENTS

*M*y brother Chuck, who did, in fact, buy a mine up near Argentine Pass, and my sister Suz, who, wisely, didn't.

Julia Gibson, Saxon Traynor, and the Big E for their insightful early draft notes and comments. Convo for his unbridled enthusiasm when there was only a prologue. Max for his grammatical wizardry borne of Latin taught by nuns. Charlie Winton for the soup and sandwiches, Julie Pinkerton for pretty much everything that got better in the writing of it, and, yes, Joan for pretty much everything else.

Chuck Kinder for teaching me how to write fiction; Colorado pioneer Elizabeth Rice Roller for her plainspoken Summit Historical Society pamphlet, "Memoirs From Montezuma, Chihuahua & St. Johns"; Douglas Southall Freeman's seminal four-volume biography, *R. E. Lee*; and Ulysses S. Grant's autobiography, *Memoirs and Selected Letters*.

The lyrics for "Sweet Betsy from Pike" (page 47), which I learned in Mrs. Knapp's third grade, were written by John A. Stone sometime before 1858, based on the English ballad "Villikins and his Dinah." The hymn "Nor Silver Nor Gold" (page 133) was written by James M. Gray and composed by Daniel B. Towner around the turn of the twentieth century.

Printed in the United States
by Baker & Taylor Publisher Services